Defiant

Lydia Finch

Author's Note

First of all, this may be cheesy, but I am so grateful to you, reader, for choosing this book! It is my first novel and was truly a labor of love. I put my whole heart into this and I really hope that comes through and that you enjoy it.

Secondly, see the end of this novel for a pronunciation guide if you would like. I also don't care if you just wing the pronunciation. I respect that and I'm not your mom.

Finally, if you would like to see more content, including character illustrations done by yours truly, a guide to the fantasy races of my world, and a guide to the many countries and cities that make it up, please head to lydiafinch.carrd.co.

Thank you again and all my love,

Lydia

Content Warning

This novel deals with themes of discrimination, revolution, and retribution. As such, it contains depictions of violence (including murder), war, death, classism, racism, homophobia, and an implied threat of sexual assault (though the assault does not occur). It also contains drinking, a significant number of swear words, and explicit lesbian sex scenes.

If you have any concerns about any other potential content or would like to ask specific questions about any of the above, please feel free to email me at author.lydia.finch@gmail.com.

Map

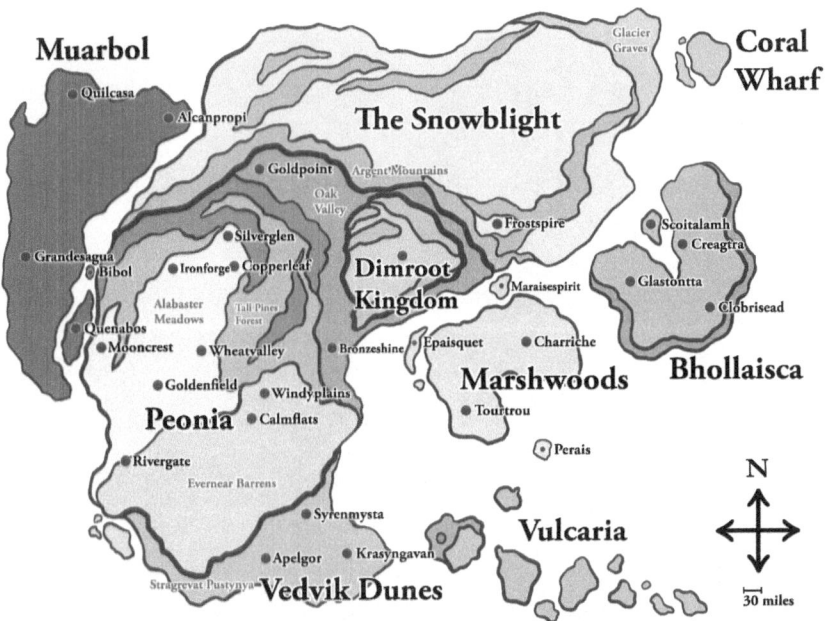

Chapter One

The fight started because Gwen punched a racist in the mouth. To be fair, *he* started it when he began making comments about the bartender's curly horns, but then Gwen *really* got it started when she punched him so hard that he went down like a sack of bricks, prompting his five big, ugly friends to hop up to defend him. She may have also snarled, "I'll show you horns, you bastards!" as she did it, with her long tail whipping back and forth like an agitated cat. Her companion, Bumble, might have then mimicked her words exactly, putting her tiny, clawed fists up with a dagger in each, which, surprisingly, didn't cool things down. Regardless of who really started it, the fight was on, and Gwen was more than ready to break some bones.

"You are gonna die an ugly death, fyrdiav trash," the man with about fourteen snaggle teeth sneered. He cracked his knuckles, a ridiculous cliché if Gwen had ever seen one, before a big hand landed on his shoulder.

"Hold up," a deep, raspy voice said from behind him. "There's five of you and only two of them. That isn't a very fair fight."

He turned to see an elemental woman, her dark skin and clever golden-brown eyes lit by a head of literal fire. It danced around her,

1

as if it were excited. She wore crisp white clothing, the short cut of her shirt leaving her midriff exposed. White boots topped with exquisite, hand-made golden armor covered in complex swirling patterns reached all the way up her long legs to her mid-thighs. She had the same style of armor on the top of her shirt and in the form of cuffs on her forearms. It was clear it was intended more as decoration than for actual protection. Gwen had never seen anything quite like it.

"What do you say I join them and even it out?" the woman said to him, winking at Gwen.

"That's still only three of you and five of us," the man scoffed. "I'd rather not send *two* women and a bird to the hospital tonight." His compatriots laughed, a hideous cackle like a pack of hyenas laughing.

She smiled brightly, taking a step towards Bumble and Gwen. "Trust me, three will be enough."

He began to retort, but the woman turned on one heel and swung her other foot up in a wide arc, connecting with his jaw. Gwen could've sworn she saw one of his crooked teeth go flying right past his greasy lips. The whole bar was frozen briefly—the only movement that of the oaf stumbling back into the arms of his friends—before all hell broke loose.

He straightened back up, spitting out what appeared to be a second tooth before blundering towards them like an enraged bull. The woman lithely side-stepped and tripped him. As the first man went down, she gripped the shirt of the second man coming at her with both hands, lifted him in the air, and tossed him across the bar.

Gwen, shocked by the woman's skill and efficiency, picked her jaw up off the floor long enough to place a solid uppercut into the stomach of the blonde man coming at her. He doubled over, momentarily distracted. Her own distraction cost her though, and Gwen grunted as his friend punched her in the center of her back. Gritting her teeth, she spun on him, headbutting him hard with her twisted horns. She then wrapped her hand in his long brown ponytail and used the leverage to fling him to the floor. His face bounced off the wood with a disgusting crunch, his nose definitely broken.

She turned back around to see Bumble jam a dagger into the kneecap of the man behind the blonde she was fighting. He was the tallest and widest of the bunch and a loud screech punched out of his barrel chest. She gleefully jammed her other dagger into his thigh before pulling both of them free and flitting back out of his reach. Gwen grinned at her and she cawed back, her dark eyes alight. She loved this shit.

Gwen grabbed Blondie's arm as he came back at her, wrenching it behind his back and pulling violently upwards. She felt a satisfying pop as his arm came out of its socket and she used the now-useless limb to spin him into Ponytail, who had just barely managed to get to his hands and knees. They went tumbling backwards, a heap of limbs.

Stepping forward, Gwen kicked her boot into Blondie's face, hearing the crackle of his nose as it shattered. "Two for two," she crowed, laughing.

Both of her men had stopped moving—they were either unconscious or they'd given up. She turned to see that the elemental woman was lifting her two victims, both out cold, to put them in a pile with Gwen's, as if cleaning up their mess. The absurdity of it had a laugh bubbling up in her throat, but she held it down. Barrel Chest was also done. He was bleeding profusely, and Gwen could hear small, pathetic whines coming from him. There was a dagger sticking out of his back and he yelped as Bumble pulled it free. She then paused, looking distastefully at the blood that had spattered on the oil-slick colored feathers on her thighs. She reached back down to grab hold of a corner of the man's tunic, using it to wipe at the blood.

"Bartender, I am very sorry for the mess," the elemental said earnestly, pulling a few gold coins from the pouch at her hip. "We will clean this up for you." She walked over and placed the coins on the counter in front of the stunned fyrdiav, his eyes wide and impressed.

"No, I think I can get it handled on my own," he said, his eyes still fixed on the pile of mostly unconscious men. He looked over to where Barrel Chest lay crying on the floor, then to the man who'd initially started the fight, still crumpled on the floor in front of the bar. "Those six were trouble anyhow—this was probably a good lesson for them." He finally looked up and made eye contact with Gwen. "You good?"

"Yeah, I'm good, Phillip," she replied, running her hand through her long, lavender-colored hair to get it out of her face. "Feels good to wreck a few assholes now and again, eh?" She walked back to the bar. "We really can help clean this up," she told him.

"Guinevere Flynn, you have nothing to worry about. It'll give me something to do," he smiled fondly. "You and Bumble are valued patrons of this bar and if that means sometimes I have to clean up after you guys destroy some over-confident drunks, then I can accept that. Plus, you did it in my honor," he added with a wink.

"You're the best, Phillip," she smiled, adding a coin to the pile. "Give Florence and the kids my best."

"Oh, I'm sure they'll love to hear about this one," he said.

She grinned at him once more before turning to take her leave. She paused as she passed the woman who had helped them and held her hand out. "Thanks for the assistance. I'm Gwen."

"Veda Aalish," she said, taking Gwen's hand.

"You didn't have to help us," Gwen told her. "We'd have gotten them eventually."

"No trouble. I'm always happy to assist a beautiful lady," Veda said, winking at her. The wink felt distinctly different from Phillip's and Gwen felt a little flutter in her chest.

"All right then," she breathed out heavily. "That's my cue. Come on, Bumble."

Bumble chittered, laughing at Gwen's discomfort. She was rarely hit on, due more to her difficult and often downright surly attitude than her looks. She also wasn't used to other women being so openly interested like that. It could get you in trouble in Ironforge—Gwen knew this well.

"Thanks again, Veda," she said as she and Bumble walked out the door.

She heard Veda come out after them. "You mind if I walk with you?" the woman asked cheerily.

"Guess not," Gwen replied.

They walked for a few blocks before curiosity got the best of her and Gwen glanced over at Veda. Her fiery hair whipped around behind her, lighting the area with its gentle glow. Her eyes glittered brightly, drawing Gwen's attention despite the brilliance around them. Her dark skin seemed warm, even though the night was chilly and she lacked a jacket. She truly was beautiful. On her back she had a large, ornate axe and a heavy backpack.

"Haven't seen you around here before," Gwen said, breaking the silence.

"First night in town," Veda responded.

"Is that all you've got?" Gwen asked, gesturing to the pack.

"Oh, yes. I'm travelling on foot, so I need to travel light," Veda smiled at her.

"What brings you to Ironforge?"

"Nothing really, it was just the next town along the way."

"To where?"

"Nowhere, I guess. The purpose of my travels isn't a destination, it's honor."

"Honor?" Gwen nearly scoffed, both at the bold declaration and the notion in general.

If Veda heard Gwen's derision, she gracefully ignored it. "I'm from Vulcaria and have come of age to take my warrior's journey. In my country, those seeking to be warriors must leave for five years once they turn twenty and seek out noble deeds to teach them the lessons necessary to become an effective and compassionate warrior," she said proudly. "We're not allowed to come back until the five years have passed or we've decided to give up."

Gwen whistled, "Damn. That's a tough order; glad I don't have to do that."

"Yes," she agreed, "but I've already learned a lot. I have a bit of extra pressure on me though—when I return, my country will decide if I'm ready to take rule," her jovial face took on a slightly worried expression.

"Wait, take *rule*?" Gwen asked incredulously.

"Yes, my mother, the queen, is preparing to give the responsibility of ruling my country over to me. I'm happy to take the title and prove my dedication to my people, but I need to be sure I'll be a good and just queen," she said.

"Wow...you're...nice for a royal. And really open about things," Gwen said awkwardly, rubbing the back of her neck. She didn't really know what to say to something like that. "We just met and you've already told me some pretty big shit."

Veda didn't seem perturbed.

"So, you don't get to see your people for five years and then you're going to go home and become a queen as soon as you return?"

"Correct."

"Well damn, that deserves a free night's sleep," Gwen said suddenly, like her mouth was talking without her brain's permission. "Why don't you come stay at our place for the night rather than paying for a room at an inn? It's small and certainly nothing fancy, but it's free." Mentally, she cringed. Because the gorgeous foreign princess *totally* wanted to come stay in her tiny apartment.

Bumble chirped happily in agreement, clueless about (or more likely apathetic towards) Gwen's internal regret.

"Really?" Veda said, her face lighting back up. "I'd be honored!"

"There you go with that word again," Gwen recovered and forced a smile, slapping her on the back.

***

The closer they got to their home, the further Gwen fell into her pit of anxiety, convincing herself that she had most definitely made a mistake. Surely Veda would be more comfortable at an actual inn. The woman had agreed, but maybe she didn't know what she was getting herself into. Gwen had said "small" and "nothing fancy", when, more accurately, she should have said "little more than a dank cardboard box, with hundreds of other cardboard boxes stacked atop and around it".

They didn't even have a guest room; where did she think Veda was going to sleep? On the fucking couch? Royalty, sleeping on the dirty old couch which Bumble had acquired years ago through unknown and definitely suspicious means.

It was too late now to back out. Gwen would sleep on the couch and Veda could have her bed...which was merely a mattress on the bare floor...but it was a bed. Technically.

Bumble opened the door to the small alley-access apartment and they followed her in. Veda had to duck slightly to get through the doorway without hitting her head on the frame. Gwen was tall, but Veda stood at least three inches taller than her.

"Well, welcome to our humble abode," Gwen said, waving one arm and feeling more bashful by the second. "I'm sure it's not what you're used to, but it's *something*." She chuckled nervously and leaned down by the couch to pick up a blanket that Bumble had let fall to the floor—and that she'd been walking past for days.

As she stood, she looked through the doorway towards the kitchen table and the profusion of papers and cups scattered there. Behind it, the sink was more than half-full of dirty dishes. The drying rack next to it contained an unreasonably tall and perilous mountain, part of

Bumble's continuous art project titled "How Many Dishes Can I Get in Here Before the Spirits Themselves Take Issue with My Hubris and Bring the Whole Tower Down".

The place was a mess.

And she'd invited royalty to it.

"Oh, Gwen, Bumble, your home is wonderful!" Veda said sincerely. She had stepped forward and was holding a hand out near a shelf covered in colorful ceramic sculptures, her eyes roving over them with delight.

"Really?" Gwen asked, surprised. She quickly folded the blanket and tossed it over the back of the couch.

"All of your belongings are so beautiful, and there are so many!" she said, referring to the hoard of baubles Bumble kept on the bookshelf in the corner, the shelves lining the walls, the windowsills, and any other flat surface she could get her hands on. There were more all over the apartment, as Bumble would pick up any pretty thing that caught her eye and bring it home. Rocks, sticks, marbles, jewelry, little toys—it was all free game and covered every inch of the apartment. "This place and these objects are clearly very loved."

"That'd be Bumble. She loves to collect stuff," Gwen said as Bumble beamed, a proud purr coming out of her.

Bumble grabbed a small bowl of colorful glass marbles from a nearby shelf and placed them in Veda's hands. "Favorite," she said, running her claws over the marbles.

"These are truly magnificent. You have impeccable taste," Veda told her.

Bumble rifled through them, choosing a sky-blue marble and holding it out to Veda. "For you!" she said.

"Wow," Gwen raised an eyebrow, honestly surprised. "She must really like you. She doesn't give her marbles away very often."

"Helped us," Bumble said by way of an explanation.

"I'll cherish this. Thank you, Bumble," Veda told her, holding the marble tenderly in her hands as Bumble placed the bowl back on the shelf. Bumble then fluttered down the hallway towards her room.

"Do you have family around here?" Veda asked politely after placing her new marble safely in her pack.

"I don't have family anywhere," Gwen said matter-of-factly from the kitchen. She'd lit some candles and was trying to tidy the room without being too rude. Veda followed her in and gave Gwen a questioning look. She didn't appear to be demanding an explanation, but was simply giving Gwen permission to continue if she wanted to. Gwen generally didn't, but Veda struck her as kind, open, and sincere.

She sighed after a moment and continued, "My parents were killed when I was an infant."

"That's horrible," Veda said softly.

"Yeah, people don't like my kind. A lot of us get put down like that," Gwen said, looking away. Veda's eye contact was too earnest and it was making Gwen feel like Veda could see inside of her.

"Your...kind?" Veda said, genuinely confused.

"Fyrdiav," Gwen said. "People think we're naturally evil creatures and that they're doing the world a favor by eradicating us. Those guys in the bar tonight were talking shit on Phillip for no other reason than that he's a fyrdiav and they figured no one would stop them."

"Well, that's ignorant," Veda responded bluntly.

"You're telling me," Gwen snorted disdainfully. "It's a common enough viewpoint in Peonia though. Not just against us, people here feel that way about most non-humans. Even the people in our government are like that. Have you heard about The Brotherhood yet?"

Veda shook her head. "Not really. In passing mostly."

"They're a Lowean religious organization that believes in the supremacy of human-kind, as humans were supposedly made in the image of their one true god. They worship this god called Starlowe, who is supposedly super nice and loving, but I can tell you that a lot of his followers aren't, especially The Brotherhood. They believe human males are the ideal and everyone else is garbage. If you're one of the luckier groups, like human females or more human-like races such as elves, you're just subjugated. If you're unlucky, like fyrdiav or aviseum," she thumbed at Bumble, who had run into the living room to grab the blanket Gwen had just folded and take it back towards her room, "you're murdered.

"It's not *technically* legal to go around killing people, but the corruption runs deep and a lot of things are just overlooked. The Brotherhood has ties to a lot of the most wealthy and influential families in the country and they're absolutely loaded too. When you have that much money and power, you can pretty much afford to hate anyone," Gwen said. "And *technically* The Brotherhood isn't our actual governing body, but they might as well be. The Council is filled with members, and they lean heavily towards Brotherhood interests."

Veda grimaced at her. "That seems like a lot of effort to put into pointless and unfounded hatred."

"Yup. Brotherhood members are actually the ones who killed my parents." Gwen surprised herself a bit as she said it; she didn't usually talk about them.

Gwen could see the question and empathy in Veda's eyes. She knew Veda was trying not to scare her away by prying, but she was curious. Who wouldn't be? Gwen thought about it, chewing on her bottom lip, but finally said, "When I was only a few months old, my parents were travelling with me through Tall Pines Forest when a group of Brotherhood members attacked them. Seeing as it was winter, I was well swaddled and covered in blankets so they didn't see me right away and my mother was able to grab me and run. She hid me inside a hollowed-out tree before they found her and she was killed. I was discovered a few days later when a farmer called some guards to come check out the bodies that were rotting on the path near his field and the sound of an infant crying within the trees. As you can imagine, I was screaming bloody murder after two days of being starving, cold, and alone. They brought me back to the orphanage in Ironforge and I lived there until I was old enough to fend for myself."

"And when was that?"

Gwen shrugged again, "Ten-ish?"

Veda actually slapped her hand to her mouth, like an aggrieved elderly woman. "*Ten-ish*?! We don't even leave our village without someone else until we're twenty! Not to sound callous, but that's...up setting. In my country, if a child loses their parents, other villagers step in to raise the child. The whole community works together to raise the best possible children, even if those children do have parents. I can't count the number of times I was disciplined by community members that were not my mother or father. From my travels, I understand that is unusual for noble children," she chuckled.

"Your village sounds lovely, Veda. Not everyone else is quite that lucky," Gwen smiled softly, no malice in her tone.

The smile Veda returned was sad. "Did you ever discover who exactly killed your parents? Were they brought to justice?"

"I mean, I know who did it, but they were certainly never brought to justice. My parents were just a random fyrdiav couple. The people that did it are worth much more than we are," Gwen said. She'd finished cleaning up and glanced down the hallway for Bumble. She could hear her rustling around somewhere towards the end of it. Gwen turned back to Veda and noticed that Veda's hair had gotten larger, burning more wildly.

"Your life and the lives of your parents are worth just as much as anyone else's lives!" she stated forcefully.

"I believe that, and you believe that, but that's not enough to change anything," Gwen said, putting her hands up in surrender before turning again to the hallway when she heard Bumble's claws tapping along the wood.

"But they should! I'm sure plenty of people believe the same, it's just not the people in power here." Veda slapped a hand down on the table, "We should go avenge your parents!"

"You are *really* forward," Gwen said, her jaw dropped open in shock. "Who does that kind of stuff? And *we*?" Bumble threw her arms around Gwen's legs when she reached her, chattering and cawing to tell Gwen to follow her to her room.

"Yes!" Veda insisted, gesturing wildly as she followed them down the hall. "I will help you! What more honorable thing could I do than assist a person in gaining justice for their murdered family members?"

"Veda, I don't know how they do it in Vulcaria, but around here we generally don't get away with murdering people that are important. People ask questions, fyrdiav get killed for their offenses against human-kind, etcetera."

"So we don't get caught. Or we take down the whole organization!" she said, excitement raising her voice about an octave.

Gwen made sure her tone was careful, "That's not possible. Listen, you seem really nice, but I'm not interested in being fodder for your honor journey. I've eked out a life for myself here and I don't want to throw it away on honor."

"That's not what I mean," Veda said, blushing. "It's not about me, I swear. I just think I can help."

"And I thank you for that, but we could all get killed. Definitely *would* get killed. I'm serious when I say these people are powerful. It's not worth it"

"Of course it's worth it!" Veda said stubbornly. "We'd be doing the country of Peonia a favor, it sounds like."

Bumble shoved Gwen into her room, where she had built a nest of blankets and pillows large enough for the three of them. She cooed, proud of herself.

Gwen looked down at her, smiling at Bumble's happy face. "Yeah?" she raised an eyebrow, "We all have to sleep crammed in here tonight?"

Bumble tittered in the affirmative.

Gwen rolled her eyes and smiled. She'd calmed down since she noticed Veda didn't seem to be reacting to their home with horror, like she'd expected. "That's not up to me," she said and turned to Veda. "Apparently this little shit *really* likes you and thinks we need to have a sleep over." She ruffled Bumble's head feathers with her hand.

Veda's mouth was open and her eyebrows knitted together, as she clearly still wanted to argue about her vengeance plan, but it seemed she was unable to resist Bumble's charm. As an answer, she grinned and lowered herself into the nest. Bumble took no time to crawl in next to her.

Gwen froze, momentarily concerned as she looked down at Veda. "Your...your hair won't, like. Light up the blankets, will it?"

Veda laughed, loud and pure, coming straight from her gut. "No, it's harmless, promise."

Chapter Two

Veda hefted Bumble onto her shoulders as soon as they stepped into the alley. Bumble wrapped her legs around Veda's neck and threw her hands out to the side with excitement.

"You don't have to carry her like that," Gwen said, rubbing her face with both hands. Sleeping on the floor in Bumble's blanket nest with two other people hadn't done her any favors and she was having a hell of a time waking up. The things she would do for that damn bird.

"But she likes it," Veda smiled, holding Bumble's legs tight to assure she wouldn't fall off while she squirmed around.

"Yeah!" Bumble added helpfully.

"And I kinda like it too," Veda laughed.

"You've known her for less that twenty-four hours and she's already wrapped you around her finger." Gwen dug her fingertips into her eyes, rubbing hard and willing them to wake up. "You also don't have to help us with the shopping."

"You let me stay for free last night and Bumble made me breakfast, it's the least I can do."

"Her cooking is terrible," Gwen said and began walking towards the street market, looping their empty shopping bags over the hilt of the sword at her hip so she didn't have to carry them.

Bumble stuck her tongue out.

"I didn't think it was that bad," Veda shrugged. "Plus, she gave me the prettiest spoon."

Gwen shook her head, knowing she was on the wrong end of a losing battle. They made their way into the crowded street, snaking through people and carts as they went from shop to shop. Ironforge was bustling on a normal day, but weekend market days were especially crowded. Gwen tried to be quick and efficient, but it still took the better part of the morning to finish the shopping. It hadn't taken long for Veda to look like a pack mule, as she'd insisted on carrying all of the now full bags *and* Bumble. Gwen didn't have the energy to keep arguing, so she'd long since just started handing them over as they filled.

Once they'd finished, Gwen led them to a park off the edge of the market to rest a bit. Though park was a strong word, considering it consisted of four benches, two tables, and approximately three-square feet of grass, with a single, scraggly tree sticking out of the center. Despite that, it was just about the greenest place in all of Ironforge. Almost every foot of space in the city was taken up by factories, stores, or the cramped apartments of those who worked them. Unlike many of the other cities in Peonia, Ironforge had no natural resources or beautiful tourist locations to speak of, so instead the people there made their living by processing the materials the rest of the country provided. As such, the city was dingy and filthy from pollution and filled to the brim with working-class folks who didn't have enough energy left at the end of the day to care about it. They were the armpit of Peonia, and yet the country would fall apart without them.

Veda set their bags down on the table and lowered Bumble onto the bench next to Gwen. She pulled one arm over her chest with the other, stretching, and watched people move around them as they went from place to place, like ants bursting from their hills. "Ironforge is so different from home. Very—"

"Disgusting? Joyless?" Gwen intoned.

"I was going to say crowded," Veda said, stretching her other arm.

"What's Vulcaria like?" Gwen asked, pulling a bruised pear from one of their bags and taking a bite.

"Well, our founders hollowed out the dormant volcano that makes up the majority of our main island and built the city inside. Hundreds of rooms carved into the sides of the volcano with thousands of twisting stairs leading up to them, all lit solely by us," she laughed, pointing at her head. "We then spread out across the many smaller islands that surround us, to make use of the fertile volcanic soil. So Vulcaria is mostly farmland. Black soil, green crops, and blue ocean as far as the eye can see."

"It sounds amazing. Sorry you have to be here instead of there," Gwen said honestly.

"I'm not sorry," Veda said, taking a seat next to her. "I love my homeland, but it's been fun to explore, learn new things, meet new people. Wouldn't have met you if I'd stayed there," she said, bumping Gwen with her shoulder.

Gwen felt her cheeks heating. "How long have you been on your, uh, journey thing?"

"This is my second year, so I'm not yet halfway through."

"That's a really long time to be away from home."

"You're right, but it's...." Veda trailed off, her attention caught on something deep within the swarming mass of people before them.

Gwen followed her gaze to see an elderly gorgon woman on her hands and knees, her groceries laying scattered and trampled around her. The constant jostling of all the people surrounding her was stopping her from standing, as her movements were slow and every bump just pushed her back down. The snakes on her head writhed in distress, but no one stopped to help her. Gwen began to stand, and Veda was already shouldering her way into the crowd.

Gwen followed her, pushing and shoving as necessary to reach the woman as quickly as she could. Veda beat her there and stood behind the woman, throwing her arms and legs wide to shield the woman with her body and force people to go around her.

Gwen dropped to one knee in front of the woman. "Here, let me," she held out her hand.

The woman placed her hand in Gwen's. There were tears in her eyes, but she smiled crookedly. She looked back at Veda thankfully, then again at Gwen before using her hand as a foundation to help her stand. Gwen could see Bumble flitting around them, picking up the woman's purchases and placing them back in her bags.

"Oh, thank you so much," the woman said, barely audible over the din of people around them. "I was beginning to think I'd never get back up."

Gwen nodded her head towards the benches they'd come from, a signal for the woman to follow. Together, Gwen, Veda, and Bumble created a barrier around her and they walked her out of the fray and into the relative peace of the tiny park, the woman's hand held tightly in Gwen's until she was safely out of the crowd.

The woman sat, lifting her long grey robe to look at the scrapes on both of her knees. "Tripped over my own feet, silly me," she said. Her snakes had calmed, curling themselves softly over her shoulders. She released her robe and brought both hands up to stroke them.

"Where are you going?" Veda asked softly. "We can get you there."

"Oh, I was very nearly home," the woman said, pointing. "Only about two blocks that way. I'm going to need a second to rest, though. My knees are killing me now," she chuckled, though her eyes were still wet with tears. "Getting old is awful."

Veda pulled the woman's hand into her own. "Can I carry you then? On my back?"

"Oh, I couldn't ask you to do that," the woman said, waving her other hand. "You could hurt yourself. Plus, I'd feel silly."

"I'm strong, I can handle it," Veda said with a wink.

"Carry bags!" Bumble said and held up her arms, the bags swinging with the movement.

"We've got you ma'am, it's no problem," Gwen added, taking a few bags from Bumble and helping gather their own.

The woman sniffed and nodded. "You girls are too kind."

Veda beamed at her before she turned her back towards the woman. "Hop on!"

Veda and Gwen's size was enough to keep people mostly out of the way and Bumble wasn't above jabbing a sharp talon into the leg of anyone foolish enough to try to run them over. Slowly, they managed to carve out a path just wide enough to get through everyone while causing only minor jostling to their cargo.

"What's your name?" Veda asked.

"Oh, I probably should have introduced myself before using you as a horse," the woman laughed. "I'm Marlys. Pleased to meet you."

"Veda. This is Gwen and Bumble," she gestured to either side with her head.

"Pleased to meet you," Bumble replied in Marlys' own voice.

They arrived at Marlys' home, which Gwen was pleased to find was a ground level apartment. She took the key Marlys offered her and opened the door for them. Veda set Marlys down gently and stuck her arm out for Marlys to use as support as she led them inside.

The apartment was small, as most places in Ironforge were, but Marlys had clearly lived there a long time. Worn paths in the wooden floor led from room to room and the furniture in the living room was faded and sagging. A small, simple carved lion's head and a dozen children's drawings were tacked to the wall beside a tall and leaning bookshelf. Veda deposited Marlys on a soft chair before going over to admire the drawings.

"My grandchildren made those for me many years ago," Marlys said with a soft smile. "Every time they visit, they beg me to take them down. Always promise to make 'better' ones, but I like them."

"I like them too," Veda agreed.

"Do you have any medical supplies?" Gwen asked. "Don't want your knees to get infected."

Marlys pointed to a room down the hall. "Couple of things in the bathroom cabinet."

Gwen gathered a small jar of sanitizing ointment and a clean rag. She turned on the sink and ran the rag under the water, wringed it out, and then returned to the living room.

"Oh, thank you," Marlys held out her hands and Gwen passed the supplies over.

They made sure Marlys was cleaned up and relaxing in her favorite chair before taking their leave, another hearty "thank you" following them out the door.

They walked back to the apartment with their own bags in their arms, evenly distributed between them now. They were quiet as they walked and Gwen considered the warmth in her belly, sending little tendrils out through the rest of her body. Most people in Ironforge would have left Marlys to struggle, as proven by the dozens of people that walked right past her. It was a dog-eat-dog city and people only looked out for themselves for the most part. But not Veda.

Gwen considered making a joke about Veda's honor quest, to lessen some of the pressure building inside her, but couldn't make herself. She knew that wasn't why Veda did it; she just saw someone in need and she helped them instinctively, without a second thought. Just like she'd helped Bumble and Gwen the night before. Something about it had Gwen feeling a little fluttery inside.

They reached the apartment and put their purchases away in silence. Veda seemed to be moving slowly, drawing it out. When they were done, she cleared her throat. "Suppose I should get out of your hair," she said, turning to Gwen with a smile. "I've stretched your hospitality out plenty."

Gwen's stomach leapt and her hand was on Veda's wrist before she'd had time for a conscious thought. "You, uh," she sucked her teeth, pulling her hand back and looking down at the floor, "don't have to go. If you don't want to. You could. Uh. Stay here, with us, as long as you'd like." She didn't know why she was so nervous and internally kicked herself at how awkward she sounded. She couldn't bring herself to look up, but felt a soft burst of warmth hit her face.

"I'd really like that," Veda grinned, taking a step closer to Gwen, then stopping short.

Gwen finally looked up and smiled back, her cheeks warm.

Bumble had wrapped herself around Veda's legs, so Veda lifted her and set her on a hip. "Stay!" Bumble said excitedly.

"Stay," Veda agreed.

Chapter Three

"So, about that revenge quest," Veda said as she shoved a piece of bread in her mouth. She was sitting at the kitchen table with Gwen, eating breakfast.

It had been a week since Veda had been with them and this wasn't the first time Gwen had been bombarded just after waking up. She had literally just crawled out of bed and sat down at the table—she hadn't been awake more than ten minutes, tops. "You're really not going to let that go, are you?" She blinked a few times, willing her eyes to focus, and scrunched up her face. It was too early for this shit.

"Of course not! I have nowhere else to be, nothing else to do," Veda responded brightly.

Gwen rolled her eyes, grumbling, and snatched a piece of bread from the center of the table. "You invite a stranger into your house and next thing you know she's plotting a couple murders."

Veda continued to beam at her, so Gwen met her eyes again. "I'm sure there are plenty of other people in Ironforge that could use your help."

"But I want to help you!" Veda smacked her gigantic hand down on Gwen's shoulder.

"What if I'm a horrible monster like they say, tricking you into doing horrible deeds? Ruin your whole honor quest by soiling you forever through my evil."

She looked Gwen in the eyes and very seriously said, "A tail and horns does not a monster make. You're a good person. No evil in you."

Her earnest nature was endearing, like she either didn't catch that Gwen was being facetious or she simply chose to ignore it. "You don't know the first thing about me."

"Don't need to." She slapped her stomach, "Good gut."

Bumble came chirping into the room, a pack in her hands, which she began to jam snacks into. "We go?"

"Where are we going? Who decided we were going anywhere?" Gwen cried incredulously. "I *just* woke up."

"We go," Bumble said, nodding and wandering off again.

"Y'all making plans without me?" Gwen said with her eyebrows high. "Because I don't remember agreeing to a thing."

"I didn't do anything," Veda said innocently, "I don't know where she thinks we're going."

"Lying isn't very *honorable* you know. To think you've turned my only friend against me." She flipped Veda off. "I knew it was a bad idea to let you two bunk together." Turning, she screamed towards the hall, where Bumble had gone. "Where the fuck do you think we're going, asshole?"

"Sylvia!" came the reply.

"I don't know who that is!" Gwen yelled back.

"Don't care!" Bumble said with a laugh.

"It didn't take much convincing for her to want to help you do this. Also, you have two friends now!" Veda pushed her chair away from the table and stood.

"See, the way you said that makes me think you actually did know what she was talking about a minute ago."

Veda said nothing.

"This isn't just some little day trip, is it? You two need to slow your roll. I didn't agree to this and I don't have anything packed. We literally don't even have a place to start because I don't know where any of these people are."

Bumble came back into the kitchen. "I have plan. Chop-chop!"

"That's not comforting," Gwen mumbled.

"Pack a bag, time to go! Pack a bag, time to go!" Bumble chanted as she marched out of the room again.

"Someone save me from those who think they're here to help me," Gwen groaned, standing up. "That little asshole doesn't let anything go once she's set her mind to it."

"That's the spirit!" Veda said, slapping her shoulder again.

***

"We've been walking all damn day. Where are we going again?" Gwen yelled to Bumble, who was being the "lookout" and hopping through the trees above them. Gwen thought she really just wanted to have fun and there was not an ounce of looking out to be had. "We are literally in the middle of nowhere."

Bumble had led them into the Tall Pines Forest that morning after almost physically dragging Gwen from their home and still they walked, many hours later. The sun was starting to dip towards the horizon, which Gwen was grateful for. It had been getting cooler as summer waned into fall, but of course it had been extremely hot the last week, just in time for her annoying friends to decide they needed to take a multi-hour trek through the woods *for no good reason*. There was little she could do about her dark pants and tall boots, but she'd long since taken her navy-colored leather jacket off, opting to walk in the lighter-colored, thinner sleeveless tunic she wore underneath. Still, sweat ran down her back and pooled at the base of her tail. She felt disgusting.

"Friend. Sylvia," Bumble said, jumping to the next tree. "Almost there. Patience."

Gwen growled under her breath and snuck a glance at Veda. She didn't seem to have a care in the world, a gentle smile on her face and a peaceful look in her eyes. She was looking at all of the plants around her, occasionally touching a leaf or a tree. A few hours earlier she'd plucked a small yellow flower and tucked it behind Gwen's ear.

"There are so many of these ones. They're beautiful," Veda said by way of explanation. Which really wasn't an explanation at all. Gwen's stomach flipped as she was reminded of the little bloom, still proudly peeking out of her hair. She resisted the urge to lift her hand and touch it.

"What's the natural plant life like where you come from?" Gwen asked her in a desperate bid for conversation, hoping it would distract her from the crisis she felt bubbling up inside her.

"We don't have trees like this. Pine trees, right?" she asked, looking to Gwen for confirmation. Gwen nodded and Veda continued, "We have the farmland, and some palm trees, but don't really have forests like this. Within the volcano it's dark and rocky. A little cold and cave-like, because the sun can barely see us at the very bottom. Nothing grows in there and I spent a lot of time within it, as that's where my family lives and we have a lot of responsibilities. Sometimes I wish I were a farmer," she said, her voice a bit wistful. "I love the open land and sunlight. I love how it makes everything so colorful and warm."

"I'm surprised you like the warmth, your body seems to give off a lot of heat—I guess I thought more heat would be uncomfortable."

Veda smiled and stopped to pick up a large, flat rock that had been resting in a patch of sun. "Our fiery bodies make it so that we can stand extreme heat easily. They also allow us to thrive in cooler environments, like inside the volcano. Temperature isn't really an issue for us, as the fire within us keeps us pretty stable. But the warmth of the sun is different. Feel," she said, holding her hand out to Gwen with the rock in the center. "This side was on the ground and is cool."

Gwen placed her hand on the rock for a moment before taking it away.

Veda flipped the rock over, "This side of the rock has been warmed by the sun."

Gwen placed her hand back on the rock and considered the warmth. It just felt like a normal warm rock to her.

Veda placed her hand atop Gwen's, where it still rested on the rock. "Isn't that so much nicer than the cold rock? And it's different than my warmth."

Gwen felt the blood rising to her cheeks for what felt like the thousandth time that day. "I guess I'm used to it," she said, refusing to make eye contact. She couldn't even feel the rock anymore, only Veda's hand on hers. Veda's warmth *was* different than the rock, that was for sure. Her touch felt like a jolt of electricity and Gwen would be hard pressed to agree that the rock was better than that.

"We're here!" Bumble yelled from a few yards ahead of them.

Gwen pulled her hand out from under Veda's and turned, nearly stumbling. Her pulse was loud in her ears. "It's about time!" she croaked, starting forward again.

Veda chuckled behind her, "You're not one for stopping to smell the roses, are you? So impatient."

Gwen flapped her hand dismissively instead of responding. She cleared her throat and ran her hand through her hair, hitting the flower, then pulled her hand away as though she'd been burned and dropped it to her side.

They finally broke from the tree line, entering a clearing with a large garden and small cottage in the center. The cottage was old, but tenderly taken care of. The squat structure appeared as well planted as the garden, like it had grown from the soil itself. It gave off the distinct impression that it was pleased to be there and thriving, despite its age. Vines grew up along its walls, curling unbidden along every surface they could reach. Even the trees around the cottage appeared to be leaning in towards it, almost protective of the peace and safety the clearing seemed to offer. A line of handmade signs were stuck in the ground at the edge of the garden, labeling the various plants.

Bumble chirped, leaping down from the trees and landing next to Gwen. She led them to the door of the cottage and knocked confidently. From inside they heard a scurrying and a high, elderly voice. "Oh, dear! Oh, oh, no!" The scuffling came closer to the door. "Who's there?" the voice called out. Then, in a high-pitched almost-whisper, clearly not meant to be heard, "I was *not* expecting company today; I don't have anything prepared!"

"Company!" Bumble mimicked louder in response. She then made a joyful buzzing sound, like a swarm of bees, which was how she said her name. The name "Bumble" had come from Gwen, at Bumble's request.

They'd become fast friends when they were very young, shortly after Gwen left Lion's Grace Orphan Home. Up until meeting Gwen, others had mostly been calling her Buzz, based on the sound of her name, or just Bird, which was both uncreative and reductive. Bumble never much cared for either of those and asked Gwen for a new name. She immediately took to Bumble when Gwen suggested it. From that point forward, when Bumble told people her name, she said it first in her way, then again in Gwen's voice, even though she'd heard it a thousand times in a thousand different voices since.

The voice calmed, "Oh, Bumble, dear! Is that you?"

The door cracked open to reveal an enormous lime green laisarnne woman in a soft and well-worn yellow dress. The wide, draped cut of its neckline left most of one broad shoulder exposed and she pulled an old lace shawl up from the crooks of her elbows to cover it. She towered over them in the doorway. If it weren't for the deeply worried look on her face and the way the baby-pink frill running down the center of her head was pressed flat to her skin with anxiety, she might have been intimidating. A thick, heavy tail wrapped nervously around her legs.

"It is!" she said, her frill standing straight back up as she relaxed. Sylvia offered a large, scaley hand to Bumble and when Bumble accepted it, she patted Bumble's hand lovingly with her other. "I hope you don't mind the mess; I was not expecting you, love."

"No mind," Bumble said. "Need help for friends. And missed you!"

Sylvia looked at Veda and Gwen finally, surprised, as if she had simply not noticed them before. Gwen, for one, wasn't sure how she could be missed. Or Veda with her literal *fire* for hair.

Sylvia had gone back to looking incredibly nervous and apologetically said, "Oh! I hope you don't mind the mess either, ladies." Her pale-yellow eyes expressed complete sincerity, as if not magically anticipating their unannounced visit was an unforgivable oversight.

"No ma'am, your home and garden are beautiful," Veda said, reaching out to shake Sylvia's hand. As large as Veda was, Sylvia's clawed hand still engulfed hers entirely. "My name is Veda and this is Gwen. Bumble told us you might be able to offer us some assistance with a problem we've got."

"I will certainly try!" she replied, nodding to Gwen and then turning to shuffle back inside. "Come, come. Let me clear this table and put some tea on."

The inside of the cottage was cluttered, but clean. Floor to ceiling bookshelves took up nearly every wall, completely jammed full of books, bottles filled with various ingredients for spell work, rocks, and knickknacks. Herbs hung drying in bushels from the ceiling. There were a few chairs in the living room, and each had multiple blankets and quilts hung across them. Gwen didn't know how long Bumble had known Sylvia, but it was no wonder she loved the woman. Tchotchke hoarders, the both of them.

Sylvia pulled open a drawer and grabbed a knife. "Luckily, I made a loaf of bread just this morning and I have some homemade strawberry jam to go with it."

"You don't have to feed us, ma'am," Gwen said as softly as she could. Sylvia seemed easy to spook and Gwen didn't want to scare her into stabbing herself while she cut the bread. "I'm sorry we showed up on your doorstep with no notice, these two just got overly excited."

"Oh, it's not a problem! What kind of hostess would I be if I left you hungry and thirsty?" When she was done with the bread, Sylvia opened a cabinet and pulled out an almost comically large jar of jam. It fit perfectly in her hand. She set it and the bread on the table before gathering mugs and the now-screaming kettle. Bumble didn't hesitate to start prying the lid off the jam, even though it was nearly too large for her to get her hands around. Veda reached over and held the jar steady for her as she did her best to wrest the lid free.

Sylvia set a steaming cup of tea in front of each of them. "This is my own brew, a lemon basil that will hopefully bring you protection and peace on your journey." Settling down in her chair, she looked Gwen in the eye and said, "Tell me about it."

Gwen stared at her, taken aback. "Who said anything about a 'journey'? Also, how do you know it's me that needs help? Maybe I'm just along for the ride."

"Your aura is very heavy currently," Sylvia smiled apologetically. "And no one packs bags like that for a day trip to see a friend."

Bumble pointedly tapped the center of her forehead with one clawed finger.

Gwen looked down, away from both of them. "What if my aura is always heavy?" she asked cantankerously.

"Oh, it is," Sylvia stated simply.

"You just met me!" Gwen snapped, her eyes meeting Sylvia's again. Sylvia looked nothing but kind, patiently waiting out the little tantrum. "I'm sorry," Gwen finally said, embarrassed.

"That's okay, dear. I'm sure Bumble can attest to my trustworthiness," Sylvia said, passing Bumble a cloth to wipe the jam off her beak with. Bumble crowed her agreement, dutifully cleaning her face.

"I guess," Gwen said, staring down at the nicks and scuffs in the table. She chewed on her cheek for a minute before finally sighing and saying, "Apparently Veda thinks we should hunt down the men who killed my parents."

"Tell me more about that."

Gwen hesitated, so Veda placed her hand on Gwen's, "You told me your story because you knew in your heart that I could be trusted. Fate brought me to you to help you. Now it's brought us to Sylvia. Bumble trusts her, and you trust Bumble."

Gwen felt her cheeks warming up again and she pulled her hand away, pretending to scratch her chin. "I suppose you're right."

She stumbled over her indecision a moment longer before saying, "They were killed by a group of Brotherhood members. They came across my parents traveling in the Tall Pines Forest and took the opportunity to murder them. I once spoke with one of the Ironforge guards that recovered the bodies and it wasn't pretty. The men responsible were never tried because they paid off the local government. And because it was only two random fyrdiav from another city, it was easily swept under the rug."

"Do you know the names of the men that did it?" Sylvia asked gently.

"Yeah, that's another thing I got from the guard."

Veda gave her a look, her eyebrows raised as if to say, "did you now?"

Gwen glared at her, "I just wanted to know who to avoid."

"I think part of you always wanted the justice the city didn't give you. We can help you achieve that if you let us."

Gwen clenched her jaw. "I'm already here, aren't I? That's a step."

Veda smiled broadly at her.

Sylvia set her cup down and waited until Gwen looked at her again. "I am talking to you and only you here—and it's important that you be fully honest with me—do *you* want to do this? Is this something your heart seeks?" She asked the question with no sense of judgement, no pressure. "Because if you do, I will help you. It sounds like these two are also committed to helping you. I have resources I am willing to expend to assist you. But none of that matters if you don't want this."

Gwen chewed on her lip. If she was honest with herself—and Sylvia—she did. Part of her had always wondered if at least a little bit of the hole inside her could be filled with the knowledge that the people who killed her parents could never harm another living being. She knew there was never going to be any justice for her parents unless she was the one that doled it out. She looked up and met Sylvia's eyes. She gave in. "I do."

Sylvia nodded. "Okay. Can you give me their names?" She reached behind herself, grabbing a small notebook and a pen from a drawer.

"Sure." Gwen rattled the names off as Sylvia wrote them down. "Regan Cole, Vito Cady, Ian Fletcher, and Zachariah Ross."

"No wonder they were so successful in paying the city off," Sylvia mused. "Zachariah Ross is one of the most influential men in The Brotherhood of Truth. Kind of the face of the organization, in a lot of ways. Very charismatic. He's personally responsible for a lot of their recruiting and has enough money to get him just about anywhere."

"How do you know?" Gwen asked.

"I know a little about a lot of things, really. When you live alone in the woods, you have quite a bit of time to yourself. I try to keep an eye on The Brotherhood of Truth in particular, though, because they've been trying to buy up my land for ages."

"Well, that's lucky for us then," Veda said. "I can see why Bumble brought us to you."

Bumble proudly puffed up her chest feathers.

"If you wouldn't mind, I'd like to tag along on your trip, for a while at least. I think it could be really helpful for my information gathering. Also, if I know as much as I think I do about The Brotherhood, we're going to need a few extra hands and I have some friends who could help us out. One is an excellent thief, like our Bumble here, and the other three are serious muscle."

"That's...a lot of people," Gwen said, trying and failing not to show how uncomfortable she was. "Do you really think we're going to need more muscle? Veda, Bumble, and I took out six men by ourselves like a week ago." She could feel the tip of her tail whipping back and forth, so she wrapped it around the leg of the chair to get it to stop.

"The Brotherhood is a well established organization. They have no shortage of minions willing to murder and pillage for them. It certainly wouldn't hurt us to have a few more people to help out," Sylvia replied.

"Or get themselves killed," Gwen grumbled.

Veda punched her in the arm for her rudeness and said, "That sounds wonderful, Sylvia."

Bumble chirped her agreement.

"You two will be the death of me," Gwen grouched, grimacing and rubbing her now sore arm.

"Where do we start?" Veda asked cheerfully.

"Well, I do believe we can start in Silverglenn. Last I knew, Avery and Jasper were over there and that's only a day's travel from Ironforge by train. We can leave in the morning. I'll send a message for Myev and Boris to meet us there," she said, now talking more to herself than them while rummaging around in another drawer.

She pulled out a small, dark purple satchel tied with a leather strap, then held it to her throat and said, "May this message reach you safely and quickly." She waited a moment, until the three beads on the satchel's tie began to glow (two purple and one blue). "Myev, Boris, I have a job for you, if you're free. Please meet me in Silverglenn as soon as possible. Take care of yourselves." She pulled the satchel away from her neck and the beads stopped glowing.

"You don't use the carrier sparrows?" Gwen asked.

"No, the sparrows aren't safe. None of the carrier birds are; The Brotherhood regularly intercepts them. They'd deny it, but they can get ahold of any message they want in any region of Peonia. Many messages do not get to who they were meant for," she said. "This is also quicker, basically instantaneous."

"Well, isn't that a handy work around!" Veda said, clearly impressed.

"It's a simple spell of mine," Sylvia looked down and laughed awkwardly, a nervous little chitter. She turned back to the drawer suddenly. "I should give each of you one in case we get separated!" She pulled out three identical bags and handed them over. Pinned to each was a set of directions written in a delicate, loopy script.

"*1. Place the satchel to your throat and imagine the receiver of your message clearly in your mind.*

2. Speak the words, 'May this message reach you safely and quickly.' If the satchel's beads are glowing, you will know it's working!

3. Speak your message. When you are done, pull the satchel away from your throat. The beads stop glowing.

4. The beads will also glow when you have a message waiting. To receive the message, simply untie the satchel.

5. The satchel may be recharged after a few uses by being left out overnight in direct moonlight."

Veda grinned, immediately pressing it to her neck and closing her eyes tightly. She said the spell before adding, "Thank you, Sylvia. You are a marvelous woman." She pulled the satchel away, popping her eyes open and looking to Sylvia.

Sylvia's satchel beads began to glow and she opened it. Veda's voice came out, as clear as when she first spoke the words.

"Well!" Sylvia then said, putting the satchel on the counter and clapping her hands once. "I'll go pack!"

As she left the room, Gwen threw Veda a dirty look and then turned her ire on Bumble. "This has gone too far now that others are involved. You're supposed to be on my side, you feathery traitor!"

Bumble only laughed and stuffed another jam coated piece of bread into her beak.

Chapter Four

Silverglenn was a town that put Ironforge to shame. Nestled next to the Argent Mountain Range and surrounded by trees, Silverglenn was as beautiful as its name. While Ironforge was an industrial city run by greedy rich men, filled to the brim with poor families and dirty vagabonds looking for work, Silverglenn was a proud intellectual community, incredibly wealthy by Ironforge standards. Known for their expansive libraries and universities specializing in spell work, the people of Silverglenn looked like they actually wanted to live there, rather than having nowhere else to go.

In other words, Gwen felt as though she stuck out like a sore thumb. With her dirty clothes, generally stand-offish demeanor, and sword strapped to her side, she looked entirely out of place among the clean-cut, chipper townsfolk. Their group looked rougher and scarier than the people of Silverglenn were used to seeing. While most just ignored them, Gwen still caught the mothers that hurried their children along when they walked by, the bespectacled men that refused to make eye contact, the people that looked over and then quickly looked away. Gwen tucked her battle worn tail closer to her body and tried to hide herself behind Veda, who seemed to be completely oblivious to how out of place they were. She waved at the children who stared at her, who smiled back before their mothers noticed and pulled them away.

Sylvia had sent a message to her friends to meet them at a little bookshop, which the sign out front dubbed Brambles. When they entered the shop, a little bell above the door tinkled to announce their presence.

"Oh, hello," a deep, feminine voice said. Gwen looked up to see a naga, her tail curled around the bottom edge of the counter at which she stood. Her brick-red scales and brown skin complemented her well-tailored navy-blue skirt and white blouse. Her hair, a few shades darker than her skin, was pulled back into a tight bun. "It's always so nice to see you, Sylvia," she smiled, shaking Sylvia's large hand with both of hers. "What brings you to Brambles today? Looking for anything in particular?"

"No, thank you, Astrid. I'm meeting with Avery and Jasper, but you know I couldn't turn down a chance to visit my favorite bookstore," Sylvia smiled back.

Astrid's pleasant demeanor darkened a little, "Oh, Jasper, that sticky fingered bastard. Though I have to say, Avery certainly does him good. Keeping him in line and such. If she hadn't married him, I probably would have strangled him by now."

"She certainly does," Sylvia agreed. "Have they already arrived?"

"They're in the back," Astrid gestured towards a doorway at the south end of the shop.

Sylvia pulled a large jar from the bag at her side. "Thanks, love. I brought you some of your favorite tea."

"You're a godsend, I was beginning to run low," Astrid said, her eyes lighting back up. She looked at the others, "If you haven't had this woman's tea, it's the best in Peonia, I swear!"

They followed Sylvia through the cozy shop until they came upon a room with a few desks and chairs in it, every surface stacked high with books. Behind one pile sat a doppelganger woman and a human man.

Most doppelgangers shifted to look human when they were in public, but this one was clearly comfortable in her own skin. She was petite and incredibly pale, almost translucent—a natural trait for doppelgangers. There was almost no color to any part of her body other than her icy blue eyes. Long, straight white hair fell over one shoulder, looking shiny and silky even in the dim light of the shop's back room. The simple canvas shirt and skirt she wore were well taken care of and her posture impeccable. Around her waist she'd tied a beautiful blue and gold sash, which was the only part of her outfit that appeared decorative rather than strictly functional. She was watching the male and smiled lovingly at him as he slumped over a book, animatedly telling her all about it.

He was thin, like her, but must have been nearly a foot taller when standing. His clothes looked about as well tended as Gwen and Bumble's, a stark contrast to his wife. His seafoam green hair fell in a disheveled mess over slate grey eyes, probably not helped along by the old, abused flat-top hat sitting on the table next to him. Its wide brim drooped in many places from years of tough love. His tunic fared little better and had clearly seen many years of hard use. It had probably started out white, but was more of a dingy grey now. The deep "v" of its neckline was spread wide—the ties that would have held it together had probably been lost many moons prior—and revealed a pale chest mottled with very old scars. It was not just his clothing and skin that had seen better days—the crooked bridge of his nose had clearly been broken before. Probably several times.

"You must have found something interesting," Sylvia said and Avery and Jasper both looked up.

"Hello, old friend!" Jasper said, standing up and throwing his arms around Sylvia.

"Hello," Avery said, her voice quiet but strong. She looked behind Sylvia, at the rest of them. "You must be our 'job'." Her face closed off almost imperceptibly and her smile tightened. Her shrewd eyes looked each of them over in turn. Gwen could tell Avery was uncomfortable around strangers, a feeling she knew well.

Jasper seemed outwardly more comfortable, smiling widely at them, but Gwen could see the tenseness in his body language. Gwen sensed that it was not that either of them distrusted their group personally, but that they were used to having to look out for each other. Strangers were dangerous until proven otherwise.

Jasper stepped back, placing his arm around Avery's shoulders. "So, what can we do for you, Sylvia?"

"Well, Gwen here is looking to take down some Brotherhood higherups," she said, motioning before taking a seat.

Gwen stood awkwardly, trying not to squirm as all eyes landed on her. Unconsciously, she wrapped her arms around her torso. Veda placed her hand between Gwen's shoulder blades in support.

Finally she cleared her throat and took a sharp breath. "I have been convinced by my friends to seek revenge on The Brotherhood members that killed my parents."

"Which members?" Avery asked.

"Regan Cole, Vito Cady, Ian Fletcher, and Zachariah Ross," Gwen said, a little emboldened by Avery's all-business tone.

"Zachariah Ross is a very powerful man," she replied. She didn't appear to be cowed by the mention of him, she was simply stating a fact. "He would be difficult to get to."

"I am aware," Gwen said, sitting down next to Sylvia.

"Nothing is impossible though," Jasper said. "What would we gain, were we to help you?"

"A favor from me, anything you'd like," Sylvia said. "You know how valuable that can be."

Gwen felt shame bubbling in her belly at the fact that she had nothing to offer.

"I would also be in your debt, were you to help my friend," Veda said, coming up behind Gwen and placing her hands on the back of her chair. "I am the princess of Vulcaria; my favors can also be quite valuable."

Jasper raised an eyebrow, whistling. "That country has books that are damn near impossible to get over here."

"You are correct," Veda agreed. "If it's books you want, books you shall receive."

"And can have hat back," Bumble said, sliding up next to Gwen with Jasper's hat on her head. No one had even noticed her taking it from directly beside him.

Jasper began to laugh. Even Avery cracked a smile. "Well done, little one. Not many are sneakier than I."

"I, uh, wish I had something to offer, but I'm just a street rat from Ironforge," Gwen mumbled, grimacing. "But if I have anything you want, it's yours."

Jasper looked at Avery, shrugged, and then turned back to Gwen. "We're in."

"Really?" Gwen asked, surprised. "That's it? You're willing to help take down one of the most powerful men in Peonia, as well as several other people from the same highly influential organization, for ambiguous favors and some books?"

"You underestimate my husband's love of books," Avery said, looking over at him fondly.

"Plus, I sure would like my hat back," he said, grinning at Bumble. She chirped happily, handing it back to him.

"It's a deal then," Veda said, holding her hand out. Jasper shook it firmly.

Avery held her hand out to Gwen, "So it is."

Gwen took it. "So it is," she replied, still somewhat incredulous.

"When do we leave?" Avery asked.

"Hopefully tomorrow," Sylvia answered. "We're about to head to The Serpent, where we'll meet with Myev and Boris. Luckily, they were close by and said they should be in town by tonight. After that, we need to come up with a plan."

"We'll clean up here and join you then," Avery said, beginning to gather their books. Jasper caught her hand as they reached for the same one and pulled it to his mouth, pressing his lips to her knuckles. Gwen turned her eyes away, feeling embarrassed and voyeuristic.

Once they were done and several books paid for, the group took their leave, heading towards The Silver Serpent Inn and Tavern. The town had cleared quite a bit as the sun began to set and everyone returned to their homes. They weaved their way through the winding streets with Sylvia in the lead.

Ahead of them, a group of three caught Gwen's eye. Two human men stood in front of an elven woman, who they had cornered against a closed storefront. One man held the woman firmly by the elbow as she clutched the necklace laying against her collarbone with her other hand. The woman was clearly uncomfortable and she tried to pull her arm free, but the man yanked her back. Veda started moving towards them, but Gwen was already stalking over, her strides long and purposeful.

"Please, it was a gift from my mother," the elven woman said, a tremble in her voice. Her pointed ears were laid back and her eyes were wide with fear.

"Well, if you don't want to part with it, we could come to another agreement," the man said, his voice filled with a slimy kind of confidence that made Gwen's skin crawl. "You're not bad for an elf."

The men ignored her approach entirely, apparently used to getting away with this sort of behavior. She reached the man holding the woman's elbow, lifted her foot, and kicked the side of his leg, hard. His knee buckled and he let go of the woman in his surprise, falling into his companion. They tumbled over each other, landing in a heap. The woman had stepped behind Gwen the second she was freed and Gwen heard Sylvia's soft voice telling her to go home.

The man who had been leading the gang of two was on his back, propped up on his elbows and in the process of getting up. His face was dark red with righteous rage and his mouth was open, words at the tip of his tongue. Gwen pressed her boot down into his groin, adding enough pressure to make her threat clear. He stopped trying to get up, his eyes flicking to hers, then to the group behind her. He closed his mouth tightly before anything that would further upset her could escape, as he was smart enough to know he was outnumbered. His sidekick scrambled to his feet and took off, his loyalty running out.

"It would seem that you've never been taught any manners," Gwen said, pressing her foot down harder. A small squeak escaped his throat. In his fall, a necklace of his own had flopped up over his shoulder. Gwen unsheathed her sword, using it to pull the chain around so that she could see the pendant attached to it. It was the Lowean symbol, a roaring lion's head encapsulated in a circle.

"Think yourself a lion, do you?" she asked, pulling her sword back a few inches and letting the necklace drop. She then placed the point of it to his chest instead, leaning forward and pressing her foot even further into his groin. He ground his teeth, but did not otherwise respond. Another smart move. "Maybe you ought to go home and pray to your god, ask him how he feels about all this. You see, I'm inclined to think that, despite what you fucks might twist it into, a loving god, such as yours is said to be, wouldn't appreciate what you were trying to do to that girl."

She stared at him, enjoying the way he shook and averted his eyes. "Lucky for you, I'm feeling merciful tonight, because this one," she thumbed behind herself where she knew Bumble would be, "would happily carve your kneecaps out and take them home as a souvenir." They'd done this bit a dozen times before and Bumble played it well. Despite being unable to see her, Gwen knew that Bumble would be spinning daggers in her hands.

"I could just take one," Bumble said in Gwen's voice.

Gwen pretended to mull it over. "I suppose he could limp home with only one functional leg. But," she pressed down on his groin one last time, this time hard enough to elicit a yelp from the man, "as I said, I'm feeling merciful." She lifted her foot off him and withdrew her sword. "Get out of here."

He immediately leapt to his feet and took off in the same direction his partner had gone.

She sheathed her weapon and turned around. "Sorry for the interruption."

"Nothing to be sorry about," Avery said with a smile.

***

They had been at The Serpent for twenty minutes or so, chatting over a round of drinks, when the door popped open to reveal a very large orc woman, laughing loudly at something. Her hair was long and curly, white in color, and pulled back in a high ponytail. Multiple braids were twined through it, keeping it pulled in tight at the sides, with another long braid coming down from behind her ear and over her shoulder.

Despite the chill of the mountain town, she wore only a pair of very short red and black shorts and a matching shirt, cropped high on her strong stomach. Scars covered her powder blue skin, marring her left eye, chest, arms, and legs. Her sky-colored eyes settled on Sylvia, and she called out, throwing her thickly muscled arms in the air, "Long time no see, my beautiful scaley friend!"

Her companion stooped through the too-small doorway behind her. Myev was large, more thickly built than even Veda, but the male orc with skin the color of a sandstorm was unbelievably huge—both tall and wide, like a brick wall with legs. He wore a simple brown tunic and pants in a traditional Vedvik style, but they seemed almost ridiculous on him, like it didn't make any sense at all to clothe a force of nature like that. His tusks were larger than Myev's and the tip of the right one was broken off. There were scars over his jawbone and through one of his eyebrows, and short, sun-bleached black hair fell over his maroon eyes as he shuffled silently in behind his rambunctious wife. To a less observant person, he would seem terrifying, both capable of and willing to rip you apart. Gwen, however, could see his eyes darting back and forth, making him appear somewhat nervous as he kept a close eye on Myev. He was formidable, but there was a softness in him.

While Myev pulled Sylvia into a tight hug, Gwen held her hand out to him. She felt a little braver now that she had a few drinks in her. "Boris, I assume? I'm Gwen," she said, attempting to convey that they were no threat to him or his wife.

His tan hand completely engulfed hers. "Yes," he said, simply.

Not sure what to do with the non-response, Gwen turned to Myev, who had hugged her way through Avery and Jasper as well. She currently had her arms wrapped around Veda, who seemed both surprised and delighted by the woman's brazenness. "I'm Gwen."

Myev took Gwen's hand and used it to pull her into a bone-crushing embrace. "Good to meet you! Any friend of Sylvia's is a friend of ours."

"Thanks," Gwen said, trying to untangle herself from Myev's hug. "We are excited to meet you as well. This is Bumble," she said, gesturing. Bumble was doing her part to stay well out of hugging range, but lifted a hand to say hello. "I hope you had smooth travels."

"Aye," Boris said.

"I suppose if you two want to take a seat, we could talk about what the job is and if you want to take it," Sylvia said, settling back into her chair.

"No need," Myev said, pulling out Boris' chair before grabbing her own. "Anything you need, we are always there for. Plus, we've been bored," she smiled, putting her arm around her husband's considerable waist and shaking him. "We'd love an opportunity to get into some deep shit, which is usually why you call us."

Boris blushed and smiled at his wife, placing his arm over her shoulder.

"Well, okay," Sylvia said. "We can tell you the details as we go then."

"Sounds like we owe you two a drink then," Veda grinned, flagging down the bartender.

The bartender was a tall elf with bright green eyes that had lit up when Veda walked into the bar earlier. When she saw Veda's arm up, her red lips had curled up on one side, almost predatory. She threw her long white and blue hair over one shoulder and sauntered over. "What can I get you, hun?"

Veda smiled brightly, placing her hand on the bartender's arm. "Another round please, my friends have some catching up to do."

"No problem," the elf said, making purposeful eye contact and smiling back. "What's your name, sweetheart?"

"Veda Aalish," she responded with a grin. "You?"

"Naiavara Aloro." Naiavara grinned in that feline way again. "I'll be right back with those, Veda." She turned and walked back to the bar in a way that suggested she was aware that Veda would be watching her the whole time.

Gwen looked into her drink, uncomfortable with the burning in her chest and the upset in her stomach. She swigged what was left in her stein and licked her teeth, awkwardly looking at anything but Veda. She wasn't sure how to take how openly Naiavara had been hitting on Veda. Perhaps it wasn't obvious to everyone, but to her it was as if Naiavara had openly propositioned Veda in front of the whole bar. She was both surprised and jealous of Naiavara's confidence. Homosexuality wasn't approved of in Peonia, at least not in the places where The Brotherhood was the most ubiquitous, though she had to admit that she wasn't the type to be particularly familiar with the culture of Silverglenn.

Gwen tried and failed to push away a childhood memory and the almost visceral pain it still brought up. She'd known she was into women almost all her life, and with no parents to guide her, she'd been unaware of the taboo nature of her attraction to a girl she'd met when she was twelve. She was out of Lion's Grace Orphan Home by then, surviving on working for what she could and stealing what she couldn't. Even so, she still visited the orphanage regularly, especially when she was desperate for a warm place to stay.

There'd been a worker at Lion's Grace, a middle-aged gnome with olive skin and soft brown eyes named Echo. She had taken a liking to Gwen during her time there and hadn't approved of the Headmistress' decision to send Gwen out on her own after she'd gotten into one too many fights with the other kids. Echo could always be relied upon to sneak Gwen back in and give her a bed for the night. It was on one of those nights that Gwen had met Willow.

Willow had been new to Lion's Grace, had only been there a couple of months, when Gwen showed back up. Willow was a human girl, her skin tanned and freckled from all the time she'd spent outside on her parents' farm before they'd died. Her arms and legs were strong from the work and she had no problem using them to show the would-be bullies at the orphanage exactly what she thought. The first time Gwen saw her, Willow had been whooping a group of three other kids all by herself, her knuckles and lips split and bloody. Gwen thought that it had been love at first sight.

She came back to Lion's Grace more often after that to visit Willow, which simultaneously pleased and exasperated Echo. "You know how much trouble I can get into, letting you in here," she'd tell Gwen, yet still she'd wrap her arms around the girl, hugging her tightly before hurrying her inside. Echo always had Gwen stay in her room with her, as it was the safest place to hide her. One night, a few months into having met Willow, Gwen lay on a cot in Echo's room, staring into the dark because she couldn't make herself sleep. Her chest was tight and her stomach unruly as she thought about Willow; the long blonde hair that she always kept pulled back out of her face, her warm, amber-colored eyes, the way she would chew on her lips when she was trying to solve a problem.

When Echo finally stirred at the first rays of light through the dingy window of her room, Gwen felt brave enough to ask her about her crush on Willow. Echo had looked panicked as she took Gwen's hands in hers and urged her in frenzied whispers to let the feelings go. "You already have so much working against you in this world, sweet girl," she'd told Gwen, her eyes pleading and her fingers moving to caress the delicate, silver lion's head necklace at her throat as if it could protect them both. "They'll kill you for that you know. Some people just disappear for feelings like that and no one ever knows what happened to them."

Gwen, never one to take no for an answer, mulled over Echo's words for a few days before deciding she didn't care. She'd found Willow outside alone and as they chatted, she gave in to the urge to kiss her. Just a quick, dry peck on the lips. Willow responded by punching Gwen in the jaw.

"What the fuck is wrong with you?" she'd screamed at Gwen, who sat on the ground holding her sore mouth with her shocked eyes locked on Willow's red, enraged face. "Why would you do that?" she yelled as a kick connected to Gwen's ribs.

Willow had kicked Gwen a few more times before finally scoffing and walking away. Gwen could have defended herself, but she didn't. She simply laid there and took the beating, Echo's words repeating in her head. *They'll kill you for that you know. They'll kill you for that.* Each kick pressed the lesson further into her bones. She hadn't ever returned to Lion's Grace after that, her shame a burning in her blood. She'd never seen Echo again, either.

Gwen had only needed to learn that lesson one more time, when she was nineteen, and she almost hadn't survived lesson two. She hadn't even kissed the woman in the shitty Ironforge dive bar—she'd just been brave and stupid and drunk enough to make her interest clear. As she laid bruised and broken in the rain-wet alley behind the bar, after the men the woman had sent after her left, after their cackles had faded, she stared at the brick wall in front of her and let Echo's warning run through her head over and over again, until it had infiltrated every bit of her foolish brain. *They'll kill you for that.*

She laid there for what felt like a century, her blood mingling with the puddles of water and spirits knew what else beneath her, before she realized death wasn't actually coming for her today and pulled herself up to limp home and lick her wounds.

Gwen shook her head, realizing she'd been staring into her empty stein while the world went on without her attention. Sylvia had been making small talk with Myev and Boris about their travels and Jasper had joined in, matching Myev's high energy easily. Gwen could feel Avery's keen eyes on her and she pointedly refused to look back.

When Naiavara returned and set the drinks down, she lingered on Veda, running her fingertips across Veda's hand where it lay on the table. Veda leaned back in her chair, body language open and inviting.

Gwen lifted her new drink to her lips, downing the entire thing and setting it back down. She mumbled something about needing air before she all but ran out the door.

She turned into the alley, walking a few yards into it before sliding down the cold stone wall to the ground. "What the *fuck* is wrong with me," she whispered angrily. She picked up a smooth rock and flung it down the alley as hard as she could, listening to it make contact with something and then clatter away.

A few minutes later she felt someone sit next to her and turned her head to see Avery. Gwen looked forward again, saying nothing. Avery allowed Gwen to pout for a few moments longer before sighing. "If you like her, you should tell her."

"What are you talking about?" Gwen tried to deflect.

Avery looked at her, one eyebrow raised, and did not speak.

"I just met her! I just met *you*!" Gwen whispered angrily, trying not to draw the attention of the loud group of men leaving the tavern. "And you know it's not *allowed*," she hissed when they were far enough out of earshot.

"Who cares?" Avery said in that pragmatic way she had. "You're intending to take revenge on some very powerful men here soon and I feel like that's considerably more likely to get you killed."

Gwen rubbed her face roughly in response.

"I never loved someone until I met Jasper," Avery finally said, her voice quiet and steady. The sudden personal admission surprised Gwen and she dropped her hands. She was looking at the wall across from them with a softness in her eyes. "The first time I saw Jasper, I was watching him have his ass handed to him. He'd stolen a book from a shop and had these four thick farm boys chasing him through the town square. Jasper was skin and bones, malnourished. I doubted he could evade them for long and I was right. The whole lot of them had barely run past the bench I was sitting on when they finally took him down. All four of them just beating the crap out of this scrawny man when one of them probably could have done the job on their own. Jasper was scrappy as hell, no doubt about that, but he clearly hadn't had a solid meal in weeks.

"Now, at that time, I was generally not one to get involved in a whole lot that didn't directly affect me, but I also wasn't interested in watching four healthy working boys beat on one sickly man, even if he was a thief. Those boys didn't so much as glance my way as I approached—obviously didn't think I was a threat. I ripped those assholes off Jasper, taught them a thing or two about a fair fight, and was on my way.

"Later that night, I was headed towards the inn where I was staying when I heard a rustle behind me. I figured it was those damn boys, back to prove that they weren't going to let a girl get the best of them. I continued on as though I hadn't heard them; figured I'd let them think they got the drop on me and then surprise them with another lesson on manners," she smiled a little, finally glancing over at Gwen before looking back at the wall.

"When I felt the hand on my shoulder, I didn't hesitate to flip the person attached to it on their back and slam them to the ground. I don't usually hide the fact that I'm a doppelganger anymore, even though people don't always take kindly to me, but back then I tried to keep a low profile. I always made sure I looked like a typical, nondescript girl from wherever I was at the time. So, I slammed the person behind me on the ground and started switching to this face, my real face, thinking I'd give that stupid farm boy a real scare and a good story to tell. Instead, I was looking directly at Jasper.

"There wasn't an ounce of fear in that ridiculous man's face as I crouched over him with my fist in his shirt and my knee on his gut. We'd been staring at each other long enough that I'd finished changing and he was smiling up at me, this dumbstruck look in his eyes, and said, 'Hello there.'" She laughed, "Just like that. That boy didn't question a thing; he was instantly in love. He tells people that that was the exact moment he knew he was going to marry me." Avery stopped for a moment, but Gwen didn't interrupt her story.

"Jasper followed me around for weeks, constantly attempting to impress me and convince me to fall in love with him. I continuously assured him that it wasn't going to happen. I was a travelling doppelganger just trying to survive and I didn't need the extra baggage. But Jasper was persistent, and I had a soft spot for him, so—against my better judgement—I allowed him to follow me from town to town. He'd steal interesting books and read them to me each night over the dinner I bought for him. Night after night he would tirelessly ramble at me about things he'd read or tell me stories about the things he'd seen in his life as a thief. He'd steal books and papers for me. I, in turn, kept him sheltered and fed.

"One night, during dinner, I looked at him and I gave in. I felt the release like something physical in my chest. Just. Letting go. Allowing the truth to be. I reached out and grabbed one of his hands, mid-story. He stopped dead in his tracks. 'You win,' I told him. I was used to spending time alone and I enjoyed it, but he made me want to never be alone again. I wanted to be with him instead." She said it like it was the simplest thing in the world.

"I wanted to go wherever he went, do whatever he did. No one else could convince me to do ridiculous, dangerous things like he could." She turned to look Gwen directly in the eyes. It was clear to her that Avery had read her like a book. "I hadn't known Jasper all that long when I agreed to be with him, but we have been together for over twenty years now. I haven't regretted a single second."

"Twenty years?" Gwen blurted, shocked. Avery and Jasper both looked fairly young.

She nodded. "Doppelgangers don't have to show our age and he wears his well. I'm telling you this story for two reasons," she looked away again. "The first reason is that I want you to know that Veda looks at you like Jasper looked at me." Gwen's heart stopped and she could feel her stomach flip, but Avery continued, as if she hadn't just said something absolutely world shaking. "This life is uncertain and what we are about to do is dangerous. You haven't known each other for long, and you're clearly used to being alone, but some people are worth interrupting our solitude for. Even if we lose them eventually. Sometimes, the joy we can feel with someone now is worth the risk of the pain we will eventually feel when they're gone. Even if it's 'not allowed'."

Avery turned, making sure that Gwen was looking at her when she said, "The second reason I told you this story is to make it clear that Jasper is everything to me. I will do anything to protect him. I will do everything I can to serve your mission and help keep you safe, but if it comes between protecting any of you and protecting Jasper, I will choose Jasper."

"And I would want you to," Gwen said honestly. "I don't want anyone getting hurt over this. It's not worth that. I'm not worth that."

"You are worth it, but I am selfish," Avery said. She wasn't flattering Gwen; she wasn't the kind of woman to do that. She was simply stating what she saw as a fact. "Your mission is noble and you deserve justice. My parents were also murdered for looking different. Jasper helped me to do what you're trying to do now, and that's why we've agreed to join you."

"I didn't know that," Gwen said softly.

Avery nodded. "Killing my parents' murderers didn't bring them back. It didn't even lessen the pain I feel, but it righted the balance of the universe some. Maybe saved someone else in the future. It proved that you cannot do something horrible to innocent people without consequences. I want to help you right your part of the universe, but if Jasper is in danger, he will be my priority."

"I wouldn't trust you if he wasn't. I'm not a leader. I don't want people on this 'team' who are going to blindly follow me. I need people who are going to make smart choices to keep themselves safe and I won't be offended if you bail ship because it gets too dangerous."

Avery nodded slowly. "You're right about some things, but I think this journey is going to teach you a lot about yourself." She stood up, brushing off her skirt. "See you inside." With that, she walked away, leaving Gwen to wonder what that meant.

***

When Gwen went back inside, Myev and Veda had just finished another pint each, slamming them down on the table and hollering. Multiple other steins were littered around them, a drinking contest clearly underway. Veda's hair glowed warmly, brighter than the dim lighting offered by the flickering wall sconces. Her eyes were half lidded in her drunkenness, her smile easy. Myev pulled her under her arm, laughing.

Myev then let her go, grabbing Boris by the hands and dragging him out to the open floor to dance. Boris smiled affectionately down at her and held her hand high above her head so that she could spin as the band's saxophone player let out a series of upbeat notes. The dwarf woman who was singing smiled out at them.

Gwen looked back to see Naiavara now leaning against their table, her hands pressed into the wood behind her. Veda stood closely to her, gesturing as she spoke, grinning and drunk-happy. Gwen felt that pull in her chest again and thought of Avery's story. Veda turned when she heard Gwen walking up, her grin growing impossibly larger.

"Gwen!" she yelled, throwing her hands out to her sides. "Are you feeling better? Avery said you weren't feeling well."

"Yeah, I feel all right now," Gwen replied, unsure of what to say now that she was there.

Veda held one hand out to her. "Dance?"

Gwen's breath caught and she glanced around the bar. No one was watching them, entirely involved their own conversations. On the dancefloor, her eyes snagged on a pair of men dancing playfully next to Myev and Boris. Fear climbed up her throat and her heart felt like it was going to leap from her chest, but Gwen pushed them both back down and nodded. Maybe she'd never learned her lesson after all.

Veda took her hand and pulled her along, laughing. Gwen caught Naiavara's smile and nod out of the corner of her eye. She made eye contact and Naiavara winked, as if to say, "I understand." Gwen smiled back in thanks and Naiavara lifted off the table, heading back to the bar.

When they got to the floor, Veda grabbed Gwen's arms and threw them around her neck, wrapping her own around Gwen's waist and pulling her in close. Her hands burned into Gwen's skin, warming the chill she'd carried in from outside. Gwen wasn't sure if she was happy or wanted to throw up or both, but she laughed brokenly as Veda released her to swing her out by her arm and then pull her back in. She then pressed them together and Gwen backed up a bit, scared, but Veda kept her grip. She took a deep breath and settled as they swayed back and forth to the rhythm, Veda leading the way.

The band let the song fade before starting up a slower melody, and the dwarf singer began to croon a low, sad tune about the love she left behind. Veda slid a hand from Gwen's waist to her shoulder blades, pulling her closer and nestling her head against Gwen's neck. Gwen could feel her smile.

"Myev may have convinced me to drink a bit too much," she said softly.

"Perhaps," Gwen agreed, smiling despite herself.

Veda was quiet for a few moments, taking in the song. Then, "I'm glad I met you."

Gwen didn't trust herself to speak, so she laid her head against Veda's in agreement and hoped that no one was watching.

Chapter Five

Ian Fletcher and Vito Cady were the only people on Gwen's list that they knew the location of, and that was only thanks to Sylvia's previously gathered information. They were also the least powerful, so Gwen kind of hoped their murders wouldn't draw too much attention, allowing them to move more easily onto the others before they were inevitably stopped.

Both men lived in Mooncrest, a small seaside town that they used the organization's influence to abuse. Despite their lack of importance to the country at large, Vito and Ian were well protected in Mooncrest as the city's co-mayors. On top of that, the human citizens of the town were known far and wide to be religious zealots, entirely dedicated to The Brotherhood and its cause.

The town got its name from its cliffsides, which were brimming with moonstone. The soft stone regularly broke off in the water as the ocean's waves hit the bluffs, causing the town to have a sort of luminous, magical quality to it. That and the warm coastal weather made it a popular tourist destination. The people of Mooncrest were used to smiling and greeting non-human folks through clenched teeth in the name of tourism money, but Sylvia had figured their group of misfits would garner a lot of unwanted attention, especially with the kinds of questions they'd be asking. As such, on the train ride over, Sylvia had given everyone but Jasper and Avery an illusion spell in the form of another one of her satchels. The spell components were contained in a black pouch and the onyx and tourmaline stones attached to the ties clinked as she passed them out.

"You sure have a lot of stuff in that little thing," Gwen noted, eyeing the bag Sylvia had been toting and from which she'd pulled the satchels.

"It's enchanted—bigger on the inside. Can't be too prepared," she said, waving a clawed hand at her absentmindedly. She then scratched her chin and neck, worried. She glanced at Avery, who had already shifted to appear human. "Girls, I'm going to need you to make your-selves look like Avery." The plan was for Bumble to act as Gwen's child and Veda as her husband. They would tell anyone that asked that they were on a family vacation with Gwen's sisters, Myev and Avery, and their husbands. Sylvia would be their grandmother. They were going to have to sell the story long enough to figure out where Ian and Vito were, kill them, and skip town.

"You need to keep this satchel on you at all times," Sylvia continued, looking at each of her associates very seriously. Gwen would've sworn she could see Sylvia's mind running a million miles per hour in that moment, her nervous eyes darting around between them. "Decide what you want to look like and focus on it hard before you press the satchel to your third eye. I've included wormwood and mugwort to enhance your natural abilities, but you need to be sure of what you want to look like when you use the spell or it will not work very well.

If you lose the satchels for even a second, the illusion will drop. If you do lose it, spirits forbid, you can recast the spell once you retrieve the satchel."

Gwen looked carefully at Avery's altered form, imagining what her sister may look like. Avery had given herself sun-kissed tan skin and black hair so that she would fit in well with the general population of Mooncrest. Her small nose remained distinctly Avery, sloping up slightly at the end. Gwen pressed her hand to her own nose, long and straight with a sharply angled bridge. She tried to think hard about Avery's nose, her pointy chin, her changed hair and skin, the dark eyes she'd given herself.

Gwen decided she'd keep her own full lips and that she'd remain taller than Avery, as Sylvia had said it would be easier to sell the illusion if it was as close to their real bodies as possible. Gwen sat with the image for a moment longer, studying it carefully in her mind's eye, before pressing the satchel to her forehead.

When she opened her eyes, she glanced over at Veda. Veda now appeared to be a tall man with dirty blonde hair and eyes the color of mahogany. Her illusion body was still as well muscled as her real one, but her chest and shoulders were broader and squarer. Though the fire of her hair was masked by the illusion, Gwen could still feel warmth coming off her. Veda looked at Gwen and gave her a big smile. She awkwardly gave a thumbs up back.

Gwen felt a poke at her side and looked down to see a child's hand reaching out for her instead of Bumble's familiar talons and she jumped a little. "Mother, candy?" Bumble said in the voices of two separate little girls. She had short, dark hair, tan skin, and a smattering of freckles across her nose. She still looked as mischievous as the day was long, an innate energy that no disguise could take away from her, as she gave Gwen a crooked grin.

"It's probably best you don't talk much, creepy little bird," she joked, ruffling Bumble's head feathers even though she could no longer see them. She thought that as long as no one touched any of them and noticed the myriad of features the disguise made invisible—her tail and horns, Bumble's feathers and beak, Veda's fire—they would be fine. Probably.

Bumble cackled back at her and ran to Sylvia, who was now a hunched over old human woman with a long silver braid falling over one shoulder. She used her staff as a cane, leaning heavily on it to sell the illusion. Bumble wrapped her arms around Sylvia. "Mother mean!" she wailed, pretending to cry.

Sylvia huffed out a breath and smiled at her, endlessly patient. She then turned to Boris and Myev. Boris had made himself appear slightly smaller, though only so much could believably be done about that, and had given himself dark brown eyes under his still black hair. His telltale tusks were nowhere to be seen. Myev had done a good job of matching Avery; her nose was still broader and she was still taller than both Avery and Gwen, but her braided hair was now a warm brown that matched her eyes and the scars that littered her body were miraculously gone. Myev's lower teeth were also hidden, but she grinned at Sylvia with her illusory human ones.

Sylvia nodded, pleased with their work. "A fine bunch of fake humans," she said.

"Got me fooled!" Jasper confirmed.

***

They stepped off the train and started towards the center of the city, hoping to find leads as to where Vito and Ian actually lived. Sylvia's information confirmed they were in Mooncrest, but not their precise address. The part of the city where the train had dropped them off was clearly a business district, filled with shops overflowing with trinkets, markets, restaurants, and little art galleries. On the surface, everything looked colorful and warm. The delicious smells of baked goods and fried meat floated around them, mingling with the briny scent of the sea. Street performers stood on nearly every corner, singing beautiful songs and dancing with anyone that would make eye contact with them.

The group was able to weave through the throngs of people easily thanks to their disguises rendering them entirely anonymous, and they worked their way towards the inn where they would be staying for the night.

The human innkeeper accepted their cover story without question when he politely inquired what brought them to the area. "A family trip, how lovely!" the man said as he took Sylvia's money, his wrinkled hands shaking slightly with age. "I really do think it's so important for families to stick together. And there's so many of you! Truly wonderful. Not everyone understands the importance of family."

"Oh, absolutely," Sylvia said, trying to keep from upsetting the man while he slowly gathered her change.

"It's mostly us human folk that get it, if you know what I mean," the man said out of the corner of his mouth, as if he were trusting them with a secret.

"...oh?" Sylvia said, clearly uncomfortable. Gwen clenched her jaw and ground her teeth together. She felt Veda's fingers find hers and give her hand a firm squeeze. It was enough to momentarily distract her into loosening her muscles.

"Other races seem to just want to go off on their own. No wonder they turn to thievery and murder," he said, *tsk*ing. "Having a strong family support really helps you get off on the right foot in life!"

Syliva let out the fakest laugh Gwen had ever heard and took her change. "Well...thanks," she said, trying to smile.

Nearby, they heard ceramic crash to the ground and Gwen turned to see a vase that had once been on a shelf was now shattered on the floor beneath it. Bumble was standing far enough away to appear like she couldn't possibly have had anything to do with it, but Gwen knew her body language. "Oh no!" Bumble exclaimed, smacking her hand over her mouth. "What happen?"

The innkeeper let out a gasp of surprise and hurried over, "Goodness! It must have been too close to the edge. I am truly sorry for the shock, sweet girl," he said, honestly believing Bumble's feigned bewilderment. He ran off to find a broom and Bumble skipped back over to Gwen's side, picking a marble up off the ground as she did and slipping it back into her pocket.

Gwen huffed out a laugh and quietly, so only Bumble could hear, hissed, "You little shit."

Bumble let out a very un-childlike cackle and ran up the stairs towards their rooms.

***

After settling their things at the inn, the group headed towards the center of the city where the poorer districts were, as they knew the people there would be the most likely to give them the information they needed. Sylvia had insisted that she keep all their weapons in her bag to avoid drawing attention and Gwen held her hand to her hip, where her sword usually sat, as she walked, feeling exposed.

Avery sidled up next to her, bumping Gwen's arm off her hip with her shoulder. "No one walks like that, knock it off."

"Maybe she has a condition dear," Jasper chuckled behind them. "Don't judge her."

Avery turned her head to stick her tongue out at him and Gwen flipped them both off with gusto.

It took them quite some time to walk far enough to escape the pretty façade of the touristy part of the city, but eventually the buildings grew darker and dirtier. Older. They started to look like they were barely hanging on, the multiple patches holding them together only just getting the job done. *Like home,* Gwen thought cheerlessly. The change was glaring, even with the sunset creeping up on them and bathing everything in a beautiful, soft orange light. People sat on the ground against the buildings or milled about the alleys, filthy and sunburnt. Some of them slept, some dug through trash cans, others just stared off with empty eyes.

In front of a boarded-up building that was once a medical office sat an aviseum mother cooing a broken song to her two children. It was a song only an aviseum could sing, a mixture of trilling birdsong and the sounds of the world around them, arranged into a sort of lullaby. They all looked painfully thin, even for aviseum, and their blue and orange feathers lacked the luster they ought to have had. Bumble reached up and gripped Gwen's hand tightly.

"Know that song," she said quietly. She breathed in deeply, steadying herself. "Hungry. Thirsty."

Gwen nodded and squeezed her hand before letting go and digging some coins out of the pouch at her hip. She then pulled her waterskin from her other side and walked towards the aviseum family. She could feel her companions watching her as she approached the family carefully, knowing they were likely to be distrustful of a stranger. She knelt, holding the items out. She didn't say a word, but tried to reach the mother with her eyes.

For a moment, the mother regarded Gwen harshly, quickly working to determine her intent. She scanned Gwen up and down before her eyes landed back on Gwen's and softened. Her instincts were good and she knew Gwen meant them no harm. The mother reached out and took the coins and water from Gwen with a quiet "thanks" as Bumble walked up behind her and grabbed Gwen by the shoulders, leaning against her back. She warbled quietly at the mother, an unmistakably aviseum sound.

The aviseum mother's dark eyes widened, clearly surprised by Bumble's human appearance. "Illusion," Bumble said in Sylvia's voice. The mother nodded and one of her children reached out before their mother could stop them, touching Bumble's arm. The child let out an impressed, "Oh!" after feeling the feathers they could not see. The mother made a sound like a metal utensil hitting a glass and smacked the child's hand away, "Don't be rude!" she chided.

"It's okay," Bumble said, smiling. She made the sound of her name and then added, "I'm Bumble." She held her hand out to the other child so that they could feel too. "You?"

The mother pointed to herself and made the sound of wind rustling through trees and then said, "Breeze" for Gwen's benefit. Gesturing to the child closest to her, the smaller of the two, she made the glass sound again, "Ting", and then she set her hand on the second child's back and made the sound of many birds taking flight, "Flutter."

"It's very nice to meet you," Gwen said smiling at them. She turned, pointing to her friends in turn and introducing them before signaling to them that they could walk closer. They all sat on the sidewalk as Bumble chattered away, garnering information about the state of the city.

Veda and Gwen tried their best to amuse Ting and Flutter, allowing them to touch Gwen's hidden horns and tail, and press their hands into the warmth of Veda's fiery hair. They gasped and laughed.

"How?" Flutter demanded after a moment. Sylvia heard the question and pulled an extra satchel out of her bag, carefully explaining it to them and letting them hold it. Their eyes were alight with excitement and they asked her dozens of questions, which she took in stride as usual. Gwen noticed Boris watching them with a soft smile on his face.

Gwen did her best to pay attention to the conversation, but despite her best efforts, she began to grow sleepy with the warmth of the setting sun on her skin and the moment of perceived safety. After a few moments, she was leaning sideways against Veda, just a bit, with the sides of their thighs pressed together. Veda slid her hand around Gwen's back and set it on the ground next to Gwen's other hip, bracketing her in. The movement caused Gwen to fall more snugly against Veda's side, but Veda didn't miss a single beat and never stopped speaking to Ting.

Gwen's heart jumped to her throat when she realized what had happened and started to sit back up before she caught Avery out of the corner of her eye wearing a small, knowing smile on her lips. Gwen blushed, but it felt almost like a challenge somehow, so she allowed herself to continue to rest against Veda. After all, Veda currently appeared to be a man, so to onlookers nothing was amiss.

The moment was short lived, the peace broken by a woman's wail piercing the air. Gwen bolted to her feet and listened a moment, trying to discern the source. To the south were the sounds of a gathering crowd. A man's voice rose above the rest, "No, please!"

Veda was also on her feet and took off running in the direction of the voice. The others followed, Breeze and her children included. Soon they came upon a large group of people surrounding a handful of guards and a fyrdiav family. A small, brown skinned fyrdiav boy was at the very center, being held down by two of the guards. One of the guards was holding the boy's arm out against the ground in front of him. Laying on the road a few feet in front of the boy's hand was a bag of flour, split open and scattered across the dirt. The crowd looked terrified, but frozen in place. Another guard standing in front of the boy pulled his sword from his sheath. Gwen could see the symbol of a lion pressed into the front of the leather armor protecting his chest.

The woman wailed again. "Please, he's a child!" she cried, struggling against the guard that held her arms.

"A child that needs to learn not to steal," the guard holding her told her.

Gwen's stomach dropped. She could see Veda's hand lift, itching for the weapons they had stashed in Sylvia's bag. She took a step forward and Gwen grabbed her arm. "We can't leap in, it'll ruin our cover," she said, her eyes darting around, trying to find a solution.

"I can't just stand here!" Veda snarled quietly.

"I want to do something too," Gwen said, "We *will* do something, but we have to be careful." Gwen let Veda's arm go and turned to Sylvia, whispering furiously in her ear.

The child's father called out from the arms of another guard, "Take my hand! Take mine!"

"What will that teach him?" the guard with the sword sneered.

"He'll learn, he will," the man's voice cracked. His face was twisted up with tears, his red eyes wide and pleading.

Sylvia walked hurriedly down a nearby alley, away from them. Gwen turned to the rest of the group, "When the chaos starts, Bumble, I need you to scream. Confuse everyone. Draw attention to where Sylvia went."

Breeze spoke from behind them, in a voice laced with anger, "We can help." Gwen hesitated a second before nodding and Breeze gestured for Ting and Flutter to hide. They scurried off, using their wings to boost them onto the roofs of nearby buildings. The fyrdiav parents were still pleading for their child, but Gwen could hear the guards losing patience. They wanted violence.

"Veda, you and I will get the boy. Avery, Jasper, get the parents. Boris and Myev, control the crowd. Keep them away from us and then stay with Bumble. Meet back at t—" Gwen was cut off by a loud explosion to the west of them. Flames bloomed above the buildings and into the sky. "The inn!" Gwen yelled, immediately pivoting and running towards the center of the crowd.

Bumble took her cue. "Oh, my god!" she screamed as loud as she could in a woman's voice.

"What was that?" Breeze added in a deep yell. Ting and Flutter joined in with a cacophony of other voices.

The rest of their group shot forward as the crowd began screaming and running in all directions. The guards looked at each other in surprise before releasing the fyrdiav family and running towards the explosion, shoving through the hysterical crowd. Veda's legs were longer than Gwen's and she reached the boy first, scooping him into her arms.

"This way!" Gwen said, motioning Veda towards a road heading east, away from Sylvia's explosion. Gwen rammed her shoulders into the people around Veda, redirecting them to give Veda a clear shot through the crowd. She could see Boris and Myev doing the same in her peripherals. "Avery, Jasper!" she shouted.

"Behind you!" Jasper's voice could barely be heard above the noise.

They cleared the edge of the crowd, picking up speed down the street. Gwen glanced back to see Jasper and Avery running behind the mother and father, keeping them safely between the two halves of their group. They rounded a few corners, running until they were sure no guards had followed.

Veda slowed down and the boy, who had his arms wrapped tightly around her neck and his eyes firmly closed, let out a gasping sob.

"It's okay," Veda said softly, "It's okay, you're safe."

The mother nearly slid into Veda in her haste. "Gabriel!" she cried, pulling him into her arms. Her relief was palpable. Gabriel began to cry in earnest, pressing his face into his mother's neck. She wept with him, running her hand up and down his back.

The father pulled both of them into his arms. "He's all right, Katya." The confidence in his voice was undermined by the way his body shook.

He looked at Gwen, Veda, Jasper, and Avery, confused but grateful. "What was that? Who are you? Why would you...." he trailed off.

"Nothing exploded; nothing is on fire. It was an illusion. We wanted to save your son and knew we had to distract the guards, so we had a friend create the fake explosion so that we could sneak you away in the chaos," Gwen explained in a rush.

"But why would you help us?" he asked, honestly surprised. His tail remained curled protectively around his wife and son.

"Just be grateful, Elliot," Katya scolded. "Quit asking so many questions."

Veda smiled, "We help because no one deserves to be treated like that. Does this sort of thing happen often here?"

"In this part of town, yes," Elliot said. "There is little punishment doled out to overtly violent guards, so long as they keep it out of the touristy areas of the city."

"Why do people stay?" Veda asked.

"We have nowhere else to go," Katya replied simply. Gabriel had finally stopped crying, now just sniffling with his face still buried in his mother's neck. "This is our home. Generations of our families have grown up here. Even if we were ready to give up, where would we go? We have no money and no one is good to fyrdiav anywhere."

The sun had all but fully set and Gwen glanced around the dim street before handing Veda her satchel, dropping her disguise.

Elliot and Katya's eyes widened as her horns and tail appeared, as her skin turned dark as midnight. She looked them in the eyes, willing them to trust her. "I know what you mean. My name is Gwen."

"That's some skillful magic," Elliot said quietly.

"I'll be sure to let my friend know," Gwen replied. "It was necessary to allow us to complete our goals here."

"Which are?" he asked.

She hesitated for a moment before taking a leap of faith. "My parents were murdered when I was an infant by Ian Fletcher and Vito Cady. I came to Mooncrest to find them. I was hoping you could tell me where they live."

"To kill them?" Elliot asked. It did not sound like the idea upset him.

"Yes."

"I won't tell you they don't deserve it," he said, looking over at Gabriel. He ran his hand through his son's hair, over his little horns. "But where two tyrants fall, there are others that will take their place."

"Isn't it better than doing nothing?" Veda asked, though it wasn't really a question.

"You're probably right," he sighed. "I just wish someone could destroy The Brotherhood and The Council as a whole. We've lived so long being stepped on, us and all the others they despise. People act like the damn Brotherhood isn't at fault, that it isn't basically in charge of this entire country. Those bastards are in every city, take up the most governmental positions. Nothing will ever really change with them in power."

"I would like to tell you that I'm capable of changing that, but I'm not. I'm only able to avenge my parents," Gwen said evenly.

Elliot looked at his wife before looking back at Gwen, steel forming in his eyes. "You deserve that much. Vito and Ian live together in the northernmost end of Mooncrest, up on a cliff. Their home can't be missed, even among those of the richer families that live in that area." He described to them how to get there, the best roads to take.

"Thank you," Gwen said when he was finished, reaching out to shake his hand firmly. "Will your family still be in danger when those guards return?"

"To be honest with you, we're always in danger. We've grown somewhat accustomed to it," he said.

"We just have to keep a closer eye on this one," Katya added, looking fondly at Gabriel. "We must remind him that it's not his responsibility to provide for this family, it's to keep himself safe."

Gwen swallowed hard past the lump in her throat and all she could say was, "Thank you for your assistance. Please, be safe." She reached out and shook Katya's hand as well, willing them to be well with every bit of her.

***

On the way back to the inn, Gwen took her satchel back from Veda and recast the spell for her disguise. Avery and Jasper walked in front of them, holding hands and chatting quietly to each other, entirely in their own world.

After a long silence Veda looked at Gwen and said, "You could, you know."

"Could what?"

"Take down the whole Brotherhood."

Gwen scoffed and rolled her eyes. "How exactly am I going to do that?"

"I'm not saying it would be easy, I'm just saying it would be worth it. It seems like folks here keep putting out all these little fires instead of stopping the people holding the torch."

"Look, I think it would be great too, but it's impossible for one person to take down a well-entrenched, country-wide organization like The Brotherhood."

"It's not just you, there's all of us, and I'm betting more beyond that!" Veda said, her voice raising. "I know you've spent so much of your life alone, but it doesn't have to be like that."

Gwen stopped and turned on her, "And what exactly am I going to be when I get all of you killed on the wild ass quest we're already on? And you want me to commit to fixing the whole country too! What am I supposed to do if they kill Bumble? Or you? Or the others? We're already risking so much!"

Veda had also stopped walking and they stood a few feet apart, glaring at each other. Her hair whipped around wildly behind her, growing larger and hotter. "Some things are worth dying for!"

"Are they?" Gwen asked, crossing her arms over her chest. "You barely know me—are you really willing to die for some bullshit heroic endeavor in my honor? In honor of a people that aren't yours?"

"Yes." Veda's voice was quiet, but stern.

"And you truly believe that somehow I, of all people, can fix this whole stupid country if I just try hard enough?"

"It'd be a start."

Avery and Jasper had stopped walking and were looking back at them, trying to keep their faces neutral. Embarrassed, Gwen put her arms back down and turned on her heel. "Well, I'm glad you believe in me so much, but that's not enough."

Veda called after her, her anger tinged with melancholy, "I wish you did too. I wish you would believe in the power of people."

Gwen brushed past Avery and Jasper, refusing to make eye contact. "Well, I don't."

***

When they got back to the inn, the remainder of their group was standing out front with Breeze, Ting, and Flutter.

Myev caught sight of them first and called out, "Took you long enough!" She made long strides to catch up to them, pulling each of them into a tight hug, one by one.

"Go team muscle," Jasper laughed, hugging her back and high fiving Boris.

"It is what we are good at," Boris replied, grinning.

Avery smoothed out her hug-ruffled shirt and took Jasper's hand once Myev had moved on to other victims. A soft smile pulled at the corners of her mouth.

"And your plan worked out," Myev told Gwen, smacking her hard on the back in congratulations.

"We made a fantastic team out there," Gwen responded, fighting off a wince.

"And you, Sylvia!" Veda hollered. "That sure was something! You are an amazingly powerful woman. I'm real grateful you're on *our* side."

Sylvia became bashful, looking down at her feet, "It was just an illusion."

"A really fucking big illusion!" Myev added helpfully.

Gwen walked up to Sylvia and placed her hand gently on the lais-arnne's shoulder. "We really couldn't have done it without you. You saved that family so much suffering."

She looked up at Gwen, her eyes glittering a little. "You should have seen their faces when they got there and realized nothing was on fire."

Veda turned to Breeze and shook her tiny hand, "We cannot thank your family enough for your help."

"Of course." Breeze patted Veda's hand sweetly while Ting and Flutter puffed their chests out, proud.

"As thanks, please allow me to put your family up in the inn tonight, or really as long as you'll let me," Veda said.

Breeze opened and closed her beak, surprised at Veda's earnest generosity. "I can't accept that," she finally said. "It's expensive."

"It won't do you any good to argue," Gwen said from behind Veda. "She gets pretty determined when she thinks she's in the right."

Veda scoffed, turning to give Gwen a sideways grin and a raised eyebrow. Gwen winked, trying to convey that everything was fine, all was forgiven. They didn't have to agree on everything and Gwen didn't want to extend the fight any longer than she had to.

"I have a request, if you'd indulge me," Sylvia said, one finger on the tip of her nose. "I could use someone to watch my home while I'm away. Water my plants, tend to my garden, that sort of thing. It's a half a day's walk from Ironforge and I could supply you with a map and the money to get there, if you'd be willing to help out until I'm able to return. I will happily pay you for all your time."

Breeze looked confused. "You'd trust us with that?" she finally asked quietly, pressing her clawed hand to her chest.

"With all my heart," Sylvia answered. "You'd be doing me a huge favor."

Breeze looked back at Ting and Flutter, who had lost interest in the adults and were chasing each other around behind their mother. She looked back to Sylvia and nodded. "Thank you."

Sylvia motioned for Breeze to follow and walked towards the doorway of the inn. "Thank *you*. My garden would be a wreck by the time I returned without you!"

Breeze chuckled and called out to the children, who ran up and grasped her dress, following her into the inn. The rest of the group walked in after, with Veda heading to the front desk to pay for Breeze's room. The innkeeper looked suspiciously at the aviseum family, but bit his tongue after seeing the dare in Veda's eyes.

Before heading to their rooms, Bumble tossed a marble at another vase while the innkeeper was distracted, feigning a scream of surprise as it shattered. She looked at the innkeeper with wide eyes, her little hands pressed to her chest. "Dangerous!" she told him. A condemnation.

"What is happening?!" the innkeeper cried before turning and shuffling off to retrieve a broom.

Bumble quickly gathered her marble before catching up to the others, laughing.

Chapter Six

The next night they worked their way through dark alleys and abandoned side streets until they came up behind Ian and Vito's unnecessarily large home. They'd decided it would be best if only Bumble and Gwen entered, as it wouldn't be particularly subtle to march an entire army into the house. The last thing they needed was to have the cavalry called on them. Veda hadn't liked the idea and had insisted she go with.

"Your head is literally on fire," Gwen had pointed out. "That'd call guards right to us."

"How little faith you have," Veda smiled, rooting around in her bag. She pulled out a dark grey cloak with tiny golden flowers embroidered along the edge. She pulled it on and tugged the hood over her head, which appeared to put out her fiery hair. There wasn't even a glow through the fabric.

"Does that...hurt?" Gwen asked, her eyes wide and her lip curled in confusion.

"No, course not." Veda laughed. She pulled the hood back down and her hair reignited. She wiggled her fingers. "It's just magic."

"Sometimes magic hurts," Gwen grumbled, looking to Sylvia.

"Mm," Sylvia nodded and shrugged, looking awkward. "Depends on the magic."

"Well, this doesn't. We created it to help our warriors hide when needed," Veda said, "so don't worry."

"Still, you should stay behind," Avery said. "We need as many eyes on the outside as we can get, in case they alert any guards when they get in the house."

"And regardless, two people are generally sneakier than three," Jasper added.

Veda grumbled plenty, but eventually agreed. The rest of them would hide in various spots all around the house, listening and watching for any sign Gwen and Bumble were in trouble. They'd also use the satchel to call for help if they needed it.

Bumble sized up the building, her dark eyes clever and discerning. She'd already helped pinpoint where the others would have the best vantages, but now she was deciding where to make their entry. She and Gwen had a lot of experience in this sort of thing—they'd been working jobs together for years that often included a little breaking and entering. Over time, they had learned sign language and devised a system of sounds and signals to assist them in jobs that required stealth. Bumble clicked her beak together twice, their signal that she had seen a potential way in, and she slinked away, dark and silent as a shadow.

Between her obsidian-colored feathers and navy-colored cloak, the only parts of Bumble that Gwen could see were the decorative strips of silver metal attached around the end of her beak and the gold and ruby necklace she kept around her neck. Even so, both were only visible when the moon hit them just so. Gwen kept her eyes on those as

Bumble scaled the side of the building, no doubt headed towards an upstairs window, which tended to be less well secured.

Bumble could not fly; her wings had been pinioned when she was an infant—a cruel practice all too commonly forced on young aviseum that weren't able to grow up with their own families—and she had learned to climb things as though she were sticky somehow. Gwen was consistently impressed, even after all their years together. It only took about five minutes for the front door to open silently.

Gwen nodded and lifted a hand, knowing the others would be watching, to tell them she'd be making entry. She couldn't help but give a quick glance back at Veda, who shot her a huge grin and thumbs up. Gwen rolled her eyes, though Veda couldn't see it.

"*Window*?" Gwen signed with her hands once she was next to Bumble again. She nodded and Gwen grinned. "*Knew it.*"

Bumble laughed quietly and turned back to the house. They entered a massive foyer decorated with large paintings in gilded frames and sculptures on dark mahogany stands. The floor was made of marble-like tiles that sparkled even in the moonlight, no doubt embedded with the stones the town was famous for. The entire room was a show of power and wealth, meant to immediately impress any visitors that entered.

They slinked their way through the home, carefully peeking into and mentally cataloging the kitchen, an elaborate dining room, a sitting room, an office, and multiple bathrooms. Towards the back of the house, a staircase led to the basement, from which a gentle snoring arose. Bumble quickly worked her way down the stairs and back again, signing "*servants*" at Gwen. Gwen nodded and moved back towards the spiral staircase that led to the upper floor.

The first room off the staircase was a library that appeared to be rarely inhabited. The books were still crisp and new, not a single binding cracked, and were likely more for show than actual use. A large desk sat towards the back window, carefully organized to look like it belonged to busy and powerful men. There was an assortment of pens, stacks of papers, and a golden stamp next to a container of sealing wax. The clean desk didn't have a single mark on it and was likely as pristine as the day it was made.

Bumble pulled out a dagger and quickly scratched a large gash right down the center of the desk, her eyes shining with the joy of property destruction.

"Control yourself," Gwen hissed, smacking at Bumble's clawed hand. She put the dagger away and placed her arms behind her back, making a big show of behaving as she walked away. Gwen sighed and followed.

Gwen was starting to get nervous. It felt strange to be here for the purpose they were, though Ian and Vito wouldn't be the first people she had killed. She'd been in several deadly combats before, not just fights but battles in which it was her life or theirs and she'd chosen her own. While her best laid intentions were always to leave her opponents alive, sometimes it didn't work that way. Some people leave you no choice.

Ian and Vito were murderers, abusers, and human monsters, but to just kill a person in their own home in the middle of the night? To not even give them the chance at a fair fight? It somehow seemed too devious—something they would do, not her. But she knew that these weren't the kind of men to fight for themselves, they were the kind who would make others fight for them, and she couldn't put anyone else in the middle of this. And in the end, did honor really matter with men like them?

Bumble elbowed Gwen sharply and signed, *"Thinking too much."*

Gwen glared at her, but she was thankful for the interruption from her thoughts. They came upon a pair of large double doors at the end of the hall and Bumble carefully opened them. On the back wall, directly in front of the door, was a huge bed with a decorative canopy towering over it. Gwen could see one chest rising and falling as a man slept. The other half of the bed, where his partner should have been, was empty.

From rumors, Gwen knew the two men slept together. People avoided saying that Ian and Vito were in a relationship, just "close friends" and "work partners", but Gwen knew better. As did most everyone else. But if Ian and Vito were quiet enough about it, they were also rich and Lowean enough to get away with some indiscretions here and there.

She grimaced and turned to Bumble, signing to her that they had to call it off. They had to kill them both at once or it would become too complicated. Gwen took a few steps back and Bumble began to shut the door, but she hadn't even gotten it halfway closed when they heard a rustle. Gwen pulled Bumble out of the doorway just as a dagger flew past her head and skittered uselessly down the hall behind them.

"Who is that?" Vito bellowed, reaching to turn on the lamp next to his bed.

It flickered on, filling the room with light before the two could back all the way out. "Fuck," Gwen exclaimed, her brain turning quickly as she tried to decide what to do. She didn't have a choice really; he'd seen them and they were not disguised because she'd wanted the men to have to look at her, the real her, as they died. It wasn't supposed to go this way.

Bumble looked at Gwen and she nodded. They stepped into the room and closed the door as Vito continued to yell. Bumble locked it behind them.

"Get out of my house!" The blonde man was scrambling around in his bedside drawers, searching for another weapon. His curly hair flopped messily about as he stopped and looked at them, realizing he had nothing and sucking in heavy, panicked breaths. "Get out! *Help!*"

Bumble pulled a dagger from her belt and deftly flung it, the tip lodging into the wood of Vito's headboard only inches from his face. He jumped and yelped.

"Shut up," Gwen snapped. "Just shut up!"

"Get out of my house!" he continued to scream, wiggling Bumble's dagger back and forth to attempt to dislodge it.

Another one of Bumble's daggers flew through the air and hit his hand, pinning it to the headboard. He screamed and Gwen walked over to the bed, grabbing him by the throat. "I told you to shut up," she said, squeezing her nails into his neck. Vito looked up at her, still panting as his blue eyes darted around like a trapped animal. The hand stuck to the headboard twitched futilely, but his right hand moved towards Gwen and she grabbed it, jerking a few of his fingers back. "Don't think about it."

"What do you want?" he whined. "I have money. I can give you so much money."

"I don't want your money," she spat, anger rising in her. This was the first time she'd been this close to him and she could feel all of her old wounds reopening, throbbing like they were fresh. Her heartbeat thrummed in her chest like a war drum. "You killed my parents."

"I'm sorry, I'm sorry," Vito gibbered, tears falling from his eyes and spit flying from his lips. "I didn't mean to, I'm sorry. I can give you money, I can pay you."

Gwen laughed without humor, "You don't even know what I'm talking about, do you? You've killed so many innocent people, how could I expect you to remember two random fyrdiav?"

"I remember, I remember!" Vito lied, trying to appease her. His chest heaved and his breath wheezed from his throat where she gripped it, tighter by the second.

"You liar," she berated him. "You don't have any conviction! You'd tell me anything to save your life." She released him and took a step back.

"I'm so sorry," he cried, dissolving into senseless whines. "Please. Starlowe help me, *please.*"

"You know what, we have one thing in common though," she said, the muscles in her jaw working under her skin. "I also don't remember them, because you killed them before I was even a year old. I'll never know what they looked like. I don't even know their names. You took that from me. Not a soul but me will ever care that they existed and I wasn't even old enough to know their names," she laughed again, the sound broken and harsh. "They were buried in unmarked graves and no one can tell me where. No one *ever* cared about them; they were just two fyrdiav."

Vito continued to blather, not hearing a word she was saying, but finally he reached up and succeeded in extricating the dagger. Desperate, he flung it at Gwen despite their closeness, the handle hitting her painlessly in the stomach.

Bumble tossed another, hitting him square in the shoulder. "Don't," she said forcefully.

Vito screamed again and they could hear footsteps coming up the stairs, voices calling out to their master.

"We hurry," Bumble said, glancing at the door. She walked quickly to the window, unlatching and opening it. She then spoke a quick message into the satchel, telling the others not to come.

Gwen nodded and looked back at Vito. He had tears streaming down his face and snot dripping from his nose. His hands shook where they hovered near the dagger in his shoulder, unsure of whether he should pull it out or not. Gwen walked forward, pulling the dagger free with no benevolence. "You're pathetic," she told him over his keening wails.

Fists pounded on the bedroom door. "Sir? Sir, are you okay? What's happening?" Gwen clamped her hand over his wide mouth, muffling another scream. "You are a coward and a bastard. Wherever your filthy soul ends up in its next life, I hope it remembers this and I hope it suffers. I hope you live every single life after this one knowing that you deserved so much more pain than you received." She pulled Vito's head back by his hair and rammed the dagger into his neck, pulling hard to drag it across. His eyes went impossibly wider before the light in them flickered out, his hands dropping lifelessly to his lap as his blood spurted across the bed.

Bumble was already crouched in the window and seeing the deed done, she turned and leapt, grabbing a nearby tree branch and then dropping out of sight. Gwen gathered Bumble's daggers and then did the same, landing gracelessly beside her friend. She could feel a thick and heavy weight in her chest, growing and stretching like it would tear her apart. She tried to ignore it as she and Bumble ran back around the house, towards their friends, who were already halfway there.

At the last moment, Gwen looked back. In the window they'd just exited, a human woman stood with her hand pressed tightly to her mouth. Briefly, they made eye contact, and the woman staggered backwards before turning and running out of sight.

***

Veda and Gwen sat together on the sand at a deserted section of the beach. Rock outcroppings surrounded them, shielding them from sight. They moved very little and spoke only in whispers, despite the seaweed and driftwood littered about being their only audience. Gwen sat in her underclothes, just barely in the water. The waves gently lapped at her legs, rolling softly up and then away again, their consistency a comfort.

Gwen's outer clothes lay spread out and wet next to them, having already been carefully cleaned by Veda. Gwen couldn't bring herself to do it at the time, as she'd been mute and almost frozen. Veda had taken on the task without asking.

"Strip down, I'll rinse your clothes," she had said quietly. "Do not argue with me." Gwen had done as she asked, unable to muster the wherewithal to argue even if she'd wanted to, and sat down next to Veda in the surf. She stared out at the moon.

Bumble and the others had gone back to the Inn, giving Gwen the space that they could tell she needed to process what had happened. Veda had come with her to help clean the blood off her clothes and skin. They had been careful going to the beach so that no one would see them, but Gwen couldn't stop thinking about the servant woman who had looked at her as they left.

"She saw us, a woman in the house. She's going to tell Ian what we look like," Gwen said, the words suddenly rushing from her mouth. It was the first thing she'd said since they had left the scene of Vito's murder.

"It's okay, we have Sylvia's disguises," Veda replied, gingerly using a cloth from her bag to wipe Vito's dried blood from between Gwen's fingers. She set Gwen's hand down on her knee and reached over to the water, dunking and wringing the cloth.

Gwen felt like she should argue, but she didn't know what to say. Instead, she allowed herself to enjoy the warmth of Veda's knee beneath her hand. The heat was soothing as it worked its way up her arm and through her body. Then Veda's hands were back to continue their methodical ministrations, slightly cooler than her knee due to the water.

Finally, "I didn't know it would feel like this. I thought I'd dealt with my feelings about what happened. I didn't know that they'd come back like this."

"There is a difference between healing our hurt and burying it deep inside," Veda said softly. "Our heart will always find a way to return to the things that wounded us if we're unable to look at them without fear or judgement and truly work through them."

"Okay, oh Wise One," Gwen smiled, making eye contact with Veda for the first time since they'd gotten there. She smiled back and then returned to dutifully scrubbing the red from Gwen's fingernails.

"I just feel like it should have been more satisfying to finally get revenge. And it felt good, don't get me wrong, but there are just so many other things inside me that I don't know how to name." Gwen paused for a long moment, the only sound the susurrus of the waves, and Veda patiently waited for her to continue. "I feel sad. I feel afraid. I feel vindicated. And I'm angry. I just felt so much righteous fury overwhelm me when I spoke to him. It felt like there was no room for anything else in my body at that moment."

"You're allowed to feel angry. Let your anger motivate you, but don't let it consume you. Don't let it change your heart," Veda said, rinsing the rag again.

"I am afraid it already has," Gwen said quietly, a confession. "I'm afraid that that's all I have ever been."

"I can assure you it's not," Veda said, squeezing Gwen's hand with both of hers and looking at her until Gwen met her eyes. "Our grief often takes the form of anger, but it's so much more. It's multifaceted and unknowable in its entirety. You are doing the best you can with the hand you were dealt."

Gwen smiled, the lump in her throat preventing her from saying anything. Instead, she looked away, back at the moon. Veda finally finished removing all traces of Vito from Gwen's skin and rinsed the rag one last time before tossing it up by Gwen's other clothes. She then turned to face the sea in all its endless breadth and lifted her arm for Gwen. "Here," she offered.

Gwen accepted, turning and pressing herself into Veda's side. They sat in silence for a long time and watched the ocean. Gwen did her best to soak in its certainty and strength.

When her clothes were mostly dry and they finally walked back to the inn, they did so with their hands firmly laced together. Veda's hand was the only tether keeping Gwen grounded. When they arrived, walking slowly and tiredly up the stairs, Veda turned to her. "You can sleep in my bed, if you'd like. Might be better to not be alone." She seemed almost bashful, a version of her that was rare and private. Gwen didn't have the energy to be ashamed, so instead she nodded and followed her to the room.

Once there, with the door locked safely behind them, Veda handed Gwen a spare sleeping tunic. "You can borrow it," she whispered, turning her back to change into her own.

Gwen's arms felt leaden and slow as she changed, but the tunic smelled like Veda and that was comforting. It was bigger than her own tunic, which also comforted her somehow; to not feel restricted at all, she supposed.

After they had changed, Veda laid down on the bed and held her arms open for Gwen, who stood uncertainly near the bedside table. Gwen nervously licked her lips, but accepted the offer and settled in. Veda's stomach was pressed to her back and her arm was draped over Gwen's waist. Having Veda's body against hers felt like lying next to a roaring hearth. Like being wrapped in an old and beloved blanket. Like home. Gwen reached her hand up and laced her fingers with Veda's, squeezing her thanks. When Gwen's nightmares and inner turbulence woke her, she was lulled quickly back to sleep by Veda's soft breaths and the gentle glow of her hair flickering above them.

Chapter Seven

The morning came and they saw Breeze, Ting, and Flutter off at the train station. While Myev distracted the children, lifting them on her strong arms and swinging them about while they hung there, Sylvia supplied Breeze with a journal she'd written over the course of the last day. It contained directions, locations of the things in her home, a list of tasks, and a surprising number of other things considering the time she'd had to write it. She told them where to find her stash of communication satchels, telling them to contact her if they needed anything, and insisted that they try her homemade teas and jams. Veda pressed a small bag of coins into Breeze's hand, ignoring her protests. After a tight hug from each of them, the small family was off.

They then headed back towards the center of the city to see if they could find out why Ian hadn't been home the night before and when he'd return. The closer they got, the higher the concentration of guards became. They seemed to be everywhere, patrolling around with deeply serious faces. There were almost no citizens to be seen, and any non-human citizen was pulled aside and questioned. Their group was left alone, presumably due to their human disguises. Guards simply nodded at them and let them continue on their way.

"I think news has gotten out," Gwen whispered to Bumble. "Think you can sneak up and listen in?" she asked gesturing towards a felineum mother and child being accosted by a group of three guards. The grey fur of the mother's tail was fully puffed up in her fear and her ears laid back against her head. She held her child close to her, protectively wrapping her arms around him. The groceries she'd gone out to get were spilling out of the bags dropped at her feet, entirely forgotten.

Bumble nodded, slinking away to hide in a nearby alley.

She returned after the guards had moved on and the felineum mother had quickly gathered her groceries and scurried off. Bumble waited a few moments before she opened her mouth and the conversation poured out. Gwen was able to put the words together with what she'd watched them do.

"'Well, someone murdered him and one of you pieces of shit knows who,' a guard snarled.

'I swear I don't,' the felineum mother said, trying with all her might to convey her sincerity.

A second guard grabbed her by the arm, looming over her and her child. 'I will kill every single piece of trash in this slum if that's what it takes,' he threatened. 'If I find out you were involved or you know the fyrdiav and aviseum that were, I will skin your son alive and make you watch. When Mayor Fletcher gets back, he'll want a front row seat.'

'I don't know anything,' the woman said, her jaw quivering slightly. 'If I hear anything, I will tell someone immediately.'

'You'd better hope that's true.'"

"Shit, we've put all of these people in serious danger," Gwen grumbled, rubbing her eyes. She felt panic tightening in her gut and traveling up her throat. "And Fletcher is going to have so much extra security when he returns."

"Maybe we should leave, come back when the dust has settled?" Sylvia suggested.

"I can't leave these people with my mess," Gwen said, shaking her head. She clenched and unclenched her fists over and over again. "I don't know what the hell I'm going to do, but I can't just leave."

"She's right," Myev said. "They nearly cut off a child's hand for stealing food on a normal day, this is just going to give them an excuse to be more violent."

"We should find Elliot and Katya. Maybe they'll have some advice?" Jasper suggested.

"Yeah, it's worth a shot," Avery agreed.

"I've got an idea to get us some information," Myev said, glancing at another group of guards rounding the intersection to the north. "Stay put," she told them and grabbed Boris by the hand, dragging him over to the guards.

"Oh, sirs? Could I ask you a question?" she inquired, masking her slight accent and taking her voice higher.

"Of course, ma'am. What can we do for you?" the guard in front asked, his body language open and unafraid.

"We're traveling from out of town and we heard there was a vicious murder last night. Is that true?" Myev cried, tucking herself under Boris' arm. "I told Allen here, I said, 'Allen, that's just awful! Who could do such a thing? And in such a beautiful city?'"

The guard gave her a look of compassion and understanding, "I hate to confirm that it is true, ma'am. One of our beloved mayors was murdered in the night. We can only be grateful that his...partner, our second mayor, was out of town."

"That's just awful!" Myev gasped, pressing her hand to her mouth. "He must be so upset to have lost his friend like that."

"Awful," Boris said in agreement.

"Well, ma'am, he is rightly furious. In fact, he's coming back from his business trip a few days early to mourn. He'll be back in town soon and we hope to have apprehended his murderers by then so that he can feel safe."

"Murderers?" Myev screeched indignantly, emphasizing the plural. "Oh honey," she turned to Boris, "perhaps we should cut our own trip short if there are multiple murderers wandering about!" She turned quickly back to the guards, wagging her hand at them apologetically, "Not that we don't trust your abilities, gentlemen, it's just so terrifying to think about!"

"We understand, ma'am, and we assure you we are doing everything in our power to find them and protect the people. Guard presence has been increased in most areas of the city. Speaking of, you really ought to not be in this section of the city. There's a large population of ruffians around here; grifters, thieves, and the like. It's much safer further up," he pointed towards the touristy areas. "We're looking for a dark skinned fyrdiav and a dark feathered aviseum. Their kind tend to stick around this area, so I suggest you go back towards the business districts, keep your distance from them."

"Well, we will certainly head back that way!" she assured them. "Thank you for your time."

Boris nodded stoically.

"Absolutely, ma'am. You and your husband stay safe and if you see or hear anything suspicious, be sure to tell a city guard immediately."

"We will," Myev said amenably before grabbing Boris by the hand and flouncing back over to the rest of the group.

She waited until the guards were well out of earshot before dropping her voice back to its normal pitch. "Well, who knew being human could get you so much information so easily?"

"It is your charm and beautiful face," Boris said, setting a finger under her chin and tipping her head up.

"You dog," she laughed, punching him in the arm. He just grinned and pulled her to his side. "Do you guys know where Elliott and Katya live?"

"Not a clue," Gwen sighed.

They began asking around, but they received nothing but cold suspicion from the citizens of Mooncrest. It was clear that they had been burned too many times and they were not about to trust the group in their human disguises. Even the other humans in the area regarded them with distrust. The tightknit community was not going to sell out one of their own to a bunch of strange humans that they didn't recognize, especially with all the overly aggressive guards milling about.

Finally, Avery slid down an alley with a short, "This isn't working. Cover me."

Gwen looked at Jasper to translate, who nonchalantly leaned against the alley wall, nodding at the others to do the same. They stood at the entrance to the alley, blocking it from sight, until Avery returned as a fyrdiav with ocean blue skin and dark hair pulled into a low ponytail. Short, goat-like horns jutted out from above serious eyes that, despite their darker hue, were undeniably Avery's.

"Stay here," she instructed in her normal no-nonsense tone. "We're drawing too much attention to ourselves. I'll be back." She reached out and squeezed Jasper's hand before walking purposefully away.

Gwen watched Jasper's face as he followed her silhouette with his eyes for as long as he could. She could tell from his tightly wound muscles that he was nervous about letting her go off on her own. The heavy guard presence was making all of them wary. Quite a few of them looked like they were raring for a fight, searching for even the slightest reason to snap.

"She told me about how you two met," Gwen said to him, trying to find a way to distract him, even a little.

"Oh yeah?" he chuckled, but was slow to make eye contact with her, still watching where Avery disappeared. After another few moments he turned his attention to her. "That's one of my favorites to tell, can't believe she beat me to it. Did she tell you I was cursed at that time?"

Gwen shook her head.

"When I was a teen, I stole a book from an extremely powerful sorceress. You know teenagers, all bravado, no common sense. I was overconfident, thought there was no way she'd catch me. Hadn't considered that there'd be consequences."

Gwen thought that even now, a less observant person might see that as a defining character trait. He seemed sure of himself, happy and unbothered by anything at all. A person could easily miss the purposeful way he situated himself in any room, always keeping an eye on any moving parts, anything that could become a threat. They'd miss the wisdom carved around his eyes, hinting at his age and the years of learning all about consequences.

"She cursed me to never be able to use anything I didn't steal. Everything I already had disappeared and anything I tried to purchase would literally turn to ashes in my hands. So, I leaned into it," he shrugged. "I went from place to place, never staying anywhere for long before I'd get run out of town or I had to bolt to avoid getting locked up. I'd become consumed by taking whatever I wanted, completely focused on stealing rare objects just because I could. Sometimes I was so wrapped up in it that I wouldn't eat for days.

"It was like an addiction and all of my thoughts were constantly dominated by planning the next heist. I didn't care about anything or anyone else. Until I met Avery. And don't get me wrong," he laughed wryly, glancing at Gwen with shrewd eyes, "at first, I thought she was just another treasure that I wanted and had to work to obtain. She was gorgeous and strong and I know now that I was in love with her instantly, but back then my desires were all very selfish.

"It was almost intoxicating that she rebuffed me at every turn. Everything I'd wanted before her, I'd managed to find a way to get, so I was more than up for the challenge. But day by day she made sure I was eating, bathing, sleeping. Sometimes we had to come up with creative ways to subvert the curse to allow me to do those things, but she took it all in stride. I think she saw me as a bit of a project at first. Like, she might as well fix me up since I wasn't going away. But she made me slow down and do the little things. Take care of myself instead of just running from job to job, one high to the next. She slowed me down, but not once was I ever bored.

"At first, I thought maybe it was because I was still trying to steal something, you know? I was still trying to win her over. Over time, though, I realized that I just loved having her around. I hadn't had much by the way of company for years, but it wasn't just that. I loved telling her stories and giving her gifts. I loved the way she smiled and the way she took absolutely no shit from anyone, especially not from me. When she finally gave in and agreed to be with me, I knew I'd do anything to be with her every day for the rest of my life.

"She spent years by my side searching for a way to break my curse. We finally managed it four, five years ago. Fifteen years she spent by my side, dealing with every consequence of my curse. When we finally found the person that was able to break my curse," he glanced at Sylvia, who was pointedly not making eye contact, bashfully focused on writing something in one of her notebooks, "the first thing I did was buy a plot of land to build her a home. Using stolen gold, mind you," he grinned, "but it was important to me nonetheless.

"Neither of us had ever had a home. We built most of that home with our own hands, filled it with every book and scroll we could find. You'd think that after a life of travel, domesticity would get boring for us, but it hasn't yet. We still travel—gotta find things to fill our home with somehow—but when we're gone, all I can think about is wanting to get her back in our bed, in our kitchen, in our garden. To watch her putter around *our* living room, watch her read a book in the sunlight streaming through *our* windows." He'd been so serious at first, opening up about his past, but his eyes had gone hazy and his smile dopey.

"I'm grateful that you guys are giving up some of that time for me," Gwen said softly after he'd trailed off.

"She's an excellent judge of character," he said. "I've always been suspicious until proven otherwise, but she can see right through people and she likes you. It's quite the compliment, really."

"I know it," Gwen agreed.

"She thinks what you're doing is worthwhile and no one has ever kept that woman from anything she thought was important. And no one has ever kept me from following that woman to the ends of the world," he winked.

They waited another hour or so, Jasper's leg bouncing in nervous anticipation, before Avery rounded the corner. "They've invited us to their home, let's go." She gestured and immediately turned on her heel to go back the way she'd come.

Jasper jumped up and chased after her, "Ah, I knew you'd do it, my love," he cooed. "My brilliant, talented wife."

Avery took his hand in hers and kissed his palm. He then used that hand to softly cup her cheek while she held onto his wrist with both hands, smiling softly. Gwen wondered what it must be like to love someone that much, that openly.

Avery led them to Katya and Elliot's house, a small, multi-story building set back from the street. It had unusual proportions, much taller than it was wide, like a teenager that had grown up, but not out. It reached perilously toward the sky like it could topple at any moment and was sandwiched between several other structures just like it.

The sharp smell of sea salt was muted here in the depths of the city, overwhelmed by the scent of rotted wood and stagnant water. It was different than Ironforge—the metallic, chemical smells of the industrial city were burned into Gwen's memory—but the smell meant the same thing. This was a poor smell; a smell of people who had settled and dug their feet in, for better or worse.

Gabriel saw them through the tiny window beside the door and rushed out, his face lit up like fireworks. He all but ran into Veda and Gwen as they approached, grabbing one of each of their hands. "This is our house," he said in that factual and proud manner found primarily in children. Like it didn't matter if it was dirty or old or less-than, it was his and that was enough to make it one of the most important things in the world. It reminded Gwen that despite everything yesterday, despite how grown up he had to act sometimes, he was still no older than eight.

He pulled the two of them up the rickety stairs and inside, the others following close behind. Myev and Sylvia had to duck to get through the tight doorway, while Boris had to duck *and* turn sideways.

The door opened directly into the family's small living room. It was little more than an extra wide hallway, but every available wall was lined with old, well-worn chairs and couches, not one of them matching another. Crocheted blankets and lovingly stitched quilts were draped over several of them to be certain there was no shortage of warmth or comfort. Various pieces of art and crafts adorned the walls, some clearly made by tiny toddler hands, but many were made by people who clearly had years of practice. Some appeared old, handed down through many generations. Heirlooms from generations of people who were talented with their hands.

"My room is over here," Gabriel announced, still holding Gwen and Veda's hands and pulling them towards a door on the left.

"Oh, sweetie, I'm sure that's not what they're here for," Katya said, walking in from what Gwen assumed was the kitchen, a damp towel in her hands.

"Oh, we don't mind if you don't, ma'am," Veda smiled as Gabriel stuck his lower lip out, pouting. "We have time."

Gabriel led them to his room, barely large enough for his small bed, a dresser, and an assortment of old, dirty toys. He held each up to Veda, who had squatted down next to him, and was chattering on about what they were and where they had come from.

Katya watched silently from behind Gwen, smiling.

"I'm shocked he's so friendly," Gwen told her honestly. "I was never that friendly."

"He says you guys are heroes. You know how it is at that age, all black and white. You're a good guy or a bad guy, nothing in between. To him you're the best people in all the world for saving him. He asked about you guys all last night, wanting to know where you went and when he would get to see you again."

"Well, I'm glad we made a good impression on him," Gwen smiled.

"I hear you did it," Elliot said from the stairs near the kitchen as he descended, the wood creaking all the way. The stairs themselves were almost entirely vertical, ladder-like.

"Well, did half of it, anyway," she confirmed. "That's what we wanted to speak to you about."

"So Avery said."

"We're concerned about your safety," Veda said from the floor next to Gabriel. She was now sitting cross-legged, her lap filled with his toys. "We noticed the increased number of guards and their already aggressive attitudes. We're afraid it will get worse."

Gwen knelt next to Veda, lifting a toy that had slid from her lap and handing it back to Gabriel. He looked pleased before blurting, "You'll protect us though, right?"

"We're trying," she told him, her heart breaking a little. How was she supposed to tell him that the awful things in the world were bigger and stronger than she could ever hope to be?

"Gabriel, can you play by yourself for a bit so that we can have an important grownup talk?" Elliot asked. Gabriel looked disappointed, but gave an obedient nod.

"I will play," Boris spoke up. Myev grinned, patting him on the back and kissing his cheek. "No good at talking."

Veda and Gwen maneuvered their way out of the room to allow Boris to squeeze into it, his hulking body taking up the bed where he sat and then some. Gabriel was not deterred, immediately launching into the same lecture he had already given Veda about his toys.

"I assume you're still here so that you can finish the job," Elliot said once they had all settled in the living room.

Gwen nodded. "We are. We didn't anticipate Fletcher not being there; we'd hoped to get them both at the same time. We also clearly didn't think through the unrest this would cause and we can't leave everyone here to deal with this alone. It's my mess," she said apologetically.

Katya waved her hand, "It had to happen eventually. Change never comes easy, you know."

"This is going to create a power vacuum, especially once we take out Fletcher," Avery said. "Who takes his place?"

"I'm not sure," Elliot said, his hand on his chin. "The mayors are generally appointed. Honestly, this might be a good time for the rest of us to rise up, take the city," he shrugged. "There have been rumblings for a while. Maybe we can amplify that, give it direction."

"I am afraid whoever is sent to take over here after Fletcher is gone will use as much violence as they need to quell unrest," Sylvia said.

"They absolutely will," Elliot agreed. "But this was coming sooner or later. We just needed a catalyst. No one was brave enough before now, but we might as well take this momentum and run with it if we can."

"No one should have to get hurt because of a problem I started," Gwen argued.

Elliot laughed. "You certainly didn't *start* the problem and you're not the only person who wants to take things into their own hands. We're all tired of being treated like shit. We're done barely surviving while these Brotherhood bastards thrive. I think I can bring together enough people to start creating a movement, to make a change after you finish what you came here for."

"There are definitely a lot of people all over Peonia that want The Brotherhood gone, but never thought they were big enough to do it alone," Jasper shrugged. "When an organization like that is so deeply entrenched in a country's government, it's not easy to extract."

"And say you manage to take over Mooncrest, then what?" Avery said, not expecting an answer. She already knew it. "The Brotherhood is everywhere in Peonia, in every level of government," she gestured to Jasper, agreeing with his statement. "They're not going to let you keep Mooncrest."

"What choice do we have?" Katya said, rubbing her forehead and eyes. "We can't keep doing this forever. We can't keep letting humans act like they're the superior race and that Peonia is theirs and theirs alone. How else do we change this?"

"You'd have the support of Frostspire," Myev said. "We've just been itching for a reason to take The Council and Brotherhood out. Those bastards have been secretly trying to infringe on Snowblight territory for years."

"How can you be sure they'd want to help?" Elliot asked, surprised.

Myev laughed. "You're looking at one of the most respected Elders in Frostspire. I sit on The Assembly of Elders. If I told them we were going to have an opportunity to snuff out The Council and Brotherhood, they'd jump at the chance. I also have connections in the Dimroot Kingdom that could potentially supply our forces with weapons and protection magic. Can't promise anything on that one, though."

"The Dimroot Kingdom hasn't had anything to do with international politics for millenia," Katya pointed out.

"No, but it's something. And Boris has connections in the Vedvik Dunes; they also aren't fond of the Peonian government."

"Maybe we can convince some of the citizens to leave before this blows up," Veda said. "My country would take them in as refugees."

"Wait a minute," Gwen snapped, her head spinning. "This is getting seriously out of hand. You guys are talking about *war*." She couldn't help but feel like she'd done this; she'd set this tinder alight and it was going to burn them all down. *"Hadn't considered that there'd be consequences,"* Jasper's voice echoed in her head. "This is not what— I didn't mean for this to happen."

"This is bigger than you," Elliot said simply.

Gwen didn't know what to say to that, so she put her hands up in front of her, like she was trying to push the whole idea way. "Well, then you can have this conversation without me. I'll finish what I started, but I have nothing else to offer," she said, standing and walking back to Gabriel's room. She had to stand in the doorway, unable to fit into the actual room with Boris in there.

She crossed her arms and leaned against the doorframe. She was still in her disguise, but her invisible tail curled around her legs, another border separating her from those in the living room. She tried not to listen as they continued their conversation.

Bumble had also slipped away at some point and was playing with Boris and Gabriel. Boris had dropped his magical disguise for the time being, his enormous bulk taking up most of the room. Both Bumble and Gabriel were climbing him like a tree, hopping around and chasing each other. Boris seemed entirely unbothered by this arrangement. Gwen watched as Gabriel slipped, falling off Boris' shoulder, and Boris caught him without looking. Gabriel righted himself and continued to climb as if nothing had happened.

After a while, Boris looked at her. He had deep set, almost sleepy eyes with dark lashes that made them look like they'd been lined with kohl. She felt like he could see right through her with those beautiful eyes, to the pit inside her.

He said, "You are afraid of the expectations of others exceeding your abilities." Peonian was not his first language, so he was a man of few words and always chose them very carefully when he did speak. Gwen could tell he was not finished, so she nodded to let him know she was listening.

"What you do not see is that they do not expect you to be perfect, just to help. To try."

"I don't know what I could even do," Gwen sighed. "I'm one person. I don't rule a country and I don't have resources; I barely have a handful of gold to my name."

"All have something to offer. Our voices. Our hope. They create more, they build. People will get hurt. And die. But more will be helped if we succeed. At least then we know we tried."

"And what if someone I love dies because I tell them we need to try to do something that I'm not sure can even be done?" she challenged. "How am I supposed to live with that?"

"You make sure they did not die without meaning."

Gwen was quiet for a long time, but Boris did not continue. "How do we even do something that big? It seems incomprehensible," she said eventually.

He shrugged. "My wife has helped win many wars and did so by putting one foot in front of the other. She follows her heart, not her fear."

Chapter Eight

It took Ian Fletcher two days to return to Mooncrest and the group spent both of those days at Elliot and Katya's house. A variety of other individuals filtered in and out, slowly spreading the news and gauging reactions about the potential for a war on The Brotherhood. Gwen remembered the guard threatening the felineum woman, her saying that she'd let them know if she heard anything. She hoped none of the people Katya and Elliot spoke to felt that way. As a group, they overwhelmingly seemed willing, though sensibly fearful.

"This revolution will begin with one of us at a time," Elliot would say, his hand on their shoulder. They would nod, offering ideas and making plans.

Eventually even Boris was dragged into the planning due to his connections in Syrenmysta. Though his main duty back home was the orphanage he ran there, he had also fought in multiple wars for the Dunes and his uncle was the Chief of the powerful city. With Boris gone, Gwen (who was admittedly still sulking) kept to her post of assisting Bumble in keeping Gabe amused. Bumble also didn't have much to add to the "grownup talk", though she wasn't against the concept the way Gwen was. Gwen was sure she'd help if there was anything the others needed from her, but in the absence of that, she did what she did best and had a good time screwing around.

On the third day of planning, the two of them had taken Gabe outside to play. The guard presence had remained heavy throughout the previous days, but Gwen noticed that they hadn't seen anyone in a while. She sat on the front stoop while the other two raced each other up and down the street, their energy seemingly endless. Gwen found it intensely endearing, though it exhausted her just to watch them.

Suddenly, a loud voice cracked through the regular din of the inner city, startling all of them. "Citizens of the lower districts of Mooncrest: all are required to report to the Southern Boardwalk within an hour's time," it boomed. The voice was clearly not particularly close to them, likely coming from the Boardwalk a mile or so away, and was magically enhanced. "This is not optional. Those that do not attend will be found and punished." Gwen could hear the rage and disdain clearly. The message was repeated several more times.

Gwen stood up and opened the front door to the shocked faces of the others. "That was Ian, wasn't it?"

Elliot only nodded, his jaw clenched tightly.

***

They walked with the flowing throng of citizens towards the Southern Boardwalk, disguises in place and Elliot, Katya, and Gabe safely surrounded by the rest of them. As they got ready to leave, Elliot had leveled a grave look at the two or three people that had been in his home, strangers to Gwen and the others. "Gather who you can and keep them close. Word may have gotten to him about our conversations. Stay safe."

As they were funneled towards the beach, guards stood on nearly every corner, pushing and rushing those they deemed to be dawdling. The shade of the buildings disappeared, leaving them fully open to the blazing rays of the sun reflecting off the waves. Gwen could see that there were at least twenty to thirty more guards standing in a loose semi-circle around Ian. He was pacing the boardwalk, his green eyes wild and teeth bared. To the side of him stood the servant who had seen Bumble and Gwen fleeing, her thin arms wrapped protectively around her middle as she shivered in fear. Each time Ian would yell out an order to one of the guards she would flinch, trying to sink further back into them.

They worked their way as close to the front as they safely could and waited for the boardwalk to fill with the indigent masses of Mooncrest. The kinship Gwen felt with them in that moment transcended the fact that she didn't know them and they didn't know her. They were united in suffering under the fists of greedy bastards like Ian. She carefully controlled her breathing to stop herself from leaping out of the crowd at him.

Once the beachfront had filled to his satisfaction, Ian cleared his throat and a guard stepped up behind him, pointing his glowing fingers at Ian. "It has come to my attention that two of you have mustered up the audacity to murder Vito Cady, your mayor. You have slit his throat in his own bed," Ian's deafening voice cracked a bit, though out of anger or fondness for the departed, Gwen couldn't tell. "Thus far, despite their efforts, the City Guards have failed to bring the perpetrators to justice. I will no longer allow these cowards to hide within this city with your mayor's blood on their hands. This is your chance, *your only chance*, to come clean before you learn to regret thinking you can hide from me. This is the only opportunity I will allow for the rest of you to stand against these murderers and turn them in."

For many long moments, the crowd was entirely silent. Not a soul stirred, no one even willing to falsely accuse one of their neighbors.

"So be it," Ian said, his rage evident despite the steady cadence of his words. "Guards." He motioned to a dark-skinned male fyrdiav in the crowd and the guards grabbed him roughly by the arms, dragging him and dropping him to his knees next to Ian. He didn't look anything like Gwen, but he was similar enough to be a target. Her breath caught in her throat and she glanced at Veda, who stared determinedly forward as she took something from Sylvia and passed it to Gwen behind her back. Her sword.

"I have been told by my cook here," Ian gestured at the woman, who was now nearly behind him and obviously desperately wishing this was over, "that the murderers were a fyrdiav and an aviseum. If none of you are willing to come forward and tell us what you know, I will kill each and every fyrdiav and aviseum in this slum until you change your mind." Ian grabbed the kneeling man by the hair and yanked his head back. The man yelped and his lips trembled with terror.

"No, you won't," Gwen shouted and stepped forward, consciously dropping her disguise.

"Well, looks like I might not have to," Ian grinned, dropping his grip on the man and kicking him to the side. He scrambled back towards the crowd.

The guards all reached for the weapons at their hips, but Ian held his hand up. "Wait. Where is your co-conspirator? I will not spare the others until I have both of your heads."

Bumble stepped up next to Gwen with a dagger in each hand, releasing her own illusion.

"You will not hurt these people," Veda bellowed from Gwen's other side, her fiery hair whipping wildly in the wind and her skin the dark mahogany color Gwen had grown to miss when she was disguised. Gwen quickly looked behind her to see that all of her friends had dropped their disguises as well, and Avery's features were slowly morphing back to their natural state.

"Oh, I will do as I please," Ian sneered.

"No, you won't," Elliot said from behind Gwen. "People of Mooncrest," he called over the crowd, "join us or leave, but this city will no longer accept the tyranny of The Brotherhood sitting down. We will no longer allow them to thrive on our land while we starve." Shouts of agreement rang out from all around, more joining in with each passing moment. "We will free ourselves or we will die trying!"

Ian cackled, a savage and unhinged sound. "Guards, take them out."

The crowd quickly devolved into chaos with the guards swarming the citizens, a surprising number of whom rushed back at the guards. Some took their children and backed away, but many of them ran forward with nothing but their fists and cries of rage. Even over the din, Gwen could hear Elliot's firm, "Katya, take Gabe. *Go*," before he ran at the guards himself.

Gwen held still long enough to see Ian back away from the fray and onto the sand of the beach. She then surged forward, straight toward the first guard between them. Their swords clashed as the guard parried. Gwen hopped back and forward again, using the momentum to swing her arms around and slide her sword under his, flinging it from his hands. He stumbled backwards a step, his eyes wide through his helmet, as she lifted her leg and kicked him square in the stomach. Even through his leather armor, the wind was knocked out of him and he doubled over. Gwen slammed the hilt of her sword into the back of his head and he dropped, the sound of her sword against his helmet ringing out like a bell.

She pushed towards Ian, taking out guard after guard. They cut at her arms, punched and kicked her, one even yanked her hair before she turned and ran him through with her sword. She didn't feel any of it. She had a singular focus on her prey. They were just obstacles.

Next to her, Myev let out a terrifying roar and Boris met her with one of his own. They stood back-to-back, stances ready as they waited for the guards to come for them. On the way to Silverglenn days earlier, Sylvia had told them that Boris and Myev had initially met on the battlefield, when Boris had used his shield to stop a combatant from hitting Myev with their axe. Sylvia said that they had battled together ever since, each of their weaknesses being shored up by the other. It made them a perfect and terrifying pair. During battle they moved almost as one, each taking down the enemies in front of them and then effortlessly moving back together to cover each other's blind spots.

She had said that there was almost a mythos surrounding Boris and Myev in their own communities, based on how seamlessly they fought together. Stories of their conquests traveled far and wide, taking on a grandiose quality that made Boris and Myev chuckle. In the few milliseconds she spent looking at them, Gwen could see why. They trusted each other implicitly, never even checking to see if their partner had their back. Instead, they dauntlessly threw everything they had into the fight while knowing instinctively that they were covered. Myev was quicker and more vicious than him, but Boris was an impenetrable force, throwing enemies off them with frightening strength. Boris was Myev's shield, and she was his sword.

Gwen looked forward again to see that Bumble and Veda stood only yards apart, clearing her way towards Ian. Bumble's daggers flew with frightening speed and accuracy, her enemies still falling as she crawled up their forms like they were stationary objects, retrieving her dagger and throwing the next before springing off the body she stood on. A guard smacked her out of the air with his arm, but she landed on her feet and bounced back at him, using her dagger to slice cleanly through his thigh and severing his femoral artery. The blood spray coated her back and several others around them.

Next to Bumble, Veda rammed her axe into a guard's thigh, bringing him to his knees with a strangled cry. Quickly, she lifted both of her arms while her axe remained buried in his leg, bringing her hands together in front of her body with a clap and then forcefully pulling them apart again. Powerful flames shot from her fingertips as she brought them to her sides, creating a half circle of flames that Gwen could feel from where she stood. Guards screamed as their clothing was set alight and they scattered, attempting to put the fire out. Veda then pulled her axe back out of the man's thigh, kicked him to the side, and continued forward.

Ian, who had initially appeared smug, was starting to worry. Only a handful of guards stood between him and Gwen now and his eyes locked on hers over their burning shoulders while he fumbled for the sword at his side.

"You've had this coming for a long time!" Gwen roared, keeping eye contact as she threw a guard to the ground, bleeding heavily from his arm and ribs where she'd struck him.

The last guards between them fell and Gwen felt sand beneath her feet as she followed Ian in his retreat towards the sea. Veda and Bumble both moved to stand behind her, working to keep the guards at bay so that Gwen could fight Ian alone.

Ian's eyes darted to each side, then he quickly turned behind himself to confirm that he was running out of places to go.

"You're much less of a talker than Vito," Gwen mocked him, and he growled in return, settling into a fighting stance. He tried to pace around her, get her back to the waves, but Veda and Bumble blocked the way. "I'm here because you hurt my family, but my family isn't the only one you've hurt," Gwen continued.

"So what?" he spit. "People get hurt, it's the way of the world. In order for some of us to thrive, some of us cannot," he said, leaping forward and swinging his sword without much grace.

"Bullshit," Gwen said, easily deflecting him. He was momentarily thrown off balance by it and she used the opening to swing her foot hard into his side. He stumbled back with a grunt, holding where she'd kicked.

He lost all patience for chitchat and came at her, striking wildly. The sand slowed Gwen's movements and she felt her feet sinking into it with the force of his blows. Before his next swing, she leapt forward, hitting him in the arm. He hissed and slapped his free hand to it, scrambling back as blood wept from between his fingers. She reset her stance and waited for him to come again.

When he did, he slipped and fell in his haste, kicking sand up around him. It was no wonder he had to have hundreds of guards to protect him. Gwen tried to move back, but he scrambled forward on his hands and knees, swinging his sword and connecting with her shin. The edge cut through her boots, through the thin skin, and slid along the bone. She ground her teeth, refusing to give him the satisfaction of crying out. Instead, she stomped down on his wrist, causing him to release his sword, which she then kicked a few feet away.

A blow to the cheek with the broad side of her sword snapped his head back and sent him reeling. Giving him no time to recover, she rolled him the rest of the way onto his back and knelt on his chest, pressing him into the sand. He scraped his fingernails at her legs, her arms, her neck, anything he could reach, trying to get enough purchase to throw her off.

Gwen looked down at his rabid eyes, the pupils fully dilated and leaving only a sliver of color in their wake. His long brown hair had slipped mostly from its tie and strands stuck to his face, wet from the tide lapping towards them.

Gwen couldn't even feel his nails digging into her skin through the rage flowing out of her. She used the hand she had on his shirt to lift him slightly and slam him back down. "Where is Regan Cole?" she yelled.

In lieu of an answer, he spit at her, hitting her in the shoulder. She set her sword down and used that hand to tightly grip his jaw, slamming his head harder into the ground. "I won't ask again."

He squirmed, bucking as hard as he could. The movement dug enough leeway beneath them that he was able to throw off Gwen's balance and slip free, scuttling backwards, further into the water. Gwen caught him as he tried to flip around and stand, knocking him onto his stomach with a grunt.

The tide reached back up towards them, completely covering his face. Gwen held him there. He spluttered and choked as it backed away. "You're running out of time, Ian," she said, her voice dangerously low.

"Fuck you," he coughed, trying to knock her off again, but failing. The best he could do was inch further towards the water, an option he wasn't keen to take.

Gwen waited as the water rolled back up over his head, pressing his cheek firmly into the sand with the palm of her hand. His struggling grew more desperate, but she didn't let up. Two more times she let the water cover him, slowly drowning him, before she came back to herself, as if she had been in a trance.

His chest heaved under her, coughing as his lungs desperately tried to expel the water in them, and fear slammed into her. She was torturing him and whether or not he deserved it, that wasn't who she wanted to be. She needed it to end before she crossed a line she couldn't come back from.

"We're done here," she told him, finding her voice, though it was creaky and hushed. She slid them both backwards and reached behind herself, still carefully holding him down, until her fingers met the metal of her sword. She pulled it towards herself and with both hands, pressed the tip to his chest. The tide now reached only his hair, swirling it around his face as he choked. Despite it all, he glared up at her.

One last time, she looked him in the eyes and then she pressed down, the sword sliding through him until it met bone. She lifted her hips off him to get the leverage to press harder, until she could feel the sword hit the grainy sand below them. He had barely enough energy left to fight, simply reaching for the blade and weakly scratching at it.

The last rattle of life shook its way out of him and finally he stilled. Gwen took a deep breath and tried to steady herself, head on her hands where they rested on the hilt of her sword, still stuck through her enemy. Behind her, the battle raged on. Slowly, she became aware of sounds again.

She crawled off him and drug him further onto the shore by his feet before turning to see Bumble and Veda looking at her. The guards paid them no mind, their numbers dwindling and still fully engrossed in the roiling mass of people on the boardwalk.

Veda and Bumble stepped forward and Veda pulled Gwen into her arms. Bumble wrapped herself around Gwen's thigh. Veda's skin warmed her and Gwen clung to her, panting. When she finally pulled away, she squatted next to Bumble and took her feathery face in her hands, rubbing her thumbs just under her friend's eyes. Gwen nodded, their eyes communicating in a way only those of old friends could, and pulled her into a hug. When Gwen released her, she stood and looked back towards the fight. "We're not quite done here."

Through the fray she could see Jasper and Avery. Both were bleeding in various places, but neither was slowing down. A guard whipped his staff around, intending to bring it down on Avery when Jasper's flat palm caught it, mid-strike, instantly halting the movement. Jasper's face was a mask of rage that Gwen had not yet seen on the usually mild-mannered man. The only indication that the guard's blow had hurt him was the guttural shout he released as he stabbed the man in his open side with a dagger.

Avery, unfazed, turned and peppered a series of laser focused punches to the guard's torso which caused his muscles to fall slack before using her telescoping staff to knock his feet out from under him. He hit the ground and did not move again. Jasper, not bothering to retrieve the dagger still sticking out of the man's ribcage, pulled another couple from the holder on his hip and released them just as quickly, striking an enemy with each one.

To their right, a burst of green light blew multiple guards off of Sylvia, sending them flying into the crowd with indignant yelps. She moved forward, kneeling next to a downed bovillum man, and her glowing hands closed around the wound he clutched on his shoulder. The flesh came together, leaving a ragged brown scar visible through his fur and the bloody tear in his shirt.

"Our friends need us."

***

By the time the final guards had retreated back into the city and the citizens had gathered their dead and wounded (Sylvia, helping as many as she could of course, had worked herself to the point of being nearly unable to stand), and found their way back to their homes to grieve, the group had catalogued their own injuries and patched up what they could.

They sat at the edge of the beach, using the water to rinse the blood off themselves. They knew they needed to get moving soon, before the guards came back, but they figured they had at least long enough to clean up since the remaining guards would likely be doing the same.

Carefully, Gwen removed her boot and washed the sand from the cut on her shin, hissing at the burn of the saltwater. That one was the largest, but she had several cuts and bruises across her body that she was truly feeling now that some of the adrenaline had worn off. She felt like a well-used punching bag.

Near her, Avery had already washed the grime off herself and was looking distastefully at the stains on her clothing. Her husband was less concerned about his cleanliness at that moment and had decided instead to take a break, lying flat on his back in the sand.

"I can heal you," Sylvia said, coming towards Gwen and swaying on her feet, the stress and fatigue making her voice higher than it usually was.

"Sylvia," Myev said, standing and setting her hand on Sylvia's shoulder, "we are alive. We can wait; it's okay." Myev had gotten her nose broken in the fight and the bridge of it sat a little more to the left than it once had. The large cut that had been caused by the impact had been carefully sewn together by Boris. Some of the blood still stained her face and teeth as she grinned. Her glacier-blue eyes sparkled. "I'm sure all of us have had worse."

"Definitely," Veda said from where she stood knee deep in the water, holding Bumble by the waist while Bumble dangled over the sea and rinsed her cloak. Bumble hated getting her feathers wet and Veda was indulging her.

Sylvia opened her mouth to argue, but Myev herded her towards the water to wash her hands before she could say anything more. She gave up and plopped heavily into the sand, allowing Myev to help her.

"We've got to get going soon," Avery said, ever the pragmatist. "It's only a matter of time before the citizens of the upper districts hear of this, if they haven't already. The guards are probably regrouping and sending a carrier seagull to The Council as we speak. No doubt they'll be sending troops from the national armed forces to put this uprising down. We can't afford to get caught in a civil war if we're going to complete our goal. We can come back and help after."

"So we're just going to start a fucking insurgency and then leave?" Gwen sighed, laying back on the warm sand. She knew Avery was right, but she was tired all the way through her bones. She couldn't even imagine standing to move from where she lay and briefly considered letting the sea have her.

"Myev, Boris, and I have already sent word to our countries asking for aid. I suspect reinforcements will be here within a week or two and anyone that doesn't want to fight will be able to relocate to Vulcaria for now if they so choose." Veda said from the water. "I thought you didn't want to be part of a war anyway."

Gwen wrinkled her nose and waved her hand dismissively at Veda, refusing to take the bait.

"We can handle Mooncrest until everyone else arrives," Elliot said from behind them, where he had returned from across the boardwalk.

Gwen craned her neck while still laying down to look at him. "Hey, did you get Katya and Gabe home all right?"

"Yes, they are safe. Packing to go to Vulcaria as we speak," he smiled and sat beside her. "We can handle what we started in Mooncrest," he reiterated. "You have a job to do. Start a few more revolutions while you're out there; we can't be the only ones if we're going to crush The Brotherhood."

Gwen blew air out hard through her lips and rolled her eyes. He punched her good naturedly in the arm.

"We could go to the Dimroot Kingdom since we don't know where Cole and Ross are and speak with my contacts there about sending help to Mooncrest or perhaps joining the fight," Myev called from where she was mothering Sylvia.

"You actually know how to physically *get* to the Dimroot Kingdom?" Jasper interjected, his eyes alight.

The Dimroot Kingdom was a large community of gnomes who had long ago hidden their land away using magical means. There was a general idea of where the Kingdom lay, but no one had ever actually found it unless the gnomes wanted them to. They were known for possessing intensely powerful magical resources, the protection of which was part of why they had hidden their entire kingdom. Gwen didn't know much about it, but she'd heard that they had some sort of symbiotic relationship with the land itself, which in turn gifted them with powers beyond the imagination of the average Peonian.

"Sure do!" Myev confirmed. "I'm good friends with their princess."

"The one that never stays safely in her castle, much to King Applewood's dismay?" Jasper asked, grinning.

"That's Ivy for you," Myev laughed. "Never much took to royal life. Her parents love her, but she's going to give them ulcers. You know much about the Dimroot Kingdom?"

"Just that I've been absolutely dying to get there for my entire life," he replied excitedly.

"You know, books and scrolls that haven't been seen by non-gnome eyes for thousands of years," Avery smiled, elbowing him gently.

Jasper looked over at Gwen expectantly.

"I don't care where we go," she said, quickly breaking eye contact. "This whole revenge trip was Veda's idea, so she's in charge."

Veda laughed from where she was now bringing Bumble back towards dry land. "Nice try, Gwen."

Myev gave Gwen a look, her eyebrows raised in question, before deciding on her own and loudly announcing, "Dimroot Kingdom it is then!"

***

They decided that with their human disguises, which they had changed to avoid recognition, they could stay at the inn one more night. Blessedly, the innkeeper didn't see them as they quietly slipped in, but they could hear him whispering furiously to someone in his office through the open door. "And they killed them! What if they kill all of us? We need to strike back...."

Avery caught Gwen's eye and mouthed, "Not your fault."

Gwen did not respond.

Once they got to the top of the steps, Veda grabbed Gwen's hand and pulled her down the hall to her room. She shut the door and leaned against it, throwing her satchel on the bedside table. Gwen followed suit.

"I wanted to check on you, see how you were feeling."

Gwen shrugged. "About the same as the last time, I guess." She was quiet for a long moment. "I just get so angry. I'm scared of myself," she finally admitted.

Veda stepped forward and took Gwen's hand in hers. "I'm not scared of you."

"Maybe you should be."

Veda shook her head, smiling. Slowly, she lifted her free hand to the side of Gwen's face, cupping it in her palm. Veda's eyes fixed her in place as she lifted Gwen's hand to her lips and kissed the knuckles.

Gwen felt like she was choking, all of her breath caught in her throat. "What are you doing?" she whispered, barely even a sound.

"Distracting you; is it working? Words don't seem to work with you, so," Veda said in a voice like smoke. She kissed each of Gwen's knuckles in turn as Gwen stood there, frozen.

When Gwen was finally able to move, it was as though everything inside of her broke at once and she lunged forward, pressing her lips to Veda's, hard. Veda met her with equal fervor, tangling the hand that had been on Gwen's face into the hair at the nape of her neck and tugging, angling Gwen so that she could kiss her more deeply.

Gwen's entire body felt consumed by her. Veda was even hotter than usual and the heat from her fingers lingered as she trailed them down Gwen's side to grasp her hip. Veda's tongue slipped into Gwen's mouth and she could hear herself breathing heavily, almost whining, but she didn't feel connected to it. She felt like she wasn't inside her own body anymore.

Then Gwen's teeth were on Veda's lips and she bit and pulled, already addicted to the sound that came out of Veda when she did. She drew Veda's hips to hers, not wanting an inch of space between them. Veda came willingly, wrapping both of her arms around Gwen, her hands burning like embers on Gwen's skin. Gwen wished they really were, wanted every bit of her body to be marked by Veda, to prove that this was real.

She placed her hands on either side of Veda's face, hoping to translate the feelings bursting from her body through her mouth. Veda seemed to understand. Finally, when she felt like she could no longer bring air into her lungs, she forced herself back and dropped her hands to Veda's shoulders. Veda still held tightly onto Gwen and her grin was blinding.

Despite that, despite all of it, Gwen still blurted, "I'm sorry, I shouldn't have done that."

Veda laughed loudly, throwing her head back. "Reynta, you are incorrigible! I started that, remember? You fell flawlessly into my trap, you fool. I couldn't stand another day of looking at you without being able to touch you. I hoped that perhaps it could help you forget some of your woes." She placed her hand under Gwen's chin and pressed gently, so that Gwen would look her in the eyes. She could only handle Veda's earnest eyes and her endearing smile for a moment before glancing down at her own hands, face burning.

Gwen sensed Veda's intention only a second before she was lifted in the air, one of Veda's arms under her knees and the other cradling her back. Gwen yelped and Veda laughed again, the sound rumbling through Gwen's own chest where they were pressed together.

"That's rude, put me down!" Gwen objected, squirming.

"Ah, settle, I intend to," Veda said, walking towards the bed.

"I'm a grown woman, I can walk to the bed myself," Gwen grumbled as Veda laid her on one of the pillows.

Veda laid down beside her, slotting her hips up to Gwen's side and bracing her head with one hand to look at her. "You looked like you might bolt." She was quiet for a second. "Which if you really want to, I won't stop you," she finally added, softly and sincerely.

"I don't," Gwen admitted, nestling a little closer to Veda's side to make her point.

Veda nodded and laid her head down, hooking her leg over Gwen's. She draped her arm over Gwen's chest and placed her hand against Gwen's cheek, running her thumb softly over her jaw.

"We should change clothes before we sleep," Gwen said after a few minutes, when the pounding of her heart had settled enough to not send the damn thing flying out of her open mouth. The buzz in her skin had lessened to a gentle hum, leaving her loose and warm.

"So tired though," Veda griped playfully.

"There's *blood* on these."

Veda let out a high-pitched whine.

Gwen laughed and moved just enough to lean off the bed and grab the tunics they'd slept in a few nights ago, which they had responsibly tossed onto the floor next to the bed, and passed Veda hers. They sat up to change, wiggling out of their soiled clothes without getting out of the bed and tossing them to the side.

Finally, they laid back down and Veda wrapped herself around Gwen again, pulling her in as closely as she could. Gwen watched the shadows that Veda's flames created on the ceiling, soaking in the feeling of their skin pressed together. The thin fabric of the tunics didn't really feel like a barrier at all and the thought was electrifying. She forcibly turned her brain in another direction.

"What does Reynta mean?"

Veda sounded like she was already all but asleep. "Reynta is the goddess who resides deep within Engadi, at the planet's core. She's the one who gave the Vulcarians the power of fire."

"So, I have her to blame for the fact that you're like a living blanket," Gwen joked, patting the arm over her chest.

Veda nodded, chuckling and snuggling into Gwen's shoulder. "You will never be cold with me around."

"I could get used to that." She spent a few moments listening to Veda breathe. "Is she your only goddess?"

"No, but she's the one I feel most connected to. In my beliefs, there are gods and goddesses for everything. The wind, the trees, the water—all these things have power and spirit in them, given to them by the gods and goddesses that oversee them."

"They're like caretakers of those things?"

Veda mumbled in the affirmative, nuzzling her nose into Gwen's hair. "Yeah, and they care for us too, like the way we're supposed to take care of animals. Cattle and deer and spiders and salamanders. All of them. We're more capable than they are, so it's our duty to care for them, to not be cruel when we fulfill our place in the chain of life. The gods do the same for us."

"Do they ever fail? We seem to fail a lot in our duties."

"Of course. The gods aren't infallible, nor are they immune to things like greed or rage; they're just creatures more powerful than us. And I'm simply grateful to them for what they do provide us with. There's so much beauty in this world, don't you think? So much to be grateful for, even when it's not perfect."

Gwen nodded, out of questions. Veda pressed a kiss to her shoulder and was snoring softly within seconds. Gwen followed soon after.

Chapter Nine

They stopped by Elliot and Katya's in the morning to drop off one of Sylvia's communication satchels. It was the one Gwen had been carrying, but she promised to stick around Bumble at all times in case she needed hers, as had Veda, who had sent hers to Vulcaria with a messenger bird. Sylvia had chosen an untrained seagull from the beach, rather than using a city approved messenger bird, and used her magic to both teach it what to do and to protect it on its long journey. She carefully explained to Elliot how to use the satchel, despite the directions pinned to the bag. As Gabe was making his rounds and giving each of them a final hug, Gwen could hear Sylvia mumbling to herself about running out, hemming and hawing over ingredients and the moon.

Boris lifted Gabe, setting him on his shoulder and walking him back towards his house to deposit him with Katya and Elliot. "Be good to your parents. Stay safe."

"I will!" Gabe promised, hugging Boris around the neck.

"Keep us updated. Let us know if you need anything at all," Gwen told them.

Veda shook their hands vigorously. "I will let you know as soon as I do what the plan is for transport of Peonians to Vulcaria. My parents should be contacting me the moment they receive the gull."

Elliot nodded, using the grip he had on Veda's hand to pull her into a hug. "We appreciate it so much."

"Be safe out there," Katya said, turning to Gwen and pressing a still warm loaf of bread into her hands. "Take it, no arguing," she said in her mom voice when Gwen opened her mouth.

She smiled instead. "Yes ma'am."

The streets were eerily bare as they walked towards the train station, save for a few confused tourists looking at the closed shops. The owners that had decided to keep their shops open appeared skittish and looked over every customer carefully, keeping their conversations short and professional.

"I'll get us tickets to Bronzeshine," Myev announced. "That'll take us three and a half days. We're going to have to walk the rest of the way though, which is another five, depending. We're going to want to stock up somewhere along the way."

***

The trip to Bronzeshine went by, miraculously, without incident. They kept up their disguises, which they'd changed one more time right after leaving Mooncrest, to be safe. Veda's new disguise had red, curly hair reminiscent of her real, fiery hair and brown eyes that glinted playfully each time they caught Gwen's. Gwen would look away awkwardly, clearing her throat or licking her lips, which would just cause Veda to chuckle. It didn't matter that she didn't look like herself, Veda's aura was the same and it made Gwen feel like there were sparks in her veins.

Bumble looked at Gwen once, knowingly, and Gwen shook her head, trying to get her to drop it. Bumble whistled, low and suggestive, before pointedly looking out the window. Gwen flipped off the back of her head.

If they listened hard enough in the places they stopped along the way, news of what happened in Mooncrest was already traveling fast. Hushed whispers, shocked expressions, and even a few angry rants met them whenever they stepped off the train. Eventually even the train's other passengers were caught up in it. The group had been shocked to learn that there had been an uprising in Rivergate as well.

Rivergate wasn't far from Mooncrest, and sat at the southern end of the White River, which separated the Alabaster Plains from the Evernear Barrens. Folks along the river, including those in Rivergate, largely worked in hydropower plants dotted along the river, which provided the richest members of Peonian society with the electricity they used to light their homes. The plants also powered the manufacturing centers in places such as Ironforge. According to the gossip, the citizens of Rivergate had successfully taken control of the plant and had stopped all power going out. This had caused mass chaos—in Ironforge especially. Things were turning quickly and Gwen consistently felt sick to her stomach at the thought of it.

Compared to the endless susurrus of the gossip on the trains, the relative quiet the woodland of Oak Valley offered was more than welcome when they finally reached it. They spent the entirety of the first day's walk in near silence, each of them enjoying the peace of the trees and creatures around them.

Veda, always delighted by a new plant or animal, would grab Gwen's hand and point it out to her in hushed tones. Gwen felt safer in the forest, away from any prying eyes, but she still got nervous when one of their friends would see their clasped hands. Their eyes would never get stuck for long though, and no one mentioned it. She knew that their friends, despite the short time she had known them, weren't the type to care about her predilections, but a lifetime of fear and hiding didn't just dissolve because she was in good company.

On the second day, Myev was already getting restless. As they set up camp for the evening, the sun just beginning to set, she clapped Boris on the back. "We should spar, my love."

Boris shrugged, no arguments, and pulled off his shirt to reveal his burly, tree trunk torso in all its glory, covered in an impressively thick layer of hair. His arms, which Gwen hadn't seen much of through his long sleeves, were also so hairy she almost couldn't see his skin through it.

Myev grinned and considered her weapons carefully; she carried both a large axe and a sword, never to be caught without a choice of weaponry. Gwen had even seen her pull several daggers out of her pack one night and she'd commented on Bumble's bow the first night they met her, impressed and lamenting that she'd had to leave her own behind so that she could "pack light". She chose the sword and walked to the end of the clearing opposite their camp. She stretched, pulling her arm across her chest, and grinned at Boris, who had grabbed his own sword and walked over to meet her. They stretched together, eyes locked, like some kind of weird foreplay.

"This should be a show," Jasper noted, setting down the book he was reading and leaning back against the tree he sat in front of. Avery, who sat next to him, hummed softly in agreement.

"I've heard stories of the two of them fighting together over the years. People talk about how they're like a well-oiled machine, working together in battle like they share a single mind. Didn't get much time to look at them the other day," he chuckled, "but can't say I disagree. It'll be interesting to see that turned against each other."

Gwen wrapped her arms around her legs, setting her chin on her knees. She glanced at Veda next to her, leaning back on the grass and propped up on her elbows. Her hair flitted softly around her face, shifting in the breeze.

"Oh!" Sylvia exclaimed, clearly already distraught at the prospect of someone getting injured. "Please do be careful."

At almost the same time, Bumble began to chant, "Fight, fight, fight!"

Myev ignored both of them, finished her stretching, picked up her sword, and fell into a ready stance. Her smirk remained, but her eyes had already grown more focused as she considered her husband carefully.

Boris set his own stance, having only a moment to prepare before Myev was on him, a series of quick blows blocked easily by his own practiced movements. Myev jumped back, circling him before advancing again. He parried and struck out with his own sword, shoving her back with the force of it as his blade hit hers. Gwen could only imagine the power it would take to knock someone as muscular and sturdy as Myev back even a few inches—if anyone could do it, it would be Boris. He clearly wasn't going to be gentle just because she was his wife and honestly, Gwen knew Myev would have been offended if he did.

Boris continued the forward momentum, swinging again and again, pressing Myev back towards the tree line. Her ponytailed hair swung wildly as she deflected each of his blows and some pieces broke free, falling across her face. She glanced backwards, realizing that by pushing her towards the trees he was working her towards a quick defeat. Her eyes snapped back to his, calculating, and on his next swing she dodged and rolled out of the way.

As he stumbled, she popped lithely back onto her feet at his side, pivoting quickly behind him before swinging at the wide target it offered. Their swords met as he lifted his arm and dropped his behind him to block her, then he jumped forward and spun on his heel.

She hopped backwards, her large teeth on full display as she snarled at him. He roared back at her while she sprinted forward again. He sidestepped her, bringing the pommel of his sword down hard on her forearm, causing her to drop her weapon. It slid away in the grass, into the brush, but she didn't spare it a moment's thought before running at him again, aiming low at the last moment. Her shoulder slammed into his legs with the full force of her body behind it, sending him reeling backwards.

Boris' eyes went wide and his enormous girth brought him quickly down, his sword bouncing away as he hit the grass, hard. Myev was on him in an instant, her legs straddling his chest and a hand around his neck, the sharp nail of her thumb pressed into the soft skin under his jaw.

He lifted his hands slightly, smiling up at her. "I surrender."

She beamed down at him, her chest heaving, before moving her hand to his cheek and pressing a kiss to his forehead. "Another?"

They went a few more rounds as the sun finished setting, each winning about an equal number of times. They were evenly matched and often luck was the decider of who took the upper hand. On their last round, Boris took the win, his sword extended straight out and the tip pressed just against Myev's neck where he had her pinned to a tree. Even in the near darkness, Gwen could see the hunger in Myev's eyes as she leered at him, looking like she wanted to jump his bones right then and there.

"We might have to give them a minute," Jasper chuckled.

But they settled, returning to their bedrolls. Boris laid back, still panting, and Myev threw herself over his side, lounging on him like a very sweaty piece of furniture.

"You're both very impressive fighters," Veda said. "I'm certainly glad you're on our side instead of against us."

"Many orcs are born and raised in blood," Myev said, glancing over from her seat very nearly atop Boris. "For a long time, people have seen our kind as only good for war. For tearing and rending and destroying. I don't want it to be that way for future generations, and I've tried to do my part within Frostspire by working towards peace for our nation, but I do have to admit that almost nothing gets the blood going like a good fight."

She laughed, but Gwen felt the guilt bubbling over inside her. She tried to squash it back down, doing a piss-poor job at best. They wouldn't be involved in war right now if it weren't for her.

"Do you and Boris have children?" Veda asked, rolling onto her stomach and pillowing her head on her arms to look at them better.

"No," Myev said, the softest Gwen had ever heard her. "Unfortunately, I am not able to bear children."

"I'm so sorry," Veda said. "I shouldn't have asked."

"Don't be sorry," Myev said. "We are friends now, brothers in arms, and it's natural to ask questions." Myev meant what she said, despite the pain in her voice. Boris rubbed her back in soothing circles. "I would love nothing more than to provide Boris with a larger family, but unfortunately I am all I can give him."

"More than enough," he said gruffly, the hand on her back not stilling.

"Boris puts a lot of love into his orphanage instead," Myev said, patting him on the stomach.

"Our son, Aiden, has visited Boris at his orphanage and says those children are downright spoiled," Jasper said.

Boris snickered, jostling Myev with the quaking movement of his massive chest.

"How old is Aiden now?" Sylvia asked. "It's been a bit since I've seen him."

"Just turned twenty-six," Avery said, a rare and tender note of pride in her voice.

Jasper smiled. "He was eight when we adopted him and we've managed to keep him alive 18 years since," he said for Gwen, Veda, and Bumble's benefit.

"Even though he's got a knack for trouble, like his father," Avery said, leaning into Jasper, "he's a good boy."

"Always welcome at my orphanage," Boris said. "Could always use an extra pair of hands."

"And Aiden is very good with the kids," Myev smiled.

Everyone continued to chat and Gwen listened silently, enjoying the camaraderie. As they began to grow tired and turn into their bedrolls, Veda's hand found Gwen's where it lay on the grass. Gwen laced her fingers with Veda's and quickly fell asleep.

***

It felt like they'd been walking forever when Myev finally stopped in a small clearing and bellowed, "Please tell Princess Ivy Periwinkle Luna Applewood that Myev of Frostspire has come to visit her." She then dropped to the grass, crossing her legs comfortably. Boris sat next to her, allowing her to lean against him.

Gwen stared at her, baffled.

"Well? Sit, sit," Myev said, patting the ground next to her, "this could take a bit."

"You just...scream into the void...and a princess eventually shows up?" Gwen asked incredulously, glancing at Veda as they sat, who seemed more amused than anything.

"Different customs everywhere you go," Veda shrugged when she caught Gwen looking at her. "I'd show up if you screamed for me," she added with a wink.

"Knowing the princess' full name goes a long way," Myev chuckled. "We're still a bit away from the actual entrance to the kingdom, but we'd never find it ourselves without waking up disoriented and miles away, missing the last few hours of our memories. This is where the Kingdom's guards begin their watch. You can't see them, but they're around and they heard, believe me."

"You'd know better than we would," Avery said agreeably, settling back on her hands with her legs stretched out in front of her.

Next to her, Jasper was practically vibrating. "This is so exciting!" he whispered to his wife, who lovingly patted his knee.

Twenty minutes into waiting, Bumble had tired of crawling up and down trees and impatiently threw herself backwards into Gwen's lap, dramatically tossing her arms out with a sigh. Gwen squeezed her feathery cheeks between her palms, raising her eyebrows at her in a way that clearly meant "be good".

Forty minutes into waiting, a soft *pop* could be heard from within the trees, startling Bumble, who had fallen asleep curled up in Gwen's lap. She sat up, wrapping her arms around Gwen's neck, so Gwen rolled her eyes and lifted Bumble in her arms as she stood.

Myev dusted the grass off her legs and turned to face where the noise had originated. Within a few moments, a very small woman stepped into existence from between two trees with another *pop*. Her skin was a warm brown and covered in freckles. Her pastel-pink hair was pulled into a thick side braid that highlighted her long, pointed ears. The robin's egg blue dress she wore was artfully made, with a highly structured bodice and many layers of skirt, which fell around her hips like flower petals, each one edged with beautiful golden embroidery. Over her shoulders sat a matching capelet held together by an intricate golden pin at the base of her throat. Her sensibly low-heeled shoes (though maybe not sensible for the forest) were also golden and glittered in the light. She looked exquisitely regal and entirely out of place in the woods.

Ivy's green eyes glittered the moment they landed on Myev and her face broke into a wide smile. "Good to see you, old friend," she said in a soft, high voice.

Myev was already loping towards the woman with her arms open wide, distressing the two guards that had come from the same place Ivy had. Before they could react, Myev had wrapped her huge hands around Ivy's waist and thrown her high into the air, laughing.

Gwen felt her hand instinctively raise in alarm, the other holding Bumble even tighter, and Sylvia let out a terrified "oh!" as they watched the gnome princess fly impossibly high into the air. For her part, Ivy just giggled, her beautiful dress rustling in the wind, before she landed safely back in Myev's arms.

"I see you missed me too," she said, wrapping her little arms around Myev's neck and squeezing before Myev placed her back on the ground.

"I have some new friends I'd like you to meet," Myev told her, still grinning and gesturing to where the rest of them stood.

Ivy's guards looked like they'd seen their own lives flash before their eyes, standing rooted to the spot with their weapons out and their jaws slack with surprise. Ivy didn't spare them a moment, instead following Myev the rest of the way into the clearing. They scrambled to follow her once they were able to regain their bearings.

Ivy shook each of their hands as Myev introduced them (the taller members of the group had to bend in half to reach the gnome, who stood just over three feet tall). Strands of Ivy's previously perfectly styled hair were falling loose from their braid as a result of Myev's excited greeting, but Ivy didn't seem bothered by it at all.

She looked calculatingly at Gwen, and then Bumble where she still resided in Gwen's arms, for a moment before stating, "You must be responsible for the uprising in Mooncrest."

Gwen choked on her own breath, unable to respond before Ivy continued.

"Some of our contacts there found wanted posters that look just like you guys. Good work over there, I'd say."

Myev's laugh rumbled deep in her chest, "Glad you approve. Have they sent the army after us yet?"

Ivy nodded with a sly smile.

"There are *wanted posters* of us?" Gwen spluttered, violently rubbing her face with her free hand in frustration.

"Oh yes, high reward if you're captured," Ivy said. Seeing the look on Gwen's face she shrugged, adding, "Not that we'd turn you in."

"Uh, thanks," Gwen tried to smile. She turned to Veda, hissing, "This is going so much worse than I could have even imagined when we started this ridiculous crusade."

"It's going about how I expected," Veda said with a toothy smirk.

"That's what we came to talk to you about, actually," Myev said to Ivy. "We're gathering forces to help with the rebellions."

"Better take you to Father then," Ivy said, straight to the point. She turned on her heel and headed back towards where she came from.

Myev and Boris followed her without hesitation, but the others stood back, unsure, as Ivy disappeared through the trees again.

"Come, it won't hurt," Myev assured them, walking through the invisible barrier herself.

Gwen watched as they went through one by one until finally she and Bumble were all that was left. A bit nervously, she stepped forward until she hit the barrier. For a moment it felt like her whole body was being gently squeezed and then she was greeted by the sound of a massive waterfall and the bright rays of the sun hitting her full force, which had previously been diluted by the denseness of the forest. She squeezed her eyes shut, giving them a moment to adjust. Bumble squirmed in her arms, likely just as stunned.

When she opened her eyes again, she could see that they stood at the edge of a crystal-clear lake, above which a waterfall towered so high that Gwen could barely see the top of it from where they stood. It was surrounded by flowers and trees, but was considerably more open than the space they'd just been in. Across the lake, Gwen could make out a bustling city, overseen at the very back by a large white castle.

Bumble elbowed Gwen and she noticed she was falling behind the others, who were following a path around the lake towards the city. "If you want to go at your own pace, you can walk you know," she grumbled, but nonetheless rushed forward to catch up.

Veda looked at her with a soft smile as they did and grabbed the hand that wasn't holding Bumble. Gwen didn't know the customs here and fear crawled down her spine, but she opted to continue holding Veda's hand. After all, it wasn't the only reason she'd have to get murdered by the government anymore. Wasn't even number one on the list—top three at best. That, and she'd eat cyanide before she admitted it, but she needed the comfort.

As they neared the city, Gwen noticed that rather than clearing out the natural flora to make space, the buildings of the kingdom were nestled within the trees, which had been magically shaped to seamlessly fit around and within the structures. Most of the buildings were crawling with vines and surrounded by flowers and small gardens. They even seemed to be magically enabled to respond to their environment. There was a line of trees on either side of the road they walked along, creating a comfortable shade over the cobblestone sidewalks. Gwen watched as a cloud shifted, allowing more sunlight to beam down upon the stone and slowly, gently, the tree branches moved to cover those spots.

The roads themselves were made of colorful stones, arranged in intricate and beautiful patterns. The buildings were all painted cheerful colors and well-tended, decorated with stained glass and small sculptures. There was a clear level of pride and love for the city that shocked Gwen to some extent; all of it was a far cry from the dark and dingy surroundings she was used to in Ironforge, where plants generally dared not grow and the buildings were coated in more soot and filth than paint. It was even different from towns like Silverglenn or Mooncrest, where most of the natural landscape was removed to make way for more buildings. There, the attitude regarding the remaining greenery seemed to be "you are allowed to exist only because we have chosen to let you," and in the Dimroot Kingdom it was "welcome, beloved friend, please make yourself at home; would you like some tea?"

Standing tall behind everything was the castle, a massive structure made entirely of shiny white marble. Flowered vines crawled all the way up the sides of the building and planters could be seen hanging proudly out of the numerous wide, mostly thrown open windows. The sun shone down on the entire city like it was particularly proud of the Dimroot Kingdom and the work it did there.

Gwen watched as a young deer drank water from a nearby fountain, standing only feet away from a male gnome who was seated on a bench and reading a book. The deer was completely unperturbed by the man, comfortable with the knowledge that he would not harm it. In fact, Gwen noticed there was animal life all around them—birds, squirrels, deer, dogs, cats, and even a few foxes—and not a single one of them seemed to feel uncomfortable with their proximity to the gnomes who milled about the city.

Gwen could tell she was not the only one awed by the kingdom. Sylvia was asking Ivy rapid fire questions about the plant and animal life in a reverent voice, which Ivy was answering without hesitation and no sign of irritation at Sylvia's seemingly endless flow of inquiries. In fact, she was clearly very knowledgeable about all the living things in her kingdom and actually seemed pleased that Sylvia was so interested. They were both entirely wrapped up in the conversation with each other.

Jasper's face was a picture of absolute delight and his attentive eyes roved over everything they could. He would stop briefly to look in shop windows, his hands reaching out almost far enough to press against the glass like a child before Avery would pull him along with a soft, "Later, my love."

Veda, who had pulled Bumble from Gwen's arms at some point, trailed behind them with the aviseum on her shoulders so that Bumble could look at things over Jasper. The four of them chatted idly as they walked, all looking exactly like a group of joyful tourists. Gwen watched them with a smile.

Myev and Boris were the only ones who seemed not to be in awe, as they had clearly visited the Dimroot Kingdom before. They ambled along arm-in-arm behind Ivy, Sylvia, and the guards. Every now and again Myev would pipe up in Ivy and Sylvia's conversation, but overall, she and Boris seemed content to just walk along quietly. Somehow, despite the—well, everything—about them, they had the vibe of an elderly couple out for a stroll.

Eventually they approached the castle gates, which opened readily with Ivy at the front of the group. Inside, dozens of gnomes wandered around doing various jobs. Many smiled at Ivy, who gave them a brief smile back before continuing her conversation with Sylvia. Gwen thought she looked slightly miffed by their interruptions, as she was truly more interested in answering Sylvia, but was covering well.

Ivy led them inside, where still more gnomes bustled about the castle, carrying trays of food, carting things to unknown destinations, cleaning various objects, and doing whatever else it was that had to be done to keep a castle running smoothly. She then took them through a few twists and turns before they reached a corridor made of highly polished marble with a plush, violet-colored rug running down the center. The walls were filled with paintings and statues on pedestals, many of which appeared to be of the royal family. All of it was so, so small. It had been easier to not notice it when they'd been outside, but inside Gwen felt like a giant towering over everything and everyone, like a monster in a dollhouse. *Is this how Boris always feels?* she asked herself.

As they approached the large, ornately carved wooden doors (large for the gnomes, for Gwen it was a pretty average sized—albeit extra fancy—set of doors) that led to the throne room, a stuck-up look-ing gnome with perfectly coiffed blue hair burst from them, nearly hitting the guards standing outside, and stalked past them without a word. Bumble, now walking for herself, made a quiet whistle and Veda chuckled. This garnered them both a stern look from Sylvia, who clearly thought they were being rude. The guards grumbled quietly, but regained their composure and kept the doors open upon seeing Ivy leading an entire horde in that direction. They bowed their heads respectfully to her as she passed through with everyone else in tow.

King and Queen Applewood sat on their thrones at the far end of the room. The King didn't notice them right away, as his eyes were closed and he was rubbing the bridge of his nose viciously with his thumb and forefinger. He was a thin but muscular man with darkly tanned skin and scarred hands that seemed as though they'd seen a lot of work, despite his status. Though his hand covered his face, a long, well-tended white beard could be seen falling onto the clean, cream-colored tunic he wore. The sunlight through the windows caught on the colorful, delicately stitched embroidery adorning the collar and sleeves of the tunic, which was tucked into perfectly pressed matching pants. Upon his white hair sat a golden crown in the shape of many twisting branches with red gemstones placed throughout.

His wife was murmuring something to him, running her hand with its long, red painted nails soothingly over his back. Her waist-length burgundy hair fell in waves over her bare, freckled shoulders. The structured sweetheart neckline of her white dress flowed into the layers of chiffon that made up the carefully draped sleeves wrapped around her biceps. The bottom of the bodice gave way to many more layers of chiffon which fell across her wide hips and down her legs. Her crown complimented the king's, with tear-shaped pearls dangling off fragile looking golden chains looped along the base.

Together, they were a stunning sight, leaving Gwen feeling like she shouldn't be dirtying the carefully maintained rugs she stood on. Between how gigantic she currently felt and their remarkable beauty, Gwen thought she couldn't possibly have felt more out of place.

The queen noticed their approach first, her hazel eyes glancing up, first with hardness at the interruption and then with instant warmth when she saw her daughter. "Ivy, my love, you know you can't just be barging in here when we're doing audiences with citizens; there's a schedule."

King Applewood looked up, his face also softening, "Though I am glad to see you again, Myev and Boris."

"We're glad to see you as well, your majesty" Myev said, bowing. "I apologize for the unannounced visit."

Gwen watched the others bow and followed suit, feeling awkward. She'd almost never been in the presence of royalty, her first royal introduction being her unorthodox meeting of Veda, who didn't exactly act with royalty-typical decorum as far as Gwen understood. She did her best to mimic Myev's demeanor, hoping she didn't look entirely like the uncultured street rat she was.

Myev began to introduce them, and Ivy stood tall (or as tall as one that small could get) and straight next to Gwen with her hands behind her back. Gwen noticed that she fidgeted restlessly, her fingers and feet in near constant, though subtle, motion. She looked impatient with the formalities and like she wished she could walk away without being scolded.

Myev finished up introductions, bowing again. "Please let me know when you have time to meet with us. There's no rush."

"I certainly will," King Applewood smiled, the skin around his brown eyes crinkling.

"We'll do dinner tonight," the Queen said. "Ivy, please help them make themselves at home in the meantime."

"Will do," Ivy agreed, pleased to be released and immediately leading them out of the throne room. "Myev, would you like to see the sculptures I've been working on?" she said the moment the doors closed behind them.

"You know I would!" Myev grinned, picking Ivy back up and setting the gnome on her shoulder.

Ivy laughed and pointed down the hall with a flourish, "Onward then!"

Chapter Ten

The front room of Ivy's chambers looked more like a workshop than anything else, with every available surface covered in the tools, clay, wires, paints, and other various minutiae she used to make highly detailed sculptures of bugs, which she then enchanted to function independently. The living sculptures puttered around the space, many lounging in and around the potted plants that also filled the room. Sunlight flooded in through the open stained-glass windows.

An orchid mantis fluttered over to land on Myev's shoulder. "Looks like Antoinette remembers you," Ivy said happily as Myev gently patted the insect with one large finger.

"Nice to see you too, Antoinette."

Bumble was instantly fascinated by the creatures, taking a special interest in a handful of bees that buzzed around a pot of red and pink flowers. She squatted by them, mimicking their buzzing and holding her claws out for them to land on. One did, crawling along her palm, which delighted her to no end. Her dark eyes sparkled and she watched the tiny sculpture with awe.

"The bees are new," Myev noted, which set Ivy off on an excited spiel about all of her creations.

Gwen looked at Veda, who watched Ivy with a smile on her face, clearly finding the gnome's endless chatter endearing. Gwen had to admit that she also found it sweet and she could tell that Ivy and Bumble were going to get along very well.

Quite some time later, once she'd mostly run out of things to talk about, a realization seemed to hit Ivy and she leapt to her feet, almost knocking over the chair she'd been sitting in. "Oh, I forgot to tell someone to have your rooms prepared, I'm so sorry!"

"No bother," Sylvia told her. "We don't need much and we're already taking advantage of your hospitality."

Ivy pointed at each of them and counted on her fingers, "You'll need...it looks like...seven rooms? I assume you two will share your usual?" she said, looking at Myev and Boris.

Myev leaned over and stage whispered while thumbing at Boris, "After the first time we visited, they went ahead and renovated some rooms to have larger doors and furniture to accommodate this big oaf."

"You also could not fit through the doors or in the chairs, my love," he chuckled.

"We're a pair too," Jasper said, holding Avery tight to his side.

"So, six," Ivy amended.

"You can put Bumble, Gwen, and myself in one together as well," Veda spoke up. "No point in dirtying up too many rooms."

Avery's eyes sparkled with mischief as she looked at Gwen, so Gwen pointedly looked away and crossed her arms, feeling a blush crawling up the back of her neck.

"Four it is then, I'll go find a caretaker," Ivy smiled, walking quickly out the door. "Be back shortly."

"Like her," Bumble said, returning to Gwen's side.

"She seems like a perfect friend for you, little one," Veda said, holding her hand out to accept the bee Bumble offered her, which was cradled in both her hands like the most precious treasure.

"She's a good friend and someone we can trust," Myev assured them. "Convincing her parents to throw their weight behind our cause will be the challenge."

***

Once the attendants had cleared away the dinner dishes, King Applewood leaned back in his chair. "Would you like to talk about why you came now?" he inquired of Myev. "I know this isn't particularly formal, but I thought maybe it'd be fine for old friends."

Myev smiled and waved a hand at him. "Of course, this is fine. I'm the last person to insist on formalities." In fact she, along with the rest of them, was sitting on the floor since the chairs were much too small. King Applewood had said that the attendants would be bringing larger chairs in just a moment and Myev had told him not to bother and promptly settled down on the floor.

"I think that's my cue," Gwen said now that things were getting serious. "I won't be particularly useful in this conversation. I'll wait outside," she told them, standing and moving awkwardly towards the door. Veda gave her a displeased look, but made no move to stop her.

Bumble followed her out the door and Gwen closed it softly behind them before setting her back against the stone wall next to it and sliding down to sit. Bumble was still holding onto one of the bees, which Ivy had graciously allowed her to keep. The gnome's eyes had lit up with happiness when she'd returned to her chambers and saw the reverent way Bumble had been cradling the bee in her claws, so she immediately insisted Bumble keep her. Ivy assured her that the magic she imbued the bee with would keep it alive at least as long as Ivy herself was, but that Bumble could always return to her if she ever worried about the bee's health or safety.

"What'd you name her?" Gwen whispered, concerned that her voice would carry into the dining room.

Bumble made a sharp sound, like two rocks hitting each other.

Gwen nodded. "A good name."

"Your language?" Bumble asked. She delighted in the words Gwen came up with for her sounds.

Gwen thought for a moment, her finger on her lips. "Thwack?"

Bumble mulled it over and then chittered, pleased with the name. "Thwack," she repeated.

They sat in silence for a few minutes and then the door opened again and Ivy slid out. She shut it and came over to sit next to them.

"I'm not big on politics either," she said by way of explanation.

"You're going to get your dress dirty," Gwen said as Ivy plopped down beside her.

Ivy shrugged. "It's not the worst thing I've done to a dress. Mother used to get on me all the time for absolutely destroying them when I'd go on treks through the forest. Just covered in mud and holes."

Gwen smiled. "My kind of girl."

Ivy gently set Antoinette down so that she could crawl towards Bumble and Thwack. "Did you name him?" Ivy asked her, leaning forward to see past Gwen.

Bumble made the rock sound again, and then translated in Gwen's voice.

"I think it suits him," Ivy leaned back, satisfied.

They were quiet again as they watched the bugs interact, but it wasn't uncomfortable.

"Would you like to see the forests tomorrow?" Ivy asked after a while.

"I'd love to," Gwen told her. "I've never seen anything quite so beautiful as your kingdom."

"We're very lucky. Very isolated, but lucky nonetheless."

"Do you get to explore the world very often?"

"Not as much as I'd like. Mother and Father worry I'll get hurt or never come back," Ivy said with clear distaste. "I love them, but I don't want to be trapped here. I'm their only heir though, so they want to keep me safe in this tiny bubble where they can teach me everything I need to know to take over some day."

"Sounds like you really don't want to."

"Not even a little," Ivy sighed.

"Why's that?"

"It's just not my...thing," Ivy said, throwing her hands up. "I don't want to be responsible for people, I don't want to tell them what to do, and I don't want to spend every day of my life being made to live up to other people's expectations. I just want to do what I enjoy and live my life for me. I want to go digging for bugs in the dirt and hang out with rabbits and talk to birds. I want to wear my pretty dresses, but not have to care if they're spotless or wrinkle-free. I want to be able to speak my mind without worrying if it's going to offend someone badly enough that they're going to begin an uprising against me." Ivy sighed. "I've just never been very good at this royal thing. There are thousands of other citizens better suited to it than me."

"Hey, I get it," Gwen told her. "Not the—royalty bit, but some of the other stuff. The idea of being responsible for an entire country sounds exhausting."

"It is. If only Mother and Father had birthed another heir," Ivy said wistfully. "I mean, technically they did, but my brother, Briar, died when I was eleven. When I was born, they thought they had the perfect little prince to stand by Briar when he took over someday, that we would be skilled and beloved rulers able to carry on their legacy. From the second I was born, there were all these expectations about who I would be. And then Briar died and I'm all by myself and I have to take on my share and his. But I'm just me and I don't want any of those expectations and I don't know how to live up to them. But they always tell me, 'Ivy, you're supposed to be here. You're meant to do something great; you just have to believe it,'" she fake retched.

"You know what?" Gwen slapped her hands on the ground before standing up and offering her hand to Ivy. "Forget tomorrow, show me the forest now. Maybe that's what we're *supposed* to be doing."

"Really?" Ivy took her hand and leapt up, excited.

"Sure, why not? We're not helping in there," she gestured towards the dining room, "so what else are we going to do?"

"Okay, we'll have to be quiet to sneak past the guards then. Don't worry, I'm an expert," Ivy told them.

She led them through the maze of the castle, carefully avoiding guards and taking them deeper and deeper into the depths of it until they came upon the entrance to an old, dusty tunnel. She lifted her hand, palm up, and produced a pink flame, bright enough to light their way. "We used to have these escape tunnels in case of emergency, back before my ancestors hid our country away. No one really uses them anymore, as you can imagine," Ivy said by way of explanation.

They traveled through the dark tunnel, Ivy's steps sure and practiced. Gwen could even see tiny, heeled footprints in the dust here and there. At the far end they found a ladder with a hatch at the top, which opened into a heavily wooded area. The hatch was disguised as a stump, nestled deep into a patch of trees. When Ivy closed it behind them, it was impossible to tell it apart from the rest of the forest.

They took a few steps and a tall section of wood and foliage lifted itself up from the rest, a soft green light flaring to life within it. "Where are you going today, little one?" they asked in a deep, scratchy voice. As the creature stepped closer to them, Gwen could see that the branches of their body formed an astonishingly tall, lean humanoid shape with patches of moss and vines interspersed throughout. The green glow came from every gap in their body, brighter by their heart and eyes and weaker as it traveled to the tips of their toes and fingers.

"Just showing some friends around, Eren," Ivy replied. She turned to Bumble and Gwen. "This is Eren. He's one of our hidden sentries, posted around the kingdom to warn of and fight off intruders. Not that we've had any of those in my lifetime."

"So about the only one causing me grief for the last several centuries has been you, little one, even though you've only been alive for 56 of those years. It's late. Your parents would be displeased." Eren said it in a way that made it clear that he knew all too well that she would not heed his warning, and he was only telling her because it was his duty.

Ivy waved him off. "We won't be out too long."

Eren sighed and nestled himself back into the trees, his light fading as he did.

"He won't tell on me," Ivy assured them. "Never has. Knows it's a lost cause."

"You're 56?" Gwen asked, a little taken aback.

Ivy waved her hand again. "If you ask my parents that's, like, twelve in gnome years."

She led them around for a while in the moonlight, pointing out various creatures and plants. There were poisonous little green and blue frogs with yellow eyes that glowed in the dark; a plant with long, dark green leaves and white flowers that seemed to constantly dance without wind; small marsupials that reminded Gwen of opossums except they had six legs and dark blue fur that glittered like the night sky; small glowing bugs in a variety of colors that balled up and rolled away if startled; and so much more. Ivy told them everything she knew about everything they passed. She said they were so different to the flora and fauna of the rest of Peonia because the magic in the Kingdom had caused them to evolve differently after thousands of years exposed to it.

Eventually they came upon a gently rushing creek from which a herd of deer as white as new snow was drinking. They lifted their heads, revealing two distinct sets of dark, almond-shaped eyes, two on each side of their faces. Ivy signaled for them to wait and stepped forward to talk to the deer, assuring them that Gwen and Bumble meant no harm. The deer seemed to understand; the largest one moved his massive head in a slow nod and returned to drinking from the water.

Gwen sat on a large boulder and watched as Bumble cautiously approached the deer and chirped softly at them, doing her best to befriend them. After about ten minutes of this, a small fawn allowed her to pet its spotted hide. Gwen grinned at the crow of joy Bumble made at her success and Ivy laughed beside her.

***

They had returned and Gwen was already passed out when Veda finally snuck into the bedroom, closed the wooden door softly behind her, and crawled under the sheets. Bumble had nested in a mess of blankets and cushions by the couch in the separate sitting area, so Gwen had stretched out in the massive bed by herself. It was the largest bed she'd ever laid in in her life and she was glad that orcs were what the gnomes had to measure against when they did those renovations all those years ago. She made room at Veda's gentle nudge and then rolled to face her. "How'd it go?" she asked groggily.

Veda smiled and ran a hand over Gwen's cheek like she couldn't help herself before answering. "I'm actually surprised at the level of interest the King and Queen have in helping us. Turns out they've been considering going to war with Peonia for years now because

Peonian forces have been constantly looking for their borders in an attempt to find a weakness to exploit."

"Checks out," Gwen grumbled, still half-asleep. She was trying and failing to keep her eyes open.

"That blue-haired guy we saw earlier? He was literally just talking to them about how they shouldn't intervene. We have excellent timing, turns out."

Gwen nodded.

"They are interested in doing more than just sending supplies; they want to provide us with weapons and maybe more if we can turn this into an actual movement, rather than just a smattering of rebellions. They want to help us organize the people of Peonia, create a true army, and turn this into something that could bring about lasting change. We've still got some work to do because they won't make this decision without the majority of their citizens backing it, so we've gotta do a vote soon. It's hard to convince a country that has enjoyed thousands of years of peace to give it up to help strangers."

Gwen hummed and closed her eyes. "I get that."

"They're going to give us a few days to come up with a good argument and then we'll present our case in the kingdom square."

"Diplomatic," Gwen noted, raising her brows though her eyelids remained closed.

Veda's thumb softly and consistently brushing over her cheekbone had nearly lulled Gwen fully back to sleep when she spoke again. "I'd really like it if you would help."

"What am I going to do?" Gwen sighed, resolutely refusing to open her eyes and properly entertain the request.

"You live in Peonia and always have. You're one of the only people here that can say that. You know exactly what kind of suffering The Brotherhood causes for the people here. You know personally the kind of damage they can do. Your story could really help show why it's worth it to join the fight."

"I don't even know that *I* think it's worth it," Gwen replied.

"Yes, you do. In your heart, you do. Even if you don't think you're strong enough to help," Veda said, cupping Gwen's neck and pulling her forward to kiss her forehead. "I may not have known you for very long yet, but I understand you better than you think."

Gwen grumbled, shrugging. Veda wasn't wrong. She would be very happy if The Brotherhood and the government supporting it was a thing of the past. She would absolutely love it if their country had a government that looked at all those who lived there as actual people. She would be pleased as punch if people like her didn't have to worry about their safety everywhere they went. If she and Bumble could get honest jobs that weren't just serfdom in pretty wrapping instead of picking up any legally and morally dubious one-off jobs available just to survive.

She just didn't think accomplishing that was something she had any right to be a part of.

Veda pulled her body closer and brushed the tip of her nose against Gwen's, then up along her cheek to press a kiss to her temple. She moved back down and softly brushed her lips against Gwen's open mouth. Gwen sucked in a hard breath, tried to cover it with a grumble. Veda chuckled quietly, laying kisses in an unbroken path all the way down the side of Gwen's cheek and neck. She then latched on over the curve of Gwen's exposed collarbone and gently sucked, teasing with the tip of her tongue before working her way up to the side of Gwen's jaw and nibbling gently, her hand tangled in Gwen's hair to hold her there.

Gwen resisted the urge to pant. She'd never been touched like this. Her whole body was on fire, every one of her nerve endings lit up like so many stars. "Is this bribery? This feels like bribery."

Veda shrugged and pressed her lips to Gwen's, softly. "Is it working?" she asked, her voice dangerously low.

Excitement had entirely overridden fear, in that locked room in a hidden kingdom where no one could find them, so Gwen made a noncommittal noise and rolled onto her back, giving Veda permission to climb atop her. She did so, both hands cupping Gwen's jaw. Veda looked down at her for a second, her smile soft and almost drunk, though Gwen had tasted no alcohol on her. She leaned back down and pressed their mouths together, her movements lazy and unhurried. Her tongue was feather-light at Gwen's lips before sliding in and exploring.

Veda's bare thighs were warm and strong around her hips and Gwen wished they'd never have to leave. The kingdom, that room, that specific bed where a gorgeous woman was touching her like she was something precious, any of it. She could have happily stayed in that moment forever.

She put her hands on Veda's sides, running her fingers up and down, then just under the hem of the oversized tunic Veda had slipped into for bed. She could feel the goosebumps she was leaving on Veda's skin and so, nervously, she slid her hands under the shirt and trailed her fingers up until her thumbs were on Veda's ribcage. She moved them back and forth, back and forth, and Veda sighed into her mouth.

Slowly, her heart beating somehow even faster in her chest, she moved her hands up further, until she found Veda's nipples with the pads of her thumbs. She was rewarded with a gasp and a buck of hips, so she brushed them across the quickly hardening buds several more times, feeling bolder with each pass.

She pinched them between her fingers and pulled gently, until they popped free. Both of Veda's hands had moved back into her hair, cupping the base of Gwen's head, and her grip tightened. Veda's own thumbs rubbed hard circles at the corners of Gwen's jaw and she captured Gwen's lower lip with her teeth, biting down.

Gwen tugged at the hem of Veda's shirt—a question. Veda wasted no time pulling the tunic over her head and throwing it to the floor. Gwen felt delirious as she gazed up at the woman above her. Veda's lips were a little swollen and very wet, shining in the firelight of her hair, and Gwen thought she might be the luckiest woman alive. She pressed her hand to the small of Veda's back to steady her as she sat up, taking a nipple into her mouth.

Veda gasped and wrapped her arms around Gwen's neck, holding her there. Gwen laved her tongue over the nipple and Veda ground her hips down into Gwen's lap, soft moans escaping her mouth. She kissed her way to the other nipple to give it the same treatment, lifting a hand to continue the work on the first.

Veda finally freed herself, somewhat reluctantly, and pressed Gwen back onto the mattress before sliding down, off the end of the bed. She then pulled Gwen down by her legs until they were pressed together again, Gwen laying and Veda standing. Gwen's tunic had gotten rucked up under her breasts when Veda had pulled her, so Veda had easy access to press her hand along the hot, wet line of Gwen's vulva beneath her underwear. She slid them off her hips, then pressed a long finger in and down, finding Gwen's clit and rubbing firm circles there.

Gwen bucked, a gasp tearing itself free of her throat. She wrapped her legs around Veda's hips and fisted her hands into the sheets, desperately trying to maintain some level of composure.

"That's it, good girl," Veda said softly, praising, and Gwen moaned, resolutely refusing to analyze what that did to her.

She dropped to her knees between Gwen's legs and pulled her even closer to the edge of the bed with one hand, her other never pausing in its careful movements. She then pulled Gwen's leg over her shoulder, opening her wide. She wrapped an arm around Gwen's thigh and then placed that hand on Gwen's fluttering stomach. Gwen wondered briefly, deliriously, if Veda could feel the butterflies there. Her fingers were spread wide and Gwen could feel every separate, scorching digit on her skin, so she wouldn't have been surprised if she could.

Veda brought her lips to Gwen's inner thigh, her hair a whisper along the tender flesh. She kissed and kissed, taking her time, until Gwen was squirming, desperate for more. There was no longer any such thing as composure and Veda seemed to like it that way, Gwen's needy mewls causing her lips to curl in an almost fiendish grin. She slid a finger inside of Gwen and crooked it, pressing up. Gwen's back arched, her hips stuttering, and she wished she had more to hold onto than the crumpled sheets wrapped around her hands.

Veda's mouth latched onto her clit, sucking and licking with purpose now, and Gwen almost screamed aloud. Instead, she shoved her forearm into her mouth and bit down hard to muffle it. Veda laughed, the rumble transferring through Gwen's skin and into her body, where Gwen would have kept it forever if she could.

There were two fingers in her now, curved and moving in time with Veda's brilliant mouth. Gwen was so close though they'd just barely started, the heat building in her core and in every tight muscle. She closed her eyes, unable to control herself anymore. "Please," she gasped, unaware she had even spoken. "*Please!* I can't, I—"

"Come on, sweetheart, you can do it," Veda said against her. "You're so beautiful, so good for me."

Gwen's breath caught in her throat as the tension inside her burst, spreading out to each of her quaking limbs. She cried out, ruthlessly biting down on the meat of one palm to stifle it, the fingers of the other locked firmly onto the hand Veda still had on her stomach.

She shook apart in Veda's arms, who whispered love into her skin as she worked her through. "That's my girl; you're perfect."

When the orgasm subsided and Gwen could breathe again, Veda crawled back up on the bed, following Gwen as she scooted back towards the pillows. Gwen propped herself up on her elbows and pressed their lips together, slick and warm. She licked into Veda's mouth, amazed and relaxed and somehow still so, so hungry for the woman above her. She wrapped a hand around the back of Veda's neck and her tail around Veda's waist, holding her as close as she could. She then dropped her hand low, beneath Veda's underwear to her own dripping wet center, where she used her middle two fingers to press and stroke her clit. Veda was close as well, every movement pulling soft moans from her mouth, and Gwen swallowed them as if they alone could sustain her.

Veda was thrusting down against Gwen's hand, her hips moving of their own accord as they chased even more friction. Finally, she pulled back from Gwen's mouth and pressed their foreheads together, both hands soft on the sides of Gwen's neck. Her hips shook and her arms trembled as she came with a low, drawn-out cry. When she had no more to give, Veda collapsed atop Gwen, who wrapped herself around her and held tight.

When she recovered, Veda pressed lazy kisses to Gwen's neck and jaw, whatever she could reach without moving. She had one of Gwen's hands held in her own and Gwen was trailing the nails of her other hand up and down Veda's strong back. Gwen still felt like she had to be dreaming. They drifted, timeless and sated, until Veda finally rolled away from her to pull the heavy quilt that had fallen to the floor up over them.

***

She would probably regret it, and maybe it was the sleepy contentedness speaking, but she thought perhaps if she did just this one thing and helped them win their argument or whatever, she could convince her friends she'd done her part for the cause. She kind of owed them, after all.

"Fine," Gwen sighed, though Veda was very nearly asleep. "I'll help."

Veda squeezed her tight, nuzzling her thanks into Gwen's neck.

Chapter Eleven

As she had predicted, Gwen regretted her agreement almost immediately. They all sat together (on chairs big enough for them) in a private chamber around a large table and everyone was staring at her.

King and Queen Applewood had given them this space to use and, somewhere else in the castle, a group of representatives who disagreed with them were working on their own list of points. The King and Queen would mediate during the debate, giving no opinion of their own so that they would not influence anyone into voting one way or another. Ivy, however, had joined their group for preparation because she thought it would be "more interesting than listening to the same stuffy politicians I already have to listen to drone on all the time." She would not be with them during the actual debate.

"Veda may have fooled me into this," Gwen finally said, crossing her arms, "but that doesn't mean I'm in charge here. Someone say something."

"You kind of are," Avery disagreed with a knowing glint in her eye. "You've lived here all your life. Myev, Boris, and Veda are here temporarily. Ivy's technically on the other side," she said, nodding her head at the gnome, who shrugged. "I was raised in a monastery on Quenabos and Jasper's from Bhollaisca."

"Got run out of there by the time I was fifteen," Jasper added, proud.

"You've lived here a long time though! And what about Sylvia?" Gwen said, pointing.

"I'm from Marshwoods originally. Plus, I'm not very good at public speaking," she said, shyly looking at her lap.

"And I'm Bumble," the bird said, cackling.

"Listen here, you little turd—" Gwen pointed at her feathered friend.

"So, that leaves you," Myev joined in, spreading her arms wide. "You get to lead our side, give our argument to the Kingdom."

"Wait a minute, I agreed to help, but I didn't agree to give the speech," Gwen spluttered.

They just looked at her.

"One of you could just...recite the speech to Bumble and she could play it back for everybody," Gwen tried.

"No thanks, throat sore," Bumble said, kicking her feet up on the table.

Gwen glared at her. "You just like to cause trouble," she hissed.

"Guilty."

"Which, as much as I love her, means she shouldn't be the one giving the speech," Sylvia pointed out.

"Gwen, we'll see how you feel when we get there," Veda said agreeably. "In the meantime, let's start making a list."

***

"I have received news from Elliot," Sylvia told them on the second day of planning. "Gabe, Katya, and a number of other citizens have prepared to leave with the envoy from Vulcaria, which Veda said should be arriving soon."

Veda nodded. After receiving the satchel and Veda's note, her parents had wasted no time in putting together a party to retrieve the refugees, headed by a warrior named Alderin. According to Veda, Alderin was one of her family's personal guards, essentially an uncle to her, and she trusted him with her life. She had been communicating with him daily and passing that information on to Elliot.

"Mooncrest is holding strong," Sylvia continued, "but I also spoke with a contact about Rivergate and it's not good. After the initial rebellion there, manufacturing in Ironforge ground to a halt, which drew extra attention from The Council. They pulled most of their forces from Mooncrest as well as hundreds more and sent them down to Rivergate to take it back. It was—" she cleared her throat, gaze locked on her hands, folded together on the table, "it was a slaughter."

They were all silent for a long, painful moment.

"The people of Rivergate were not prepared for the viciousness of the response and they stood no chance." She took her shaking hands off the table and placed them in her lap. "The Council wanted to make an example out of them."

Gwen felt sick. This was exactly the kind of thing she was afraid of. The Council had more resources and stronger armies than they could even dream of. They were only a handful of people, running around like headless chickens. Sure, the citizens of Mooncrest had control now, but it was only a matter of time before they, too, were beaten back down.

"We have to do something to build support immediately," Myev said. "Organize this thing into one force. We won't make a dent if we can't coalesce the small groups spread across the country; it makes us too easy to put back down. Even once the forces from the Dunes and Frostspire have gathered to help, we need a cohesive plan or it'll be like picking off fish in a bucket. Sylvia, do you have contacts that you trust to help us build a network over which we could pass information? You know some very skilled people."

"A few come to mind. Let me reach out to them, see if they're willing to help," she replied.

"I'll reach out to Aiden, since he already has a satchel," Jasper said.

"I've got a few friends spread here and there that I bet would help if we could find safe ways to contact them," Myev said. "Do you think we could make more of your satchels and enchant a few more birds, since the carrier birds aren't safe?"

"You wouldn't need to enchant new birds if my country votes to help," Ivy added. "We have safe birds of our own, already magically bred to have traits that help them avoid being captured or compromised. Invisibility at will and things like that."

Sylvia nodded, impressed. "I'd need supplies to make more satchels, and a few extra pairs of hands since it would be slow going on my own," she looked over at Ivy, her face tentative. "Ivy, you're good with magic, aren't you?"

"Yeah, I'd love to help," she smiled, looking excited to be asked.

"If only we were close to my home, I have plenty of supplies there," Sylvia fussed.

"I bet we have them here," Ivy interjected. "I could use some of the money I've secreted away during my travels to buy anything we can't forage, even if the kingdom votes not to help. I can help as an individual, not as a princess."

"We could never ask you to do that," Sylvia said quickly, raising her hands, "your help with the magic is more than enough."

Ivy waved her off. "This is the most exciting thing that has happened here in decades. I want to help however I can."

The others continued to talk about people they could contact, things they could do, as Gwen sat silently entrenched in a shame she had a hard time putting words to. They'd begun this journey for her and it had snowballed into all of this. It had grown so large, much too heavy for her to carry. Too heavy for any of them. Every day they were pulling more and more people into the weeds. She couldn't help but feel responsible.

"We're asking people to die," she almost whispered. "We're asking people to die for this." She looked up, her eyes desperate.

Myev, who was sitting next to her, reached over and placed her hand atop Gwen's on the table. "People are already dying." Gwen met her eyes and tried to understand. "They've been dying for nothing at all; dying just to serve some rich assholes who don't care about them in the slightest. At least this is something."

"I wasn't sure in the beginning either, but our friends are right." Avery told her. "If we have even a little bit of power to help change this, shouldn't we try? Even if we fail?"

Gwen was quiet, chewing on the inside of her lip until it bled, so Myev continued. "You're right, Gwen. People will die. Probably a lot of people. It's horrible, but it's a fact. If there was a way we could do this without violence, without death, you know that we would. And you know that we will minimize suffering wherever we can. I am not naïve enough to believe that The Council will be careful about civilian casualties, but we will do whatever we can. Unlike the Peonian government, the things we want to do are *for* the people and we will always take that very seriously.

"All of this has proven that there is a strong desire in the Peonian people to free themselves. Anyone who wants to actively join the fight despite the risks will do so of their own free will; we would never force them. But some people cannot stand up for themselves, and it is our duty to fight for those who cannot fight for themselves."

"Some things are worth putting your life on the line for," Boris said simply.

Veda was holding Gwen's knee under the table and she gave a firm squeeze. Gwen nodded and after a moment, her friends continued their conversation. They were right, of course—people made their own decisions. If this wasn't something people really wanted, they wouldn't help. She tried to shove the shame down as deep as she could and refocused on the conversation.

"After all this, when we leave Dimroot," she said when the conversation came to a natural lull, "we go to Rivergate. We go see what we can do to help."

Veda's smile was blinding.

***

"So, you're from Marshwoods?" Gwen asked, carefully cutting another bunch of lemongrass and sliding it into the relatively small basket at her feet.

She had offered to go out with Sylvia and Ivy after dinner, feeling the desperate need to get out of the castle, away from all the responsibilities determined to crush her into dust. Before heading out, Sylvia had given them a small lecture on sustainable foraging, but even so, she, Sylvia, and Ivy each had two baskets with them, the majority of which were already full after stopping in several locations to harvest. They needed to gather as many components as they could so that they could be dried before the next full moon, only a few days away.

Sylvia hummed in the affirmative. "Born near the Maraisespirit, which my mother used to say was why I had a natural affinity for magic."

Marshwoods was a swampy cluster of islands, just east of Peonia. Gwen had heard it was an incredibly magical place, somewhat like Dimroot Kingdom, but Marshwoods magic was wilder, harder to tame. All she'd ever heard of Maraisespirit was that it was supposedly the most magical and spiritual place there, which Gwen found impressive considering she'd also heard rumors of Perais, an island that locals said split off from the mainland long ago and traveled wherever it pleased, sometimes swallowing ships whole on its way. That sounded pretty magical. And terrifying.

"Why'd you leave?" Gwen asked, taking a fistful of dandelions from Ivy to add to her basket since Ivy's were both already full.

"Wasn't wanted there," Sylvia said softly. "My mother was the only person that ever really understood me and after she died, my family said I was too fragile to survive there. Unable to do what it took to come out on top of the food chain and provide for myself."

Gwen snorted in disbelief before she could think better of it. "You're literally the most self-sufficient person I've ever met. I saw your garden, your house. You're doing just fine for yourself."

Sylvia's laugh was high and tinkling, like a breeze through wind-chimes. "Thank you."

"Their loss, really," Gwen said earnestly.

"My family tended to see their relationship to the land and magic as adversarial, instead of cooperative. To them, it had to be tamed with violence, to be controlled and abused into submission, so that it always knew who was in charge. If a magical creature infringed on your property, you killed it. It didn't matter if it meant you harm or was simply being an animal, you killed it because it dared exist where you didn't want it to. I could never do that. I tried to make them understand that the strongest magic is created through building a relationship with the world around you and the energy that runs through everything, which first and foremost requires you to be respectful. To understand that you are not better or worse than a toad or a tree or an ant. We are all part of this dance together."

"That kind of thinking is why we do so well here," Ivy added. "Every being can have access to magic with practice and the right tools, but those who have a deeper natural connection to the world and its energy tend to be more powerful. Though we get an extra boost here 'cause there's miles upon miles of caverns beneath us filled with bahen."

"What's that?" Gwen asked.

"A crystal that absorbs and magnifies magical energy. Because we have such a symbiotic relationship with our land, the bahen allows us to draw from that energy for our magic without even having to mine them and use them directly. It's like a consistent, ever re-filling battery, right under our feet."

"Think of the bahen as another tool," Sylvia said. "If you're using the energy of the bahen, you don't have to rely only on the energy in *you*. It's why I use spell components like these," she pointed to a basket, "in my magic. I can get more powerful results combining their energy with my own, instead of draining myself dry relying only on my energy. The bahen allow the people of the kingdom to create amazing results with minimal drain on their own magical energy."

"And that's why Peonia wants so badly to find us. If they could mine all those crystals...." Ivy shuddered and elaborated no further.

Sylvia got a bright glint in her eye, suddenly excited. "Gwen, I know you've never practiced magic, but you should still be able to feel the strength of the bahen. Sit, sit!" she directed, setting the basket aside. She sat cross-legged on the ground with her hands on her knees, palms facing upward. Ivy sat too, facing Gwen with her big, enthusiastic eyes. Her ears twitched as she smiled. Sylvia motioned for Gwen to do the same.

Once Gwen had, she continued. "Close your eyes and just breathe for a moment. In through your nose, out through your mouth. What can you hear around you?"

"Uh," Gwen scrunched her closed eyes. "Crickets. Wind. My breathing. A bird of some kind. I don't recognize the call."

"Good. What can you smell?"

Gwen refocused her thoughts on her nose and took a deep inhale. "Lemon—the grass probably. Forest-y...stuff."

"Focus and break it down, try to find each individual smell," Sylvia directed gently.

"Okay, I also smell, uh. Wet, like, dew. Like the night smells sometimes." Gwen focused as hard as she could, trying to sort and separate everything in her brain. "I smell myself. My leathers and that fancy soap Ivy gave us to bathe with."

Ivy giggled, "It's lavender."

"Lavender then," Gwen amended.

"Good," Sylvia praised. "Continue to breathe deeply and relax. Allow yourself to become part of the landscape."

Gwen swayed a little, gently moving her upper body back and forth an inch or two, just because it felt good. She listened. She smelled. She thought about her place in this giant, unfamiliar forest.

"What do you feel?"

"The ground under my butt. The grass and flowers tickling my tail. The breeze in my hair. The weight of my hands where they rest on my knees."

"What do you feel inside?"

Gwen was stumped for a second, but she sucked a deep, loud breath in through her nose and tried to clear her mind. "My breath in my nose. The muscles contracting in my chest. My heartbeat, just a little." She looked deeper, focusing on the tiniest details, and was surprised by what she found. "A—a buzzing? I guess? Just under my skin."

"That's it," Sylvia whispered reverently. "That's the magic. That energy under your skin and in your blood and in your bones. It's in you, just as it's in everything else."

Gwen focused on the energy, feeling it vibrate through her body. She shivered and Ivy chuckled again.

"Here," the gnome said in a near-whisper. Gwen cracked an eye open as Ivy sat a fat, yellow dandelion in her palm. "Focus the energy on that. Envision the energy in you flowing into the flower, mixing with the energy already in it, and then the flower floating up from your hand. Imagine it slowly lifting away from you, what that would feel like."

Gwen closed her open eye and did as she was told. For a long minute, she could just feel the slight weight of the plant on her skin. A sticky spot where the sap inside had leaked out onto the stem. A breeze rustling through and gently shaking the thin petals. She imagined the energy as a ball of light in her chest, because the buzzing was strongest just behind her sternum. Her energy was purple, unlike Sylvia's green or Ivy's pink. She then imagined it funneling slowly down her arm, past her wrist, into her palm, and into the flower. She imagined the flower glowing with that light, until it covered the entire flower. She imagined it lifting. Slowly. Just a little bit.

And then the weight in her palm, as slight as it was, was gone. In its place was only the warm humming of the energy. She opened her eyes and the dandelion hovered—just an inch or two, but it hovered—cloaked in the soft purple light she'd imagined. She couldn't help but crack a grin, so wide it pulled at her cheeks and crinkled her eyes. She'd never done anything like this before, hadn't known she could. She allowed the flower to drop back into her palm.

She looked at Sylvia, then at Ivy, and they both smiled back. Sylvia looked like a proud mother and she clapped quietly. "Knew you could do it."

"Thank you for teaching me," Gwen smiled.

After a few long moments of companionable silence, Sylvia gave a soft grunt and used her staff to help her stand. "Back to work, I suppose."

Gwen gingerly tucked her dandelion into a basket.

***

The kingdom square was packed with people and Gwen felt her knees shaking as she looked out at all of them. She stood at a podium on one side of the stage, opposite the gnome they'd seen stomping from the royal chambers on their first day in the Dimroot Kingdom. His name was Aretas and apparently he had been a staunch and very vocal proponent of staying out of the affairs of other countries for a very long time. Gwen nervously listened to him rattle off reason after reason why the Dimroot Kingdom should remain hidden and neutral, regretting her choices more and more by the second. He was intelligent, well spoken, and factual. She was...her. King and Queen Applewood sat in the center with Ivy between them, periodically interjecting with questions. Aretas answered them all without a second's thought.

"The Peonian government has spent years searching for our borders to no avail," the blue-haired man said. "They search because they hope that they can invade us, take our sovereignty from us, and make us cogs in their ever-growing machine. The resources we have here in the Dimroot Kingdom are rare and powerful, gifted to us by this special land for protecting and cultivating it. Peonia wants to use these gifts for their own gain, but it is precisely due to the strength of our magic and the technology made with it that they cannot find us.

"If we allow that magic outside our borders, they could turn it against us and use it to destroy our beloved kingdom. Who knows the destruction they could wreak in the world with the full power of our magic behind them? Their greed and violence know no bounds, so what makes us think it would be a good idea to even inadvertently empower them to those ends?"

"What will we do if they eventually find and breech our borders anyway, as their own technology advances?" Queen Applewood asked.

"We will do what we have always done," Aretas said, "we will ruthlessly exterminate any threats to us using the considerable networks of magic, warriors, and sentinels at our disposal."

"And if they find a way past our sentinels? If they reach any of our settlements?"

"I have the utmost faith in our highly trained guards, your highness. We have never cut corners with their training, even though it has been thousands of years since they have faced an outside threat within our borders."

"Is it not sometimes better to go on the offensive, eliminate threats before they arrive?" King Applewood mused.

"As of yet, they have never gotten close enough to finding us that I believe that to be a necessary action," Aretas told him. "Our protection measures have thus far maintained a 100% success rate since their implementation."

The King nodded and gestured for Aretas to continue.

"We have remained safe for all these millenia because our ancestors knew that staying completely invisible to violent colonialists like Peonia was the best way to assure our safety. I ask you, people of the Dimroot Kingdom, do we want to take the chance of losing all that we have?"

The crowd clapped for him as he bowed slightly to end his speech and then looked expectantly at Gwen. She cleared her throat, looking down at the papers they had prepared, and willed herself to begin.

"First, I would like to take the time to thank King and Queen Applewood, as well as you, the citizens of the Dimroot Kingdom, for allowing us to speak on this matter." Her voice was a bit wobbly, so she took a breath and tried to steel it. "I know that this decision will not be easy for you and I hope that I am able to help you understand why we have come to your kingdom with this plea. My friends and I," she gestured to where they sat off to the side, "are happy to answer any questions you may have at any point in time.

"Ostensibly, Peonia is an oligarchy and is run by a group called The Council. The Council consists of fifteen members, each coming from the familial line of one of the original founders of the country. These families are the wealthiest in Peonia and make all of the decisions for the country with little to no regard for the health and safety of the rest of the citizens. Anyone that knows anything about Peonia knows that it has been shadow-run by The Brotherhood of Truth since its inception, a cult-like organization that believes in the superiority of the human male. Thus, The Brotherhood has fostered a society built on the subjugation of all other races and genders. Most, if not all, of the members of The Council are proud members of The Brotherhood.

"Peonia has had a history of colonialism that has not endeared it to most other countries, including yourselves. They regularly try to expand their borders into the surrounding countries and use the Peonian citizens' labor, skills, and physical resources to do so. This is not something a large portion of us support, but it is not something we have been able to stop. I come from the city of Ironforge, where most of the weapons and machinery used in the Peonian army are made. I can assure you that most of the workers in the factories of Ironforge work there solely because they must, to feed and house their families. Many of us are caught in an inescapable cycle where we must choose between working at painfully low wages doing back-breaking work, or starvation and homelessness.

"Many people, especially those that look like myself or like many of my friends, have a very hard time getting jobs at all and must lie, cheat, and steal to make it to another day. We do not thrive; we are barely surviving. The lucky among us have become experts at clawing our way through just to get by. Those that are not so lucky are gone. They die, sometimes horribly violent, demeaning deaths, and despite that, it is likely that no one with power will care enough to do anything about it."

She sucked in a shaky breath, her heart thundering in her chest. She'd thought about leaving this out, speaking about things in an abstract, less personal manner, but she knew her testimonial would lend credence to the cause. They hadn't written this part down ahead of time—no one was going to force her to share her story—so she just began, allowing the dam to break in her chest. "When I was an infant, my parents were murdered by several members of The Brotherhood of Truth. They were traveling through the Tall Pines Forest, minding their own business, when they were attacked. My mother managed to break away for only a moment and ran through the forest with me in her arms, desperate to save her child's life. She hid me in the hollow of a tree before being slaughtered, only a stone's throw away from the tree. I was found days later, thanks to a local farmer who had heard my cries.

"I will never know the sound of my mother's voice. I will never get to see my father's face. I do not even know their names. All of that was taken from me before I had the opportunity to create even a single memory of them to hold onto," her voice broke, but she continued. "There is no record of them. I do not know where their bodies ended up. I do not know where they came from, where they were going, or why they were going there. Do I have grandparents somewhere out there? Do I have any family at all? Did my parents own a home filled to the brim with things that made them smile? Did they have beloved friends? Pets? Hopes and dreams? I will never have answers to any of these questions because The Brotherhood was able to erase my parents entirely with their money and power. For all I know, the only person in the world that cares that they once lived is me, and when I die, there will be no one. They will be well and truly forgotten.

"But my story is not unique. I am not the only child in Peonia who grew up with nothing and no one. The orphanage I grew up in was filled with children whose stories mirrored mine. We are only fyrdiav, we are only aviseum, only laisarnne, only orcs, only doppelgangers. Only unimportant and disposable. Why should anyone care about us?" She felt her voice rising, her fists clenching where they sat on the podium. "Well, we care about us. We care about each other. And we are tired of allowing the government of our country to treat us like we are not living, sentient beings with hearts and souls."

She returned to her notes. "Our rebellion is in its infancy. The rebellion in Mooncrest happened only two weeks ago. It is simply a spark, a single city that grew tired of being abused, but from one spark, a fire can grow, and an entire forest can be destroyed. Our fire is already growing. We want this spark to be the first step in a very necessary change. We are just starting out and we have a long way to go. I will not pretend that the road ahead of us is not filled with darkness, uncertainties, and fear. Nonetheless, we have come to you to ask that you help us destroy a government that has taken us for granted for centuries. That has treated us as fodder for their bloated, parasitic empire. To create a new one that treats both its citizens and neighbors with respect."

The silence when she was done was deafening, as though every one of them was holding their breath. Finally, Queen Applewood cleared her throat. "And how can we do that? In what ways can we help your cause?"

"The Dimroot Kingdom is filled with brilliant minds and incredible resources. Having your Kingdom as an ally would be invaluable in the fight against The Brotherhood of Truth and The Council because the native Peonians have very little. We have only our determination, skills, and unbreakable spirits. To combine that with your aid, we could actually stand a chance," Gwen replied. "If nothing else, we ask that you send supplies such as food, water, and medicine. If you are willing, weapons and magic. We are not asking you to drain your amazing kingdom dry to help us; we will do whatever is within our power and rally as much support as we can within our own borders. We are not looking only to your country, either. We are asking for the help of our neighbors from the Snowblight, The Vedvik Dunes, and Vulcaria. We already have confirmed aid in various forms coming from these countries."

"Why should we help? What is there for us to gain?" the King asked.

"I *could* say you should help because it would benefit your kingdom. That you would be safer if you weren't constantly under the threat of attack by the Peonian government and our civilizations could live in harmony, but we both already know that's true. The thing I beg you to remember as you decide, though, is that the Peonians are people too. We are only asking that you lend your hand however you can to help us create a society like your own for our people. To take a decisive step on the right side of history. I would never suggest you sacrifice your own people for ours, but don't we all have a responsibility to help take care of each other as living beings sharing this planet? Isn't creating a more just world a benefit to all that inhabit it, regardless of borders?" She was using words suggested by the others as responses to questions, but as she recalled and recited them from memory—she felt them burning in her blood.

The King nodded and the Queen gave her a smile, her eyes alight. She could see where Ivy got that look. Gwen turned and looked out at the crowd, the nodding heads, those mumbling to their neighbors behind their hands, and felt powerful somehow. "I'm not here to trick you or to force any of you to do anything. I am here to tell you the truth, lay out what we see as the facts, and then let you make the decision you think is best. We will accept whatever you choose."

The King and Queen asked a few more questions before they stood, taking the stage to explain that the citizens would have three days to decide their position before the vote would take place. After that, they would count them and announce the results. The King reminded them that he, his wife, Aretas and his assistants, and Gwen and her friends would all be available for questions during that time.

Gwen took her seat next to Veda, who was grinning at her. "What?"

"Proud of you," Veda bumped her shoulder with her own.

"Thanks," Gwen mumbled in return, staring at her own lap, cheeks warm.

***

Gwen led Veda through the secret passage Ivy had shown her, out into the woods. She reached down and clasped Veda's hand to help her out of the hidden stump door, and Veda didn't let go once she was on solid ground, lacing her fingers with Gwen's. As they passed him, Eren cracked his eyes open. Before his inner light could even reach its full brightness, he nodded once and closed them again.

They explored the nearby forest, Veda as amazed as she always was with everything around her, and Gwen tried to share the things she remembered from Ivy's stories. Eventually the tree line broke into a small clearing with patches of flowers and shin-high grass. Towards the center, bathed in moonlight, was a smattering of short moss surrounding a large boulder.

The space around the rock was just large enough to rest in, so Gwen pulled her jacket off, tossing it to the side. They were deep in the mountains and the night was chilly, but Veda's warmth would stop her from feeling it at all. She wanted to curl into Veda, skin on skin, and allow it to melt her—the stress, the fear, all of it. She sat and patted the ground next to her. Instead, Veda moved to sit behind her, pulling Gwen back into the space between her legs and against her chest. She wrapped her arms around Gwen's middle and rested her chin on Gwen's shoulder.

Somewhere else in the forest, Ivy and Sylvia were creating more communication satchels from the herbs they had gathered. Sylvia had had to use magic to help them dry the last little bit, and as she looked at the herbs and stones and cloth bags their little team had gathered, she'd done an anxious little sigh and said, "It'll do!"

Bumble had gone with to make the satchels, forever curious, and when Gwen and Veda had snuck away from the grand hall, Myev, Boris, and Jasper had been many flagons deep into a drinking contest. Gwen couldn't help but smile at the thought of Avery's exasperated yet fond face as she watched her husband get clumsier and more animated with each drink. Even he knew he wasn't going to be able to beat Myev and Boris, but he didn't seem to care. That didn't seem to be the point.

Veda pressed a soft kiss to Gwen's throat, just under the turn of her jaw, and Gwen hummed and ran her fingertips over Veda's arms in return. She swept Gwen's long, lavender hair to the side and continued kissing down the back of her neck and across her shoulder. Gwen's eyes fluttered shut and a tight, feverish knot grew in her stomach, reaching its tendrils up through her chest. She felt as though something inside her might burst at any moment. Or that it already had, filling her with something lighter than air.

She turned in Veda's grasp, lifting herself up onto her knees, and pressed Veda back onto the moss. She stared down for a moment at Veda's golden-brown eyes, somehow even brighter than the halo of her hair, before reaching down and running her finger along the slope of her nose, over the soft cushion of her lips.

"I think I love you," she said, before she could even fully think the thought. It fell out of her mouth entirely unbidden and for one sharp, terrifying moment, she thought maybe she'd made a mistake.

But Veda simply grinned up at her and wrapped a hand around the back of her neck, pulling her down. "I love you too."

When their lips met, Gwen sighed shakily, her breath stuttering in her throat. Veda swallowed the sound and pressed their lips more firmly together. Gwen knew her heartbeat was pounding fast as a hummingbird in her chest, but her fingertips pressed gently to the skin of Veda's neck confirmed that she wasn't the only one. She did love Veda. It didn't matter how long she'd known her; Veda had changed her life in so many ways.

Soon they would return to Peonia, with or without the help of the Dimroot Kingdom. Soon they could be part of a full-scale war, if they weren't crushed before then. Soon they would continue her quest for vengeance. Tonight, however, there was nothing for them to do but wait, and with Veda's breath against her skin, so very sweet and alive, Gwen found it hard to worry about any of that.

Chapter Twelve

Three days passed in a blur of faces as they spent hours upon endless hours speaking with citizens of the Kingdom. Gwen didn't always know what to say, but she found that being her honest self usually went over pretty well—people seemed to appreciate that she would give it to them straight. Avery and Jasper received about the same response. Veda and Myev's infectious, extroverted personalities endeared them to most of the people they spoke to while Sylvia's deep well of worldly knowledge answered a lot of the questions the rest of them couldn't. Bumble and Boris spent most of their time distracting and playing with the children (Gwen very maturely did not vocalize her envy) while their parents asked questions. Overall, she thought it was a good group effort and went better than she could have expected.

The day after the vote, King and Queen Applewood took the stage in the town square once again. Gwen sat on one side with her friends, Aretas and his team on the other, as they had been during the debate. Avery, the most math minded of them, had spent the morning with the King, a member of Aretas' group, and a handful of royal employees as they worked through the votes. The sun was high in the sky now, the day already half over, and Gwen tried not to fidget under its heat.

"Our team has spent the morning tallying your votes," the King explained. "This process was overseen by a representative of each group and myself, to assure fairness and honesty. A decision has been reached. 73% of the citizens of The Dimroot Kingdom have voted to assist Peonia in their fight against their government."

The crowd began to murmur and emit scattered cheers, some citizens pleased and some not. Gwen's heart was beating loudly in her ears and she sat as still as she could, trying to let the news sink in. Veda set her hand on Gwen's shoulder and shook it softly, a congratulations. In her peripherals, she could see Myev nodding, pleased. Finally, Gwen looked up and made eye contact with Aretas, whose jaw was clenched so tightly she thought he might crack a tooth. She quickly looked back down at her feet.

"What that will mean exactly will take more discussion, but we will begin by providing resources," King Applewood continued. "We will be sending food, water, and medical supplies to Mooncrest, Ironforge, and Rivergate at this time and we will send more to other locations as it becomes necessary. We will be working with the Peonian group," he gestured to Gwen's friends, "as well as their allies to accomplish this.

"I am deeply proud of this Kingdom and your desire to help others who are suffering. I am pleased to know that your empathy and kindness extends to our neighbors outside of our borders as well as those within them. This decision will mean an ongoing discussion and your voices matter. We are prepared to listen to your ideas, opinions, and concerns. Thank you all."

The crowd clapped politely as King Applewood left the stage. Gwen hurried off after him, feeling the heavy weight of thousands of eyes upon her.

***

"Holy fuck," Gwen whispered as they stepped out of the boundary of the Dimroot Kingdom and back into the Peonian forest, the breaking of the magical barrier causing a soft *pop* in her ears. "I'm so glad to be out of there. Aretas and his death glare were getting old. No offense," she glanced apologetically at Ivy.

They'd spent the last two days making plans for how to get supplies from the Kingdom to the places that needed it. The talks were boring and Gwen had little to add, seeing how she had few powerful connections, so instead she got to spend two straight days focusing on trying not to make eye contact with Aretas across the table, who looked at her like she had personally shit in his shoes. His disdain for the others was also clear, but since she'd (unwillingly) taken the lead in the debate, she received the largest portion of his ire. He didn't hate her personally, Ivy had assured her, just what she stood for. Which, unsurprisingly, did not help, but she was grateful to Ivy for trying anyway.

"Hey, I get it; I'm glad to be out too," she laughed. "I didn't actually think my parents were going to let me go."

Myev had told Gwen about the argument she'd been made witness to, in which Ivy had floated the idea to her parents of going with the Peonian party to Rivergate, and it had apparently gotten quickly and irreversibly emotional. They'd always been extremely protective of Ivy, as both their daughter and the Dimroot Kingdom's only heir, so the idea of her leaving the safety of the Kingdom and entering what was rapidly becoming an active warzone didn't fly easily.

Ivy had taken Myev with as a buffer, knowing her parents would be a little better behaved if there was a witness, but Myev said she could physically feel the vein in the King's forehead getting ready to burst as he tried to keep his cool while he argued with his daughter.

"His face was so red he looked like he'd gotten the worst sunburn of his life and the Queen kept, like, aggressively reorganizing her skirts, as though she needed to take her frustration out on something and how dare the cloth be touching her at that exact moment," Myev whispered to her the night before they left. "Ivy gave them some line about," she gave big, dramatic air-quotes, "'how can I expect to learn to rule this country properly if you won't even let me defend the things we believe in' and 'in order to lead our people someday I'm going to need real world experience'. I think that's what got them in the end. Hard to argue with her when she's using their own words and goals against them, even if they knew deep down that she was just doing it to get what she wanted."

When they'd given their goodbyes at the waterfall that morning, Queen Applewood's eyes were wet and her bottom lip wobbly, and Gwen could swear she'd heard Ivy's bones creak as her mother squeezed her as tightly as she possibly could.

"We'll keep her safe," Gwen told the king, hoping she was appropriately conveying how seriously she was taking this.

King Applewood was quiet. Gwen didn't miss how, for just a fraction of a second, he clenched his jaw to stop the slight tremble in it. "I know," he finally said, without a hint of the emotion he'd almost let bubble to the surface. "I know."

Ivy seemed to be bursting with excitement as they walked, a wide grin plastered on her face and her hands constantly moving. She touched her dress, the plants they walked by, Antionette where she sat perched on Ivy's shoulder, anything within reach. She settled a little over time, but as they all got ready to lay down for the night, she still had more energy than she knew what to do with. Thus, she volunteered for first watch with Gwen. She pulled out a small piece of wood and began to carve it, so Gwen watched her work in the firelight.

Antoinette and Thwack were in a small woven basket Ivy had brought along to help carry them, as they weren't exactly quick movers, which she'd padded with little scraps of cloth and leaves so that they had a space to bed down and rest. Bumble had curled herself protectively around the basket as she slept, giving Ivy a break from pet duty.

Gwen's nerves hadn't fully settled all day, despite being away from the Dimroot Kingdom and the responsibilities thrust upon her there. Perhaps because they were headed straight towards bigger responsibilities, more dangerous ones, and they only had a handful of days to prepare. She knew it was the right thing to do, but she didn't know exactly how to help once they got to Rivergate. She didn't know how to tend to the wounded, rebuild decimated communities, or how to strategize and plan a war. The only thing she knew how to do was fight, and they'd already done that. And the whole country was currently worse off for it.

Lying only a few feet from Gwen, Sylvia sat up briefly before huffing and settling back down. The movement caused a break in her obsessive thoughts, and she used the brief reprieve to try to actively push them away, at least enough to let her sleep a little after her shift. She watched the light of the fire glint off Ivy's knife and tried to just breathe. She tried to remind herself to take each day as it came, since it was her only option anyway.

***

Gwen immediately resented the awareness crawling its way through her brain. She felt like she'd been asleep for half an hour, tops. The sunlight burning through her eyelids told her it was morning though, so she sighed and sat up. Most of her friends were still asleep. Boris was snoring loudly with Myev snoring almost as loudly next to him. Between them and beneath their blankets was a small lump, which she knew was Ivy. After their watch, Ivy had tried to go to sleep wrapped up tightly in her own nest of blankets, her tiny, freckled nose the only thing visible. After a few minutes away from the direct warmth of the fire, Gwen could see the blankets trembling.

"You okay?" she whispered, nudging the blanket pile gently.

"Not used to camping," Ivy chuckled through her chattering teeth.

"It gets awfully cold in the mountains at night, especially now that we're getting into fall, and there's not enough of you to generate much warmth," Gwen joked. "Do you want one of my blankets?"

"No," Ivy said quickly. "There's not much of you either, is there?"

"I'm at least twice your height," Gwen told her.

"But just as scrawny as me."

"Fair. But I also have her," she said, thumbing back at Veda, deeply asleep and curled around her back. "I'm plenty warm."

She heard Myev stand and start shuffling around the others, towards her and Ivy. She and Boris were on watch and she must have heard their whispers. She reached down without asking and gathered up the entire lump of fabric with Ivy in it. "Come on then, you little chipmunk. Closer to the fire and closer to my body heat. I'm warm anyway."

"Because your home is in a solid block of ice!" Ivy squeaked back, digging her way through the blankets to press herself against Myev's skin. Myev tightened her arms around her little bundle and went back to her post.

Now, despite the deep displeasure caused by the prying claws of the sunlight, Gwen smiled at Ivy no longer shivering and sleeping soundly between the two massive orcs.

"Oh, fiddle," she heard Sylvia mutter.

Gwen stood up and stretched, heading over to where Sylvia was cooking something on the fire. "Need help?"

Sylvia was chewing on her thumbnail, the claw clacking against her teeth. In her other hand, she held a wooden spoon, which she was using to frantically stir a thick, dark liquid that smelled like elderberries and... something floral? Not exactly breakfast.

Gwen had noticed Sylvia growing more and more agitated as they walked the day before, her eyes darting around nervously every time the woods made a sound, which had not helped calm Gwen's own sense of impending doom. She had asked her what was wrong, but the laisarnne had only shrugged. "I'm not sure yet," she'd whispered back, "but something isn't right."

Even though she had also been on high alert, Gwen hadn't seen a single thing during their travels or her watch, and it seemed like no one else had either.

Sylvia pulled her hand from her mouth and placed it on Gwen's shoulder. Gwen looked over, waiting for her to speak, and then she heard Sylvia's voice in her head, though her mouth did not move. *"It's that raven to your left, about twenty yards into the forest, high up in the trees. Be careful when you look, don't make it obvious,"* Sylvia told her. *"It's all by itself and it's been following us since about midday yesterday."*

Gwen glanced over without turning her head, searching for a small flash of black. She opened her mouth to reply, but closed it again quickly. *"Are you sure?"* she thought back, hoping the mental link went both ways.

"Yes. If you catch it in just the right light, its eyes glow blue," Sylvia told her. *"I've been sensing a very negative magical presence and that's where it's coming from. I'm certain."*

"What do we do?"

Sylvia nodded at the liquid in the pot in front of her. *"I don't have all the ingredients I'd like so it won't last very long, but if we get everyone to drink a bit of this it should cloak us for a while. Long enough to change our route and hopefully lose it. Start splitting it among those bowls while I wake the others."*

Gwen nodded, grabbing the wooden spoon from Sylvia and quickly scooping the liquid into the bowls.

"Good morning!" Sylvia said to Jasper and shook him gently by the shoulder, her voice higher than normal. Her hand remained fixed on him, and Gwen watched him blink, face contorting as he tried to wake up enough to understand the mental messaging. His eyes cleared and he nodded, woke Avery so Sylvia could pass her message, crawled out of their blankets, and made his way to Gwen.

Sylvia moved on to the others, touching each of them in turn. Slowly, they all made their way to her and drank the concoction. Gwen took a large gulp herself, resisting the urge to cough as it slid thickly down her throat. The floral scent had been peonies, she now realized, and she felt like she'd taken a hearty swig of an old woman's perfume.

They finished their "breakfast" and waited, looking at each other without speaking. Sylvia considered each of them in turn, her scaly eyebrow ridges knotted together, and then motioned for Gwen to put her bowl down. She grabbed her hand and mentally told Gwen to grab Veda's. One by one, they linked hands. From far away it might have appeared as though they were praying.

"Okay, pack quickly. We have about fifteen minutes before the spell kicks in and we need to be moving by then. Once we leave camp, follow me."

In her mind, Gwen heard the various noises of acknowledgement from the others before everyone broke away and began to gather their things. Sylvia was still muttering to herself and Avery put a comforting hand on her back in between rolling her and Jasper's blankets up and shoving them in her pack. Ivy seemed jittery, but was doing her best to gather her things as quickly as she could. Myev, who had finished packing in minutes with military efficiency, gently pushed her aside and took over. Ivy went to put out the fire instead.

Veda pulled her magic cloak out of her pack and slipped the hood up over her head, hiding her fire. She then hefted her pack onto her shoulders and grabbed Gwen's hand, prying her fingers off where they were clasped, white-knuckled, around the straps of her own pack. Gwen hadn't noticed how tightly she had been gripping it. She held both of Gwen's now-free hands in her own and gave her a look that somehow conveyed concern *and* told her it would be okay at the same time. Gwen tried to smile back in thanks, but the skin on her face felt stretched too thin with worry. She threaded her fingers through Veda's, grateful for the comfort anyway.

They began to move, following Sylvia. After a bit, she assured them in little more than a whisper that they were fully cloaked for the time being, but everyone kept their mouths tightly closed and their steps careful. Gwen looked around for the raven, every creak and flutter of wings drawing her eye. As far as she could tell, it hadn't followed them, but they had no way to be sure. When night fell, they set up a small camp without a fire, huddling together for warmth and chewing nervously on dried meats and crackers. Although none of them had seen the bird anywhere throughout the day, they only spoke when necessary. They barely slept.

They started walking again before the sun had even fully risen, after drinking another batch of Sylvia's cloaking mixture. "This is the last of my ingredients for this potion," she told Gwen, chewing a hole in her bottom lip as she gave them each a bowl with less in it than the day before. "I really hope we've lost it."

"Me too."

For two more days, they didn't see the raven at all.

On the third day, they felt safe enough to make a fire when they camped. It was getting colder at night and Myev's warmth wasn't always enough for Ivy. Veda had tried to help, also curling protectively around Ivy while they slept, but her body cooled considerably when her fire was out and she had been wearing her cloak at all times.

After they built the campfire, Veda removed her cloak for the first time in days and tugged Ivy into her lap, holding her tight. Bumble was also violently cold, though she tried not to show it, and Veda called her over too so that she could wrap her long arms around both of them. Gwen bundled them all in the biggest blanket they had, hoping it would be enough.

Gwen sat down next to the others, all as close to the fire as they could get. Even Myev had pulled out her heavier jacket as the sun faded away. She knew very basic survival magic since she'd grown up in The Snowblight, but even that was no replacement for a good, warm coat.

No one wanted to talk. They were exhausted from barely sleeping or stopping to eat the last few days. No one knew where the raven had come from, or what harm it meant, but they all knew it was serious. Not one of them doubted Sylvia's gut instincts or her ability to read auras.

It wasn't long before they'd all crawled into their blankets and fell into fitful sleep. Everyone except Gwen. "I'll take first watch," she said, leaving no room for argument. No one had the energy to argue with her anyway.

After Bumble and Ivy were safely nestled between Myev and Boris, Veda came over and leaned back against the log Gwen sat on, between Gwen's legs. She crossed her arms on one of Gwen's thighs and pillowed her head on them. She was asleep in minutes.

Gwen was grateful for the extra warmth. She'd felt frozen all the way down to her bones the last few nights, in a way that made it feel like she would never be truly warm again, and somehow Veda knew without asking. Still, she knew it was more than the weather making her bones feel like ice beneath her skin.

She looked across the sleeping bodies of her friends and a protective fondness bloomed unbidden in her chest. If someone had told her a few months ago that she would go on a long, treacherous journey with a group of complete strangers and that within days she would feel compelled to protect each one of them with her life, she would have laughed in their face. Despite everything, despite how prickly and mean and frustrating she was, they liked her. They believed in her. What started as a job had turned into something more, for all of them.

***

It had been five days since they'd seen the raven. Everyone was still on edge, but a little less so. Still exhausted, but a little less so. The return trip was taking them longer since they'd had to take an alternate route, but they were only half a day's walk from Bronzeshine. The idea of getting to sleep on the train instead of on the forest floor had all of them feeling a little optimistic.

It was still freezing cold, so Veda and Gwen sat side by side under a single blanket, leaned back against a tree for their watch. The nights had been quiet and they enjoyed the time to simply be, together. They talked quietly about Gwen's time at Lion's Grace, about great heists her and Bumble had gone on, about Veda's childhood on the sunny beaches of Vulcaria, and her journey away from home. They'd been traveling together for well over a month now, but they'd had barely any time to just get to know each other.

A soft hiss behind them cut Veda's story short and she looked around, trying to find the source. Gwen did the same. It was a forest filled with animals, so sounds were common, but something about the hiss wasn't right. There wasn't another sound, but Gwen turned back to Veda and tried to nod her head to signal that she'd take a quick look around the camp, yet found herself suddenly frozen. She could only move her eyes. She stared at Veda, panic hitting her like a punch to the gut as she realized Veda couldn't move either. A soft mist floated just above the ground, barely visible.

Then, all around them, movement. Gwen tried desperately to turn her head. All she could see was the faintest shuffling of figures cloaked in black, moving into their campsite. She guessed there were at least half a dozen based on sound alone. Something small walked closer to her and she tried to look, straining her eyes as hard as she could, begging her body to just work, to just *move*.

"Hello there," a male voice said. "Awfully clever, to whip up a cloaking spell like that. Awfully clever, but not quite clever enough. You made it a little more difficult, but we found you again anyway, didn't we? I wasn't planning on doing this here, was hoping to trail you to Rivergate, but you and your friends are trying my patience. I thought we better lay some ground rules."

Suddenly her neck moved, snapping her head forward to face the voice. It was the raven, its blue eyes burning into her. Now that she had been forced to look forward, she could see that none of her friends were moving either.

"I imagine you're wondering who I am, speaking to you through this bird. I couldn't expect you to remember my voice, after all, since the last time you heard it, you were an infant. But I think you'll figure it out. You're not all that bright, but you're also not a complete fool. I want you to listen closely. I want you to remember every word I say today, for your own sake. Make sure you never forget."

Zachariah. Fear had shot through her veins the second he had begun to speak, like a million tiny shards of ice, and she knew. She didn't remember him, no, but it was like every ounce of her flesh knew anyway. Knew exactly how afraid she should be. She tried to tense all of her muscles, to move just a single inch.

Nothing.

"Stop tiring yourself out," the raven mocked. "You're going to be paralyzed for some time. Might as well just relax and enjoy the show. Had you played your cards right, we never would have had to meet again. You could have lived the rest of your pathetic life in relative peace, but instead you thought you could get away with killing two of my men and starting your feeble little rebellion."

The figures had fully infiltrated their campsite, at least one figure for each one of them and then some—it was hard to tell exactly how many because of the darkness and her inability to move her head. Only one of them was moving, walking through everyone and surveying them. The others waited.

"I'm here to provide you with a lesson. The only reason I'm leaving you alive is because I expect you to do your part in putting an end to the ridiculous insurrections you've caused. Spread the word, if you will. Do you have any clue how many people you have gotten killed? How many more will be crushed like insects if this continues? You obviously don't care *enough*, running and hiding as you've been, so I figured I might need to bring your lesson a little closer to home."

The moving figure stopped at Sylvia. The hood of its cloak moved slightly as it looked towards the raven and beneath it, Gwen could see that eerie blue glow. "Not that one," Zachariah said through his raven. "She's just a batty old lizard, nothing special."

The figure moved on to Avery and Jasper.

"A changeling and a human, sharing a bed," Zachariah said with an air of disgust.

The figure took a few more steps, reaching Myev and Boris. Between them, Bumble and Ivy. Gwen's eyes raced to them, to the figure, to the raven, back to them.

"Now this is interesting," Zachariah said as the figure crouched next to Myev. "I recognize this brute. Likes to think she's something special because she's in charge of those savages to the north. Perhaps her death would serve as a warning to them as well."

The figure pulled a dagger from its belt and plunged it into Myev's torso.

"She's paralyzed too, but rest assured that she can feel everything. We've knicked her thoratic aorta. Not enough to kill her right away, just enough to keep things interesting for a while. In the time it takes for her to actually bleed out, she will be in an extraordinary amount of pain. She will feel every second of it and know that there isn't a thing she can do to stop it. And so will you." The raven stepped a bit closer. "Stay out of our business."

The figure pulled its dagger out of Myev with a sickening squelch and stood. The raven took flight and the figures receded back into the forest.

Gwen could see darkness spreading over the blanket covering Myev. She felt like she was screaming, her throat on fire, but no sound would come. Tears slipped down her cheeks and landed on her collar. Next to Myev, Boris' whole body shook, but nothing more. Gwen knew he was fighting the paralysis with everything he had, but it wasn't enough.

Myev didn't move at all.

The inside of Gwen's head roared like a tsunami breaking on the sand. She felt like she couldn't even think or breathe, trapped in the most unrelenting agony she had ever felt. Her body was no longer hers, but instead a cage, keeping her away from her dying friend. She only knew how to fight and she couldn't even do that.

Ten minutes passed before Sylvia rolled over and pushed herself to her hands and knees, swaying. An incomprehensible, guttural noise worked its way out from between her clenched teeth. She crawled to Myev, collapsing with her hands over Myev's belly. Her hands glowed green and Sylvia screamed, piercing the silence. Her magic wavered, the light flickering. Something was wrong, but she continued trying. Gwen could see every muscle in her body straining, even from where she sat trapped by the tree. Still Boris shook, the muscles in his throat straining as though they might snap.

Five more minutes passed and Sylvia was able to sit up, her hands still glowing and pressed tightly to the sopping wet blanket draped over Myev. Boris had managed to move his arm just enough to lace his fingers with Myev's. They were still shaking.

Another five minutes and Gwen could feel her fingers begin to move, clawing at the dirt. Next to her, Veda was panting. She had gotten one arm back against the tree and was trying to push herself up. Gwen could hear a keening coming from the blankets between Myev and Boris. Sylvia and Boris were both sobbing, a cacophony of "it's not enough, please, no, please, it's not enough, she's fading, something is wrong, no, no, not her". Gwen couldn't even tell whose voice belonged to who.

Twenty-five minutes after Myev had been stabbed, Ivy was able to crawl out from under the blanket. Her clothing was soaked through, blood smeared across her face and matting her hair. She threw her hands atop Sylvia's, adding her own magic. She was wailing. Gwen and Veda had managed to get to their knees and were slowly crawling towards their friends, their hands ripping up tufts of grass as they pulled themselves forward.

Within thirty minutes, Bumble had crawled free. She collapsed in a ball at Myev's feet. Boris had managed to get to his knees and had curled his body over Myev's, his hand on the side of her face. He was speaking to her in a language Gwen didn't know. It sounded like a prayer. Avery and Jasper had managed to sit up and Jasper had thrown himself into Avery's arms, hiding his face in her neck. Her hair fell like a veil over the both of them as she held him.

Thirty-five minutes. Ivy and Sylvia pulled their hands back. Myev's chest rose and fell. Shallowly, but it rose and fell. She had not opened her eyes. Boris had not stopped praying.

"The poison," Sylvia babbled. "The blade was poisoned; it weakens the effects of my magic. It's all I can do. It's all I can do. We have to go; we have to get her somewhere else. It's all I can do." She pulled out a communication satchel and spoke her spell, begging for help into it with a cracking and wretched voice. Something about another spell, about teleportation, about any cost, about not enough power, that she would do anything, that she needed more. When she was done, she put her glowing hands back on Myev's belly and continued to try.

Two hours after Sylvia's plea, there was a crack of thunder and a hole ripped out of thin air. A woman came through it—Astrid, from the bookshop in Silverglenn. "I'm so sorry, it took me time to gather the ingredients. I was as quick as I could be, I swear," she said to Sylvia, passing over a large glass jar of ointment.

Sylvia mumbled a thank you, almost unconscious of it, as she tore the lid off the jar and scooped out the contents. She spread it over Myev's now bared torso where they had pulled the blanket off, sticky with blood, and used the last of their water to clean around her wound. When they had, they could see dark tendrils, reaching out from the skin around the gash.

Collectively, they held their breath, crowded around their friend. Her skin was pale and she hadn't so much as twitched in the last two hours, but finally the salve seemed to melt into Myev's skin and slowly,

slowly, the wound began to stitch itself back together. Better, it didn't come right back apart, like it had every time Sylvia or Ivy had tried. Myev's breathing got a little deeper, a little less labored.

"I have several carriages coming," Astrid said. "I'm not strong enough to get that big of an object through a portal, but I have contacts in Bronzeshine and they're coming as quickly as they can."

"Thank you, thank you," Boris told her, his voice thick. "I cannot thank you enough. I will find a way to repay you."

"Don't," Astrid shook her head. "I've heard what you guys have been doing, for all of us. Consider this me repaying you."

No one spoke during the time it took for the carriages to arrive. They packed quickly and then surrounded Myev again, afraid to be more than inches away from her for long. Bumble was in Gwen's arms and she in Veda's. Avery and Jasper were wrapped around each other like they'd never come apart again. Ivy was staring blankly into the trees, her bloody hands like dead fish in her lap. Sylvia vacillated between hiccupping cries and stony silence.

When the carriages rumbled up, they stood, watching as Boris and Sylvia carried Myev to one carriage and laid her on the floor inside. Boris and Ivy crawled in after her, each of them holding one of her hands.

Gwen carried Bumble to one of the other carriages, following Astrid and the others. Bumble was crying again and Gwen squeezed her tightly to her chest. She didn't let go the whole way to Bronzeshine.

***

It seemed like all anyone had been doing since the attack was counting the minutes, hours, days—but it took four more days for Myev to wake up. Sylvia had continued to tend to her in a small inn owned by one of Astrid's friends—a drakoso man named Oskar—, doing everything she could to make Myev healthy again. She explained that magical healing didn't usually just fix what was wrong in an instant. "Magic is like first aid. Small cuts, burns, things like that, those I can take care of easily, but deeper wounds aren't so simple," she explained. "I can stop bleeding; I can stabilize you so that you won't die. I can nudge your body in the right direction and give it a boost, but it still has to go through its own processes."

Myev's situation was also complicated by the magical nature of the wound. Zachariah had done something to thwart exactly the kinds of interventions they were making. Half the techniques Sylvia tried didn't work at all and the others did half of what they should have. It would take time, and Sylvia couldn't guarantee Myev would be quite the same ever again.

For the first day or two, Sylvia kept her unconscious using a magic powder she'd concocted. "I can't have her waking up and moving around until her wound is more thoroughly healed," she explained, sprinkling a small amount of the powder across Myev's pale face. "She could re-open it easily or cause more damage."

Boris looked distraught but said nothing, as he clearly trusted Sylvia implicitly. So he waited. They all waited.

Gwen didn't think Sylvia had slept more than an hour or two since the incident and the color of her scales was dull and faded. Her tail just dragged along the floor behind her most days now, as she lacked the energy to keep it up. Ivy helped as much as she could, but healing wasn't her strength; she'd never needed it before. And this wasn't a normal wound. The responsibility fell so fully onto Sylvia and they were all frustrated by their uselessness.

"Myev is strong and she *will* be okay," she told them each time she left the room. She always sounded less sure than she wanted to.

Gwen caught her in a rare moment alone as she stood outside Myev's room, her eyes closed and her face heavy.

She walked over and placed her hand on Sylvia's forearm. "Are *you* okay?"

Sylvia looked up, considered lying, then sighed and settled on the truth. "I'm doing my best. Remember how we talked about running out of magical energy? The tools are doing nothing and I've been going full bore for so long now, I—I'm afraid I'm hitting empty," she looked up with watery eyes. "I don't want to fail you guys. I can't fail her."

"You could never fail us," Gwen said, pulling the larger woman into a hug. She seemed small and fragile despite her size. Sylvia sniffled, wrapping her arms tightly around Gwen's shoulders. Gwen could feel her body shaking. "Take a break," she ordered, putting on the most authoritative voice she could.

"I can't, I—"

"You are going to take a break," Gwen told her, punctuating every word. "I am going to go get you a warm mug of tea and a bowl of whatever the hell Oskar has cooked up for the inn today, and then I'm going to find Ivy and the two of us are going to watch over Myev while you eat," she pulled back from Sylvia to look her in the eyes, a bit hard with the height difference, "the *whole* bowl, and drink the *entire* cup, and then nap for *at least* six hours, preferably more. I will accept no less."

Despite everything, a grin pulled at the corners of Sylvia's mouth. "Yes ma'am," she replied quietly.

***

After the four longest days of their lives, when Sylvia finally came out of Myev's room and gave all of them a teary-eyed smile, they knew that meant she'd healed enough to be able to wake. Ivy was in the room like a lightning bolt.

"Rough few days, Princess?" they heard Myev croak.

Ivy had crawled up into the bed and was curled into Myev's side. Myev held her there with one weak arm, the other claimed by Boris. "Hey guys," she smiled, her eyelids still droopy and purple, like bruises. "Sorry for the scare."

"Don't you ever do that again," Jasper tried to command through his watery grin.

"Mm, won't make it a habit," Myev agreed.

Sylvia explained what had happened to Myev: the magical poison, how it rendered much of her magic useless, the ride to Bronzeshine, the state of her health. Myev listened without saying much, barely conscious as it was.

"I can't, uh, I can't just make you guys stronger against magical effects—that takes years and years of practice and exposure, but I have this," Sylvia said, pulling a necklace from around her wide neck. It was a faded red leather cord with a handful of black, blue, and purple beads on it. An iron nail was bent around the center, making several tight curls over the cord. "I've worn it most of my life; it was given to me by my mom, who taught me how to do magic before she passed. It's protective, fluorite and obsidian and iron. Makes it harder for magic to affect you. I think it's what made it so I could move before anyone else." She held it out to Myev, her eyes on the ground. A few tears hit her scaly foot. "I only have the one, but if you'd had it, maybe...." She cleared her throat, "And I'm...I'm sorry I couldn't do more to—to stop it."

Myev reached out, curling Sylvia's fingers back over the necklace. "No, old friend. *You* were our protection. That necklace," she pointed, "helped you recover faster, I'm sure, but you are also stronger than you think. There is so much power in you and if you weren't there, I wouldn't have made it. Don't you ever dare think you didn't do enough."

"But I—"

"Ohhh!" Myev moaned loudly, dramatically, "I'm too sick to argue, I can feel my energy just draining away!" She closed her eyes, threw her head to the side, and let out a loud sigh.

Sylvia cracked a wet laugh and Myev opened her eyes with a grin.

She squeezed Ivy where she was still plastered to her side. "And thank you, little one. I felt you before I lost consciousness."

Ivy nodded, unable to bring herself to speak.

Sylvia pulled her necklace back over her head. "Well, if I can find more stones I can make—"

"Sylvia," Veda said gently, cutting her off. "You can't protect us from everything. You just can't. You are not responsible for what happened. We can find your stones, but please don't run yourself ragged. You've been giving everything you've got the last few days and you look like you're about to fall over. You can rest. We want you to rest."

Sylvia closed her mouth, her lips wobbly. She swallowed hard. Finally, she nodded.

Chapter Thirteen

They weren't safe in Bronzeshine. Most of the citizens they passed there, at least the vocal ones, had thus far either rebuked the rebellions popping up around Peonia or remained staunchly neutral. They seemed afraid that the rebellions would affect the lifestyles they led and were not willing to take the risk of muttering even the slightest positive notion about what was happening. Astrid's friend Oskar was sympathetic to them and had been nothing but kind during the time they'd spent there as Myev recovered, but he had a business to run, and they'd all overheard enough from the patrons of the inn to be wary. They'd been using Sylvia's disguise satchels most of the time, but the magic in them was starting to weaken with the overuse and the situation wasn't sustainable. They couldn't stay much longer.

The problem was that they couldn't move very far or fast with Myev in her current condition, especially not to Rivergate, which was both half the country away and an active warzone. She became furious whenever it was mentioned, but she couldn't walk for very long with her wound still healing and she certainly couldn't fight. They could only go places they could reach by train, and they could only go there if it was safe.

"Leave me behind then," she'd snapped one night as they discussed it.

"Absolutely not," Boris growled, and that was the end of that.

They needed to go somewhere they could keep a low profile until Myev was well enough to make the trek to Rivergate. As much as they wanted to go help the people there right away, Myev was the priority, whether the woman liked it or not.

"What do they think this violence is going to accomplish?" Gwen heard a dwarven man say one evening in the inn's dining area. "They can't expect to fight the government over petty bullshit and get away with it."

His wife nodded, running her hand fretfully through her wheat-colored beard. "I'm just glad your sister lives here and not in one of those places, though Ironforge is too close for comfort. I don't like that we're even here visiting; who knows how far the trouble could spread. Maybe we should convince her and Dalen to come back to Goldpoint with us. I know they'd hate to leave the shop, but it'd be safer there."

Can't go to Goldpoint, Gwen noted mentally, though that seemed obvious to her. It was the richest place in Peonia and thus most members of The Council lived there in their ancestral mansions. While perhaps they wouldn't expect public enemies numbers one through eight, plus Ivy, to be right under their noses, it wasn't a theory Gwen wanted to test.

"She knows how to defend herself, should those ruffians show up at her door," the man continued.

Can't go to Ironforge, she thought, briefly losing track of the dwarven couple's conversation. Ironforge was one of the towns already embroiled in the conflict (even if it wasn't as bad as Rivergate), which was one point against it at the current moment, but she also knew that there were plenty of people who would turn them in without a second thought if it meant protection for themselves. They couldn't risk it.

Gwen tuned back in as the couple's conversation got more heated, the man's voice rising. "Why can't those...those *monsters*," the man spat, as if the word was poisonous, "just accept their lot in life and leave the rest of us alone? Their lives aren't nearly as bad as they think they are."

Gwen felt the hair on her arms bristling and she clenched her fists, trying to focus on the feeling of her nails digging into the meat of her palm. *Those monsters.* Not people, *monsters.* Veda looked at her from across the table, her eyes begging Gwen to just stay under control. She reached over and placed her hand atop Gwen's. "We have to be careful," she whispered.

"Better than they used to be, at any rate," the dwarven woman added. "Used to be that all those non-human looking types were killed on sight, but now they're allowed to be members of polite society."

Gwen stood up quickly, her chair scraping along the floor, and stalked off towards her room before anyone could say a word to her.

***

Veda gave Gwen about twenty minutes to herself before coming to find her in their room. She opened the door to see Gwen sitting at the bare, uneven desk with her hands laced together under her chin, staring intently at the dingy grey wall.

"You're brooding," Veda said, tossing her disguise satchel onto the bedside table.

Gwen sighed, glancing over. "I'm not brooding."

Veda walked up behind her and pulled Gwen's chair back a few inches, so Gwen growled, irritated, and straightened her back out to stand. Instead of allowing her to do so, Veda threw a leg over her and settled down in her lap, wrapping her arms around Gwen's shoulders. "You're brooding," she repeated.

Gwen's breath still caught in her throat at the closeness, despite everything, and she looked up at Veda with her mouth agape. Veda grinned at her, fully aware of the effect she had on her.

Gwen closed her mouth with a snap.

"But thank you for not starting another bar fight, as much as they deserved to be punched," Veda continued.

Gwen sighed again, this time in resignation, and placed her hands on Veda's hips. "They really did, but you're right. We need to be careful."

"I'm usually right," Veda winked, and Gwen rolled her eyes as hard as she could. "We can probably leave soon anyway," Veda said. "Myev's doing better and she's getting antsy too. Just another day or two. We'll find somewhere else to go."

Gwen nodded, looking petulantly at the floor to Veda's left. Veda placed a single finger under her chin and lifted, forcing Gwen to look her in the eyes. She said nothing, just watching for a long moment, before leaning in and giving Gwen a soft, sweet kiss on the lips. "We're going to be okay," she whispered. "We're going to get there as soon as we can and help, I promise."

Veda kissed her, again and again, until all of the tense energy drained out of her and she reached her hands up, holding onto either side of Veda's face. She slid her tongue past Veda's lips, causing her to make a noise of contentment. It didn't take long for their kisses to become more heated, desperate almost, and Veda pulled away to stand.

Gwen made a noise of disapproval and Veda chuckled. "So impatient."

She leaned down to pick Gwen up and then set her on the desk, shoving her back into the wall as she crowded in to kiss her more deeply. Quickly, almost clumsily, she undid the buttons on Gwen's jacket and broke their kiss only long enough to pull it off and her shirt over her head, throwing them both behind herself without looking.

"You're one to talk," Gwen shot back, and Veda just grinned at her. It was her favorite smile in all the world.

The boots were next and then Veda was back, her tongue swirling around Gwen's in a way that had her lightheaded. She wrapped her arms around Veda's neck, holding them together as Veda's hands dropped lower and around, to the button of her pants above her tail. Veda undid them and began to slide them down her hips, so Gwen lifted just enough for her to pull them the rest of the way off and send them in the vague direction of the shirt.

Veda bit Gwen's lip, pulling it with her teeth and then letting go with a pop. She planted a trail of kisses lower and lower, until she was kneeling in front of the desk. Wrapping her arms back and around Gwen, she grabbed onto her ass and pulled her forward until she was perched on the edge of the desk. She then spread Gwen's legs wide and moved in, kissing and licking and nipping along her inner thighs.

When her tongue finally made contact with Gwen's clit she bucked, slapping her hands down on the desktop behind her for balance. Her strong nails dug into the wood, scratching it as her hands flexed and unflexed to Veda's rhythm. Veda flattened her tongue, swiping it from bottom to top and back again, tasting as much of Gwen as she could. She then reached up to put both hands around Gwen's waist and hold her still while she used the tip of her tongue to truly target Gwen's clit, her attention there both worshipful and unrelenting.

Gwen threw her head back and squirmed, unable to hold still, yet unable to move much in the other woman's grasp. Her legs were spread as wide as they could go over the edge of the desk and the soles of her feet searched desperately for purchase, anything to give her a foundation strong enough to press back against Veda, to find just that slightest bit more friction.

As she got closer and closer, every muscle in her body tensed in anticipation. She was shaking, causing the lopsided desk to clatter against the floor in her wake. Finally she came, crying and arching her back, as Veda worked her through the aftershocks of her orgasm.

Veda pulled back and looked up, her chin wet and shining. "I love you," she whispered, her eyes bright.

"Are you sure you want to love a monster?" Gwen asked, because she couldn't help herself.

Veda stood again and grabbed Gwen's chin firmly between her thumb and forefinger, smashing their lips together. She tasted herself on Veda's mouth and all her thoughts, all her worries, were lost in it, so hungry and reverential on hers. Completely drowned out in the sting of teeth and the soothing swipe of Veda's tongue after. In the firm pressure of Veda's fingertips on her face. In the warm press of her body against Gwen's.

She took her hand from Gwen's cheek and slid it around to the back of her head, gathering Gwen's hair and using the leverage of it to pull her head back and latch onto her throat. She sucked a bruise there as her other hand traveled back down, between Gwen's legs. Gwen whimpered, unable to hold it back, as she pressed inside, her thumb resting on Gwen's clit. She was almost over-sensitive still, but Veda was gentle, pumping her fingers in and out, curling them to hit all the right places. Somewhere in the back of her mind, Gwen wondered how many times Veda was going to force her to come before she was satisfied.

Veda brought her mouth back up to Gwen's ear. "Do I appear even slightly unsure?"

Gwen sobbed out incomprehensible noises as Veda's hand worked, her fingertips scrabbling over Veda's arms and shirt as she tried to find something to hold onto. She tried to formulate a snippy response, maintain even an ounce of her dignity, but couldn't get her mind to focus. Why was Veda still dressed while she was fully naked, being taken apart bit by bit? It didn't seem fair. But if this was the punishment for her surly attitude, she was never going to lose it.

"I love you too," she finally choked. "I love you."

Veda rewarded her with another searing kiss. "If you're a monster, you are mine," she said against Gwen's lips, "and I am yours."

***

"Do you think you can make it to Windyplains if we leave tomorrow?" Sylvia asked Myev as they all sat around her bed.

The orc snorted and then glared, her arms crossed firmly over her chest. The longer she was on bedrest, the more irritable she got. "It's not even a day's ride! I'm not made of eggshells; I think I can handle a train ride to the next town over."

Boris reached out and uncrossed her arms, then pulled one of her hands to his mouth to kiss the knuckles. "We do not think you are fragile, my love. You almost died."

"I've almost died hundreds of times," she waved her other hand dismissively.

"So we'll go to Windyplains and meet with Nihal then," Sylvia confirmed, choosing not to acknowledge her friend's attitude. The woman was truly a saint and they were all lucky for it.

Nihal was another friend of hers, because she honestly seemed to know just about every single person on the entire continent of Peonia and then some.

"How do you know so many people?" Veda had joked. "I'm beginning to think you're creating them yourself."

"I am *very* old," Sylvia said, entirely seriously, as she scrubbed her hands up and down her face. She was still exhausted, but her scales had regained their color.

Nihal had information about a Brotherhood hideout stowed away in the woods near Windyplains, which he'd gleaned from a man named Pavlin that he'd met at a tavern. "It's been abandoned, according to Pavlin," he told Sylvia via satchel, "but it was in use up until very recently, so there may be records or papers there, something useful. Couldn't hurt to check it out."

If they couldn't currently go running into the thick of the burgeoning war effort by heading to Rivergate, they figured they could at least gather some intel. That, and Gwen thought Myev might start tearing off heads soon if she wasn't allowed to do *something*.

***

Windyplains was a small community that lived in the shadow of their fancier and flashier sister to the south, Calmflats. Calmflats was a tourist city known as an oasis within in the empty, quiet expanse of the Evernear Barrens, world renowned for their extravagant gardens and relaxing spa treatments.

Windyplains, however, was known only for the violent winds that ripped through the area, making it impossible for the folks there to do much of anything. When they tried to grow crops taller than a foot or two, the winds came and tore them up, blowing them away to spirits only knew where. If they built anything more than a story or two tall, the powerful wind knocked it right back down. Any time they reached higher than the bare minimum, tried to become more than just a dot on the map, the wind quickly took care of it. The mythology was that the town itself was cursed long ago by a spiteful witch that some of the citizens had wronged.

A large portion of the citizens there commuted to Calmflats for work, and those that didn't mostly worked nearby ranches or the handful of service jobs available in the small town. As such, it was filled almost entirely with quiet, simple folk who were unlikely to care much about the rebellion. From all Gwen had ever heard, they tended to keep to themselves until something threatened their community and, for the moment, the rebellion had not shown up on their doorsteps. Gwen sincerely hoped their arrival would not change that. Not yet.

They headed straight from the train station to one of the local taverns—even towns as small as Windyplains had several. In fact, in Gwen's experience, it seemed that small working towns were almost exclusively made up of taverns and churches. Get off work, go spend most of your hard-earned money at the tavern, then head on down to church to repent for the sins you committed while drunk out of your mind. Rinse. Repeat.

The tavern was decently busy, despite the somewhat early afternoon hour, and most of the patrons were crowded around a back table. Raucous laughter filled the room and Gwen watched as an air elemental man spit out his drink onto the person next to them. The ale-covered bovillum growled and wiped his hands on the first man's shirt, who was profusely apologizing. All was quickly forgotten, though, as both were pulled back into the story being told by the dwarven man in the center of the circle.

"So, there I was, trapped in that godforsaken tree by that stupid giant acid frog and he's hitting the tree over and over again with his tongue, which is starting to burn away due to the aforementioned acid. I'm mostly grateful that it's not my leg he's slobbering his murder juices all over, but I know I'm not going to last much longer up there 'cause the tree's already starting to lean. I try to aim my bow, which, as you can imagine, is hard with the tree shaking like a sinner in church."

Gwen found herself impressed by the way he didn't seem to need to breathe whilst telling his story.

"But I steady myself, tune into the frog's rhythm so that I'm moving in time with him, aim, and shoot. You wouldn't believe it, but I swear to ya that the arrow went right through his eye, dead center through the pupil, and he dropped like a sack of bricks. As he does, the tree gives one last heave and I feel myself falling. After all that I'm not about to get pancaked by a damn tree, so at the last moment I have to drop my bow and leap, grabbing onto the next tree with all my might. I don't know if you can tell, but I've got pretty short arms to work with," he lifted them and shook them for emphasis, "but I managed to catch and hold somehow. However, my bow, my favorite bow, fell right into that dead fucker's open maw and I couldn't do nothing but watch as it hissed and spit in that acid 'til there wasn't a piece of it left. That bow was a gift from my ma," he sighed. "Ain't trusted a frog since, I tell ya."

He looked up and caught sight of Sylvia as they walked closer and immediately hopped off his stool to stomp towards her. He wrapped his arms around her thighs, the highest he could reach, and squeezed tight enough to make her squeak. "Syliva, old girl, how are you?" he bellowed.

"Good, Nihal, thank you," she replied, quieter than him, and pressed her hand to his upper back. "It's been a while."

"Yes it has!" Nihal stood back, hands on his hips, and took in their crew. Gwen took him in as well. He was an older man with tanned and wrinkled skin, which crinkled up around his brown eyes and all but covered them completely when he smiled. His long red hair and beard were shot through with white and filled with intricate braids, not unlike Myev's. Many of the braids ended in beautifully carved decorative beads. His clothing was an eclectic and colorful combination of pieces from a dozen different cultures, giving him the appearance of being well traveled. Based on his story, he probably was—Gwen knew frogs like that only existed in the rainforests of Muarbol.

Nihal turned and walked back to his seat, quickly downed the rest of his drink, and then burped. "Well, let's get going then, so we can chat." A few disappointed "aww"s came from the crowd. "Oh don't be that way, I'll be back tomorrow," he assured them as he grabbed his coat from the back of his chair.

They followed him outside and he pointed, leading them towards a dilapidated inn a few buildings down. To Gwen's surprise, he was quiet the whole way, like he no longer had to be putting on a show.

Nihal led them into the inn and up the steps to his room. They all filed in, squeezing body after body into the tiny space. Boris sucked in his tummy and carefully shut the door before loudly letting go of the air he was holding and falling back against it. "Did we have to do this in a closet?" he asked, which earned a hearty laugh from Nihal. Myev leaned back against him and he wrapped his arms around her shoulders.

"Sorry pal," Nihal replied, "this is about the most private place I can think of, if we keep our voices down."

"What did you have to tell us?" Sylvia asked, straight to business. She seemed uncomfortable with the tight space as well, her tail wrapped tightly around her legs to avoid bumping into anyone with it.

Gwen's own tail was twisted around Veda's waist, who was once again holding Bumble on her shoulders, since the bird would take advantage of any opportunity to be carried or held.

"Few days ago, the tavern was surprisingly dead, only a handful of other people besides myself." Nihal began. "One of 'em, told me his name was Pavlin, came up to me and began a conversation. Told me he was a resident of Rivergate who'd lost his wife in one of the scuffles down there, so he decided to get the hell out of there. We chatted a while, and I made my allegiances pretty clear. Eventually told me that he'd heard from a friend that there was a cabin up here, in the woods, that's actually a secret entrance to an abandoned Brotherhood hideout. Said he could lead me to it, but he wasn't brave enough to do anything about it himself, in case there was anyone left down there. Said I seemed like a pretty connected guy and maybe I could pass the information on to the right folks."

"How do we know the information is good?" Avery asked.

"Don't, per se, but the cabin does exist. I went up there the day after to see if what he said seemed legitimate. He told me about how to access the secret entrance, and I saw where it was, but I didn't try it because I don't know what's down there. I'm not about to take on a whole Brotherhood sect by my lonesome if it's not actually abandoned."

"Makes sense," Gwen replied. "We could check it out soon, see what we can find."

"We need to make sure we're prepared for anything," Sylvia said, worrying her lip with her teeth. She became quieter and looked down at the floor. "And I don't think Myev should go, just to be safe."

"Wait a damn minute!" Myev hissed angrily, trying and failing to keep her voice down. "I'm fine now! I'm standing and walking and all that without falling apart, aren't I?"

"Sylvia is right," Boris said, matter of fact.

Myev whirled in his arms, glaring up at him. "Don't you dare," she warned.

"She is right, love," he repeated, more gently. "This might be a good one to sit out. Just to be sure."

"I'm a fucking decorated war veteran who has seen more combat than anyone in this room, even you," she snarled, pushing her finger into Boris' chest. "I've seen things folks could barely imagine, but I take one measly stab wound and you people think I can't do it anymore."

"We don't know what's in that hideout," Sylvia pleaded, "and I don't want to put you in harm's way until you're completely healed. You could easily open your wounds and start bleeding internally again."

"It is not that we don't think you can take it, it is that we cannot stand the thought of losing you," Boris told her. "*I* cannot lose you," he added softly, meant just for her. "We can sit it out, you and me. Just this once. There will be more important battles to fight."

She continued to look up at him, her jaw clenched and lower lip jutted out, but her eyes had softened. After a few moments she took a deep breath. "Fine," she gritted out, like the word itself was causing her pain.

"I'll stay back too," Sylvia said. The "to keep an eye on your condition" was unspoken.

"I'll stay with Sylvia," Ivy piped up. "I want to learn more about healing, since we're probably going to keep needing it. With the war and all," she added bluntly.

"Veda and I can go with Nihal, scope things out," Gwen said. "Bumble can stay behind, too," she added, almost as an offering—*see, not everyone is going*. "We don't want to draw attention to ourselves with a huge group."

"We'll go with you guys, though," Jasper said. "Just to be cautious."

No one had any more argument in them and the room was quiet.

"Sounds like a plan," Gwen finally said, clapping her hands together. "Let's get out of this cramped ass room."

*****

Sylvia came bursting out of the inn's kitchen door, mumbling to herself. "What kind of kitchen doesn't even have cinnamon? Honestly!" Her eyes caught on the group of them playing cards at a table—Gwen, Myev, Avery, and Jasper—, and her eyes brightened. "Would you guys mind doing me a favor?"

"Sure, what's up?" Gwen spoke for all of them, at least partially because she was tired of losing. She was pretty sure Jasper was cheating, but he only ever grinned slyly when she accused him, and she never could catch him in the act. Regardless, she maintained that it was statistically impossible for him to win as often as he had been.

"I need cinnamon, because somehow the kitchen doesn't have any, but I also need pyrite, for a spell. Nihal mentioned I could purchase pyrite from a friend of his and I was going to ask him to get me some, but he's wandered off and I can't find him. The grocer is on the opposite end of town, so I was hoping someone could go get one and someone else the other, to save time."

"We can go get the rocks," Jasper said, gathering up his cards.

"And I can get the cinnamon," Gwen agreed.

Sylvia grinned and began digging in her bag for her money. "Myev, why don't you go with Gwen? A little walk might be nice."

"Am I allowed to walk, Doctor?" Myev said peevishly.

Sylvia took this magnanimously, recognizing it as the childish lashing out that it was. Like an alley cat hissing at a dog who had it cornered—she could spit and growl all she liked, but it was clear who had the upper hand.

"Some fresh air should do wonders for your health *and* your attitude," Sylvia said coolly.

Gwen held back a snicker. Jasper did not.

Myev had the good sense to look just a little cowed as she pushed back from the table. "Let's go," she grunted at Gwen.

When they'd stepped outside, turning towards the shops, Myev shoved her hands in the pockets of the light jacket she wore. "Sorry you're stuck with the invalid."

"Oh, shut the *fuck* up," Gwen replied before she could think better of it, laughing.

A grin pulled at the corners of Myev's mouth and she snorted, once. "Fair enough."

They walked in companionable silence until a happy, familiar voice called out behind them. "There's no possible way I'm seeing Guinevere Flynn in the flesh right now!"

Gwen turned, her blood immediately turning to ice at being recognized, to the grinning visage of Echo, from Lion's Grace Orphan Home. She was bounding down the steps of a battered but well-loved church. She wore a long skirt and a thick, puffy sweater that swamped her slight frame. Around her neck was the same Lowean lion necklace that Gwen remembered so well from her time at the orphanage, the one Echo would rub between her fingers when she was nervous.

Gwen stood there, stunned and unable to move as her heart split in two halves—the first overwhelmed with the instinct to run and leave Windyplains immediately, the other with the bone deep desire to pull the older woman into a tight hug. She hadn't seen her in at least a decade.

"Don't look at me like a rabbit caught in a trap," Echo said, catching up to them and wrapping her arms around Gwen's legs. "I'm not going to turn you in."

"You know?" Gwen finally said, clearing her throat. She put her hands on Echo's shoulders to return the hug as best as she could. When did she get so tall and Echo so short?

"Of course, news travels fast enough." Echo stood back and looked up at Gwen, still smiling. She looked so much older now, her face deeply lined and her hair greying in wide swaths.

"But you're not going to turn us in?" Myev asked, cautious.

"Absolutely not, you're safe with me," Echo said, putting her hand out. "Echo Little Thimble. I used to look after this one when she was young."

Myev took Echo's hand, which absolutely disappeared beneath Myev's fingers. "Myev. Good to meet you."

Echo turned back to Gwen. "Should have known you'd never stay out of trouble."

Gwen smiled nervously, all teeth and knotted eyebrows. "Yeah, I guess. What are you doing here?"

"I'm the pastor of this church," she said, gesturing at it. "Left Lion's Grace a few years after you did, been here ever since. It's a good community."

"You're not mad at me?" Gwen blurted, unable to contain herself.

"Oh, Gwen," Echo took one of Gwen's hands between both of hers. "Violence is always a tragedy, but the way people have been treated in this country all this time is even more so."

Gwen's muscles eased a bit. "It's good to see you," she said, uncharacteristically softly. "Been a long time."

"I may be too old to do much to help you, but you always have a safe place here," Echo patted her hand before letting go. "Where are you off to?"

"We've been sent on a very important shopping mission," Myev said.

"Mind if I walk with you?"

Gwen looked at Myev, who said, "Of course not," with a polite smile.

More than half the people they walked past smiled at, nodded at, or said hello to Echo as they went by. It was clear she was a popular figure in her community.

"Are all of these your parishioners?" Gwen asked after the millionth hello. As much as she was happy to see Echo again, she couldn't help but feel the endless eyes Echo drew to them—there was no guarantee anyone else that happened to recognize them would be as kind about it as Echo was. She tried to keep her face shadowed in the hood of her jacket.

"Not half of them," Echo said. "I can have friends outside my job, you know." She poked Gwen playfully in the side. "Glad you appear to have made a friend."

"Several friends," Myev answered for her. "The rest of us are just busy running other errands."

Echo smiled, her face so truly pleased that it pulled at Gwen's heart. If she'd ever had a positive adult presence in her life, it was Echo. "Several friends. Good on ya'."

Gwen grumbled a "thanks", her face heating with embarrassment.

"Got a girlfriend yet?" Echo asked, so casual, like just hearing the words wouldn't basically kill Gwen on the spot.

Which they almost did.

She choked, then coughed, a high-pitched panic sound rising from the deepest part of her gut to escape out of her mouth, which she miraculously managed to quell. Echo had clearly changed her opinions on that subject, which was great, but Gwen also hadn't quite figured out how to talk about the fact that she had a *girlfriend* just yet. Hadn't even *called* Veda her girlfriend. *Girlfriend*. Spirits above.

Myev was grinning at her.

"Uh. Y-yeah," Gwen said, her voice a full octave higher than normal. Her face was so hot she thought it could melt right through a glacier.

Echo giggled, actually giggled, and patted her on the back of the legs. "Good for you. What's her name? She cute?"

Gwen sucked a deep, noisy breath in through her nose and consciously willed her eyes to be just a *tad* less wide. She knew she looked like a panicked prey animal, the whites of her eyes fully visible and her nostrils flared. *Is this what having family is like?* she wondered. She'd heard they'd ask you lots of embarrassing questions if you didn't visit often enough, but it had never been an issue up until now.

"Veda." She kept her answer short to minimize the chances of her voice cracking.

"She's the princess of Vulcaria," Myev added. Helpfully. "Gorgeous. Absolutely stunning."

Gwen resisted the urge to punt her across the road.

Echo whistled. "A princess! How'd you manage that?"

"Bar fight," Gwen responded before she thought better of it.

"Now that's a story I *have* to hear."

***

That night—after dinner with Echo, after promises to visit and bring Veda so Echo could meet her, after Gwen had died 87 separate times of embarrassment—Sylvia gathered all of them in the common room of the inn. Finally, she had received all the components she needed and she held in her hands the result of all their hard work—a flask filled with a liquid of some sort, the color of rust. She could see the stones Jasper and Avery had gotten sitting at the bottom.

"Give me your weapons," she instructed those that would be going to the cabin in the morning. They did so and one by one, she gently coated them in the concoction. The potion glowed briefly on their surfaces before fading as the magic was absorbed by them: wood, leather, and metal alike.

"This will empower your weapons to be stronger against magic and magical creatures," she explained. "It only lasts a day or two, but that's good enough for now. If someone like Zachariah is down there waiting, you need all the advantages you can get. It's clear he has some very powerful magic up his sleeve after our last run in."

Myev grumbled something under her breath and Boris gently hit her with his shoulder. She crossed her arms and looked away.

"I beg you though," Sylvia continued, "if you meet with him there, run instead of fighting. I don't think any of us should take him on with anything less than the full group."

"We should be fine, but if shit gets too serious, we'll get out of there right away," Gwen assured her.

They retired to their rooms for the night and as soon as they had changed into their nightclothes, Veda lifted her and tossed her on the bed, crawling up after her. She had a *thing* for picking Gwen up and Gwen had learned it was easier to just accept it. Veda gave her a soft kiss and then wrapped herself around Gwen's body as Gwen pulled the blankets over them. As it got colder every night, she was extremely grateful that she got to sleep with a woman built of fire.

"The lady I had dinner with tonight used to be one of the caretakers at my orphanage," Gwen mumbled after many minutes of comfortable silence. "I hadn't seen her in a long time. It was good catching up. She wants to meet you."

"That's awesome, I'd love to," Veda said, nuzzling into her collarbone. "Echo, was it?"

"Yeah," Gwen confirmed. Her stomach turned a little as she prepared herself to ask a rather stupid question, but her mind wouldn't let it go. "Are you my girlfriend?" she asked quietly, in a rush.

Veda laughed and Gwen could feel it rumble through her bones. "I'd like to be, if you'll have me."

"Yeah," Gwen smiled, relieved. "Just checking."

"You think I go to war for all the pretty girls?" Veda joked.

"Actually yes, I do," Gwen elbowed her. Then, after a moment, "How are you never afraid? What if someone wanted to hurt us for—for this?"

"I'd cut their legs off," Veda replied, matter of fact. "Arms too, if it was necessary. Plus, I'm afraid of many things. Just not this."

Gwen snorted in disbelief. "Like what?"

"Spiders."

Gwen cackled. "Mmhmm."

"I'm scared of not being a good leader—of letting my people down," Veda said more quietly.

"That's fair. You're so..." Gwen struggled to find the right descriptor, "normal, I guess, that sometimes I forget you're a princess."

Veda laughed. "Your country's idea of princesses and mine are very different, I'll give you that."

"If it helps, I think you'll make a great leader when you go home," Gwen said, her heart leaping a little at the thought. *Home.* In her mind, the word in relation to Veda translated to *away from me.* Because this was not Veda's home and never truly could be.

Veda smiled, which Gwen couldn't see, but could feel on her skin where Veda's face was pressed to her chest. "Thank you. I'm also afraid of being alone," she continued. "I've lived in such a close community all my life that stepping foot on the shores of Peonia all alone was terrifying. I had to figure out how to make my own way without the support of my family, which I'd always had up until then. I'm afraid that I'll never make it back home—that I'll die out here, alone."

"You're not alone now."

"No, I am not." Veda lifted her head to look at Gwen and bit her bottom lip, worrying it with her teeth. Gwen waited her out.

Finally, her voice low and vulnerable, she said, "The first few years out here, I went from place to place pretty quickly. I'd go anywhere I had heard there was trouble, and I would stay for a few days to help solve the problem, to learn how to serve others and become a warrior and leader like I'm supposed to. But then I would finish the job and it would always become clear that I'd fulfilled my purpose and because I was an outsider, and because of the nature of my journey, I was not meant to stay. So I'd go, and I'd find another problem to solve, and another and another, always dreading the moment when it was over and I had to leave. When it would just be me again, waiting for the time that I could go home and stop feeling quite so unmoored."

She closed her mouth, warring with herself about whether or not to say the next thing. She'd laid her head back down and her gaze was now fixed on the hem of Gwen's shirt, which she picked at with her fingers. "Sometimes I'm scared that the reason I pushed you so hard to get involved with this rebellion was to give myself a reason to stay with you longer. If we had more to do than just track down your parents' killers, you would have a reason to keep me around and I wouldn't have to go. I'm scared I pushed you for selfish reasons and that it was wrong and cruel of me."

Gwen was floored and her mind raced, trying to find a coherent way to respond. She finally settled on, "I don't think that's true at all."

Veda didn't respond. Gwen hadn't seen her so vulnerable and unsure before. She reached down to grab Veda's hand, gave it a firm squeeze.

"Hey."

Veda looked up at her, her eyes a little miserable.

Gwen used the pad of her thumb to flatten out one worried eyebrow. "I don't care about you just because you're of 'use' to me, you know that right? And I don't think you pushed me because you were selfish, I think you pushed me because you knew in your gut that it was the right thing to do. You've been right this whole time. I just wasn't ready to see it at first." Gwen swallowed hard. "I also, uh. I don't want you to go either. When this is all over. I don't want this—us—to have an expiration date."

Veda was a little watery eyed now. "That's good to hear."

"Maybe, um. If you'll let me—at the end of this—maybe I can go with you. Home," Gwen said, blushing all the way down to her toes. It felt a little too much like a proposal, like *I can't live without you,* but as long as Veda was being honest, she might as well do the same.

"You'd leave your home for me?" Veda asked, breathless.

"This place never really felt like it was meant for me anyway," Gwen gave a wry chuckle. "I'll go ahead and try to leave it a little better than I found it, but maybe I was meant to go somewhere else." She refused to meet Veda's eyes, afraid that somehow it would cause this precarious-feeling bubble to burst. Veda hadn't said yes yet, so no was still on the table. If she looked her in the eyes, she might come to her senses and tell Gwen that she'd taken it too far.

"I could give you the most wonderful home," Veda said so earnestly that it made Gwen's heart thump once, hard, in her chest before flinging itself up her throat. Veda continued, "I'd love to have you come with me. We'd love to have you in Vulcaria."

Gwen smiled, relieved and excited and floating a little. "You sure?"

Instead of answering, Veda lifted herself up off Gwen's chest and kissed her, ardent and jubilant. Her hair had flared to nearly twice its normal size. Gwen kissed her back, grinning into it.

"And Bumble, too, if she wants," Veda finally said when she pulled back.

Gwen laughed. "Yeah, I think we're stuck with her."

Chapter Fourteen

Nestled deep within the trees and up against a cliff face was an old cabin. A shack, really. There were no windows and the wood siding was so worn that much of it was barely holding on. The whole building slumped in on itself like it wished it could just melt into the ground and be done with it.

"Here? Really?" Gwen said before she could think better of it.

"I know," Nihal chuckled, "looks like nothing at all, but just wait. There's more underneath," he waggled his fingers mysteriously.

Nihal turned the doorknob and pushed, but the thing barely budged, the poor wood trapped by the drooping frame around it. "Shouldn't have closed it last time, I guess." He gave the door two hard shoves before it finally popped open with a loud creak and pop, as if it were crying out with relief at its freedom.

They entered after him and looked around the single room of the cabin. In one corner sat a long-neglected fireplace coated in soot. At the back of it lay the corpse of what appeared to have once been some sort of rodent, but it had long since turned into dark jerky. Next to it was an old iron stove and across from that there was a small, bare bed.

Any blankets, pillows, or personal items the room once held were long gone.

Nihal was rustling around by the bed, lifting the thin mattress, touching the logs that made up the wall, lifting the mattress again. "Gotta be here somewhere," he mumbled, scratching his chin. Gwen watched with her eyebrows raised as he bent down to touch deep gouges on the floor, presumably caused by the bedframe. He then yanked the bed loudly away from the wall and squatted to inspect the floorboards beneath it.

"Ah-ha!" he whooped after a moment, straightening out to stomp his foot hard against the floor. One of the boards pressed downward with a click. A section of the floor in the corner lifted, revealing a trapdoor. Nihal reached down to triumphantly throw it open and Jasper crinkled his nose at the sound the trapdoor made as it hit the wall.

"Any chance we had of being sneaky is gone. Between that, the bed, and the door, if someone's down there, they definitely know they've got company," he lamented.

Avery patted his arm soothingly.

Nihal had already drawn his sword and was partway down the stairwell. "Guess we better follow," Gwen said, unsheathing her own weapon.

Veda shrugged and pulled her axe from her back, heading after Nihal. "Guess so."

They descended into pure darkness, the stairway lit only by Veda's hair. She had brought her cape, but they needed to see somehow so she wasn't wearing the hood. On the wall at the bottom of the stairs were a series of torches in metal holders. Veda created a flame in her palm, pulled a torch free of its holder, lit it, and passed it back. Avery took it with a nod of thanks and used her torch to light a second for Jasper. A third was handed to Nihal.

"I can see fine," Gwen told her as she reached for a final torch. "We have plenty, don't worry about it."

"Stick by me then, just in case," Veda turned to her and winked.

Gwen responded by rolling her eyes and pushing gently on Veda's mid-back. "Will do, Living Torch. Let's get moving."

They followed the corridor at the bottom of the stairs until they reached a large room filled with seating and low tables; a gathering area of sorts. Some of the chairs were knocked on their sides, as if those who had been in them had left in a hurry. Cups still half filled with liquid and moldy, partially eaten food sat atop many of the tables.

"Pavlin's tip must've been correct," Nihal grunted. "Ain't nobody here now."

Three doors led deeper into the hideout, two at the back of the room and one to the left. Jasper was already at the leftmost one, jostling the lock with a set of picks he'd pulled from his pocket. The door opened to what looked like an office. A few papers were strewn across the desk and floor, hastily tossed in the search for something else. The cabinets and drawers in the room hung open, mostly empty.

Avery held a paper to her face, reading it in the torchlight. "Some of these are letters," she glanced up at Gwen, "this one is addressed to a guy I don't recognize, from Regan Cole."

"So, The Brotherhood was definitely here at some point," Gwen said, picking up another piece of paper. It had Zachariah's name on it.

They searched the room and found little of use, but Gwen gathered the stray papers anyway and put them in her bag. They moved on to the first door in the back of the sitting room, which was unlocked. It was a kitchen and the smell of rot hit them the second the door was open. Gwen swallowed hard to fight her gorge rising and covered her nose with her hand.

"This is—this smell is too strong to just be food," Nihal said.

Gwen nodded in agreement, stepping forward to look at the abandoned food atop the large counter in the center of the kitchen. It was mostly baked goods and cheeses, but the room smelled of blood and meat with a sickly-sweet note underneath it all. Noticing a dark stain creeping out from the edges of the counter, she rounded the side and gagged hard, closing her eyes a moment to get the reflex under control. Between the counter and the stoves were a pair of canieum, their necks dark, gaping maws, slit from ear to ear. She could see the white of their vertebrae shining out of the mess of gore their throats had become. Their open eyes stared out at nothing at all. Gwen grit her teeth hard enough to hurt. She noticed their hands were touching, as if they'd sought out one last second of comfort as they died.

Behind her, Nihal let out a ragged breath.

She'd seen plenty of bodies and had slit Vito Cady's throat herself. If she had stuck around to look at him after she'd done it, she imagined he would look a lot like the two canieum. The senselessness is what got her. They had no weapons on them, nothing to fight with. Likely, they'd just been cooks, not warriors of any kind. Likely, they'd been ambushed from behind and killed without warning. She turned and stalked past Nihal, out of the kitchen. Her friends looked at her with questions, but she merely shook her head and opened the last door, which Jasper had already unlocked.

"Dead folks," she heard Nihal say behind her. "Murdered."

They entered another long hall dotted with doorways. Gwen felt Veda's warm body come close behind her, her hair causing shadows to dance along the corridor. She put her hand on Gwen's shoulder, so Gwen lifted her own to set it upon Veda's and squeezed her thanks. They had to continue.

The first few rooms were yet more small, ransacked offices that yielded nothing at all. There was barely enough room in the offices to store anything, so clearing the rooms would have made for quick work. The papers and envelopes that were left were mostly blank and empty save for a few letters, which they gathered up. Further doors revealed a communal bathing area that smelt of putrid, stagnant water and several storage areas filled with the basics. They rifled through them anyway, but found nothing of interest.

Past that, stairs led up to four lavish bedrooms filled with expensive looking rugs, tapestries, couches piled high with cushions, and grand four-poster beds. Nothing remained to denote who each room might have belonged to. At the end of the hall, they found several rooms that had been servants' quarters, each containing more corpses that were spread across the rooms like tossed garbage.

"They couldn't even make it out of here with all of their papers because they spent too much time doing this," Avery whispered, her voice pure steel.

"I'm sure they were afraid of what the servants would reveal if they escaped," Jasper said, pulling a blanket off the bed and placing it over the body of a fallen cyclops man. "Those bastards thought this the most prudent solution."

Finally, at the very end of the hall, there was a single metal door with a small window in the top third. Veda brought her face close to the glass and scanned the room. "It seems empty," she said, "but it's so dark in there that I can't tell for sure." She jiggled the handle. "Locked."

Jasper picked the lock and took a few steps into the room, holding his torch ahead of him, with Avery on his heels. The rest of them entered behind her. Despite their torches and Veda's hair, the tunnel of a room yawned so far back that the darkness seemed endless, like the light couldn't touch it even if it wanted to. Carefully, they stepped further in. Why lock the door to an empty room?

"Maybe they took everything?" Nihal offered.

"Something feels wrong," Avery shook her head. "There's something here, but I don't know what."

Deep within the darkness a growling rumbled forth and Gwen ground her teeth. "There it is," she whispered.

She motioned to the others and they all began to back up towards the door as the growling grew closer. It seemed to be coming from all around them, bouncing off the walls and getting louder by the second. They were almost at the door when half a dozen creatures came forward into the torchlight. Stark white skulls—from something Gwen had never seen, something with horns and long, sharp fangs and too many eye sockets—seemed to float in the air. As she kept her eyes trained on them, she realized that what held the skulls aloft were bodies made of some sort of smoke, shadows, even. The dark, shifting mass was formed into the rough shape of some huge, four-legged beast. The creatures' jaws moved in jerky movements as they snarled and snapped, the one in the lead leaping at Avery and Jasper.

Avery's torch hit the floor as she pulled her staff and it connected with the skull, a loud crack ringing through the room. The spell Sylvia had put on it flashed with a bright green light and the creature hissed, backing up. Two daggers flew from Jasper's hands, also glowing as they floated within the shadow creatures for only a moment and then dropped through them to the ground. Another stuck in the center of one of the skulls, but the creature shook its head a few times until it was dislodged. The daggers seemed to hurt them during the time that they were touching the beasts, but they didn't stay long and it was simply not enough. The creatures backed up only as much as necessary to keep out of Avery's range, slowly flanking them and considering their next attack.

As a group, they tried to resume their slow retreat towards the open door. The creatures lunged again and Veda's axe made ephemeral contact with the body of one, sliding through and hitting the stone floor hard. She kicked at its skull, making contact with a dull crack. It backed up, growling, but didn't need long to recover before slinking towards her again.

"I know what these are," Avery said, "they're the perfect watchdogs for an underground lair like this. Their only weakness is sunlight. Even with the spell on our weapons, they won't do much. Not enough to kill them." Quietly, almost to herself, she whispered, "This was a trap."

"If we can be quick, maybe we can shut that door to hold them off for a few seconds and run," Gwen said, looking behind her. "Get behind me and I—"

"I'm already in front," Avery cut her off. "Go."

"Avery—"

"Go," she repeated more firmly. "I'll hold them off. Turn and run and don't look back. I'll be right behind you."

"I'll help," Jasper said, more daggers in hand. He kicked at one, trying to back the beasts up and give them more room.

"Your daggers aren't doing as much damage as my staff," she told him. "I need you to run."

Jasper studied his wife's back, his shoulders tense. "No," he finally told her. There was something in his voice that made Gwen nervous. "It's better than nothing and I won't leave you."

"Jasper," Avery warned, a crack in her voice betraying an anger Gwen had never seen her show. Avery was always the epitome of composure.

Something felt wrong, but Gwen bit her tongue and motioned to Veda and Nihal to move. Slowly, they backed out of the room, one after the other. For every step they took back, the creatures moved forward, following. Every few seconds one would leap and Avery would knock it back, the ruthless strikes of her staff the only thing keeping them at bay. Gwen wished more than anything that they'd brought Sylvia or Ivy with them. Anyone with any kind of magic to push these horrid creatures back into the darkness they'd come from.

When Avery and Jasper were the only ones left over the threshold to the room, Avery spoke again. "Jasper, I need you to go." Her voice wavered, just a bit.

"No," he told her again.

"We both know they're going to get through that door in seconds if we all run and they're faster than us," she said, pleading. "It was a setup. We fucked up and it's too late, you know it. I can hold them off long enough for the rest of you to get out."

"No, I won't leave you. Ever."

Gwen realized what was happening only a millisecond before Jasper dropped his torch, turned, and slammed the door. She heard the lock click just as she hit the door with her body, her fists slamming into the little window. "What are you doing?!"

"Tell Aiden I'm sorry and we love him," he yelled.

He retreated until he was back-to-back with Avery, now surrounded. She turned her head towards him and even in the flickering, dying torchlight, Gwen could see the grief and rage etched on her face.

She was screaming his name when the creatures surged forward, overtaking them.

Gwen's own throat was already raw from the howls ripping themselves out of her as she threw herself against the door, trying with everything she had to get through it. Jasper's torch went out and the blitzes of light on their weapons were the only thing she could see of her friends.

"We have to go!" Nihal yelled, his voice shaking. "She was right, those things will tear right through that door!"

"No, I can't leave them!" Gwen shrieked.

Veda moved her out of the way and brought her axe down hard on the metal door. It bounced back, barely making a mark. She tried twice more, even her axe and strength useless against the reinforced door. She cried out helplessly.

From inside the room, Avery's voice burst through, like it took everything in her. "Go! Please!"

"Don't let their sacrifice be in vain," Nihal said. His voice was shaking, but his hand was firm on Gwen's arm, pulling. He grabbed Veda with his other.

Veda's face was a mirror of the agony Gwen felt as she reached out and grabbed her hand. Gwen squeezed her eyes shut and bit her lip so hard she tasted blood. Slowly, she turned around, feeling like she was moving through thick syrup, as if she were in a dream.

They ran, following Nihal, and every step they took felt like a betrayal. Every breath in her throat was like a thousand shards of glass. Her whole body rejected each inch they moved away from their friends.

They ran, skidding around corners and leaping up the stairs. It wasn't long before they heard the horrible screech of metal being ripped apart as the beasts made it through the door behind them. It meant her friends were dead. Gwen wanted to scream, wanted to turn around and let them have her too.

They ran, and she could sense the creatures gaining on them as they rushed up the stairs into the dilapidated cabin above. They hit the grass outside, the sun shining mercilessly down on them, and she finally turned back to look. The creatures stood just inside the open cabin door, out of the reach of the light and unable to follow. She didn't even care.

She dropped to her hands and knees in the dry grass, a sob tearing itself free from her throat. She wailed, the keen pulling every ounce of breath from her lungs. Veda was kneeling beside her. She had her arms around Gwen and they were shaking, her tears falling hot onto the back of Gwen's neck.

Gwen dug her fingernails into the grass, glaring back up at the creatures. They howled and bit at the air, furious at losing their prey. Above the door sat a single raven. It looked at her, an unnatural blue glow in its eyes.

"I see you survived. How unfortunate," the raven said in Zachariah's voice. "Though not all of you, it seems."

Gwen could only roar towards it, unable to even stand through the grief weighing her body down.

"This place has been abandoned for some time now, as its location had been compromised," the raven told them, "but I knew it would be the perfect bait for an ambush. All I had to do was have an associate slip a little clue to your allies and I knew you'd be on it like flies to honey. After that it was simply a matter of leaving you a trail of breadcrumbs until you were right where I wanted you."

Distantly, she registered the sound of fists hitting a tree, over and over and over again. Nihal.

Zachariah cackled. "I knew you'd never be able to resist, that you wouldn't heed my warning. Knew that once you were in my web you'd just keep going, hoping you'd find something, especially after seeing what I had them do to the servants. You'll never learn, you'll just keep going until it gets you killed. Or your friends," he added flippantly.

Veda was screaming at the bird, but Gwen couldn't say a thing, could only stare at her hands buried in the soil. He was right, after all. She got Avery and Jasper killed. They started doing this for her and they died for it. She dropped her head to the ground and rocked forward, feeling like she couldn't breathe anymore. Didn't want to.

Even long after the raven was gone, she remained frozen there, until Veda pulled her face into her hands and made her look her in the eyes. The sun was beginning to dip towards the horizon. "We have to go, before the sun is gone and they can follow us."

"But Jasper. Avery. They're—they're still—" Gwen said, shaking her head.

"We'll come back. I swear we will," Veda promised.

With her help, Gwen stood, and though it killed her, she began to walk away. What was one more betrayal?

***

Sylvia knew something was wrong the moment they walked back through the door of the Inn without Avery and Jasper. Gwen's mouth opened and closed, but nothing would come out. Tears filled Sylvia's eyes and she pulled Gwen into her arms, holding her as tightly as she could. She could hear Veda trying to explain what happened, but she wasn't listening.

She felt Bumble wrap her arms around her legs and she was making a sound not unlike a caw, but it came out in a broken, wretched way, like she couldn't hold all the hurt inside her and didn't know what else to do with it. She felt so many pairs of arms wrap around them with her in the middle, Veda and Myev and Boris and Ivy and even Nihal, and she began to cry again. Deep sobs wracked her whole body, rippling outward to the others. They held on, mourning their fallen friends and trying to find any bit of comfort they could in each other. Gwen didn't deserve any of it.

***

Dawn came and they returned to the cabin. The creatures still stood just behind the sunlight coming through the open door, waiting. A surge of hatred filled Gwen and she wished she could tear them apart with her bare hands.

"Ready?" Ivy asked Sylvia.

Sylvia nodded, breathing deeply and lifting her hands towards the doorway. A moment later a ball of light as bright as the sun burst from them and into the cabin. The second it was through, Ivy lifted her own hands and a transparent, magical wall filled the entrance to the cabin, blocking it. The creatures howled, scrambling forward and hitting the barrier. Ivy held it and Sylvia grew her ball of light until it filled the entire cabin.

In their fear, the creatures didn't even think to go back down into the dark depths of the lair. They just kept hitting the barrier, again and again, until their movements slowed and they slumped to the ground. They were only animals. Horrible, terrifying things, but animals nonetheless. Their shadowy bodies melted into the wood of the cabin floor, leaving only a pile of skulls. Once they moved no longer, Ivy dropped the barrier and shot one last burst of magic towards them, destroying the skulls in an eruption of shrapnel.

As a unit, they entered the cabin and worked their way down through the abandoned hideout until they came across the shredded door at the end. Pieces of metal littered the hall. Gwen stepped on them without a care, walking until she stood before Avery and Jasper's bodies. Bile rose in her throat and she felt herself hit the ground, but the pain in her knees was nothing at all. It was distant, like she wasn't a part of her own body anymore.

Avery's long white hair was splayed around her, blood spread through it and sticking it to the floor. Jasper's body slumped over hers like a puppet with its strings cut and his thin hands were tangled in the fabric of her tunic. Avery's arms were wrapped around his neck, holding him to her.

She stared for what felt like a lifetime, burning their mangled bodies into her mind, before she heard someone speaking. "Gwen," Veda's soft voice finally broke through, like it wasn't the first time she'd called her name. She placed her hand on Gwen's back. "Please don't look anymore."

Veda's hand felt like a hot iron on her skin, branding her guilt into her bones. Her touch made everything real. Every part of Gwen was shaking and she was holding her jaw together so tightly it hurt. Now she could hear Sylvia whimpering softly and disconsolately behind her. The hushed voices of Myev and Boris trying to soothe her through their own tears. The small, trembling gasps coming from Ivy. Nihal stood in the doorway, head turned away from it all, barely even breathing.

Bumble gently lifted Gwen's arm and tucked herself under it, burrowing into her side. Gwen pulled her into her lap, hugging her close and seeking her forgiveness. "I did this to them. I did this. I'm so sorry," she rasped.

"Didn't," Bumble said into her chest. "Didn't, no. No, no, no," she cried, unable to form another thought.

"Gwen, please," Veda repeated.

"This is my fault," she whispered, closing her eyes as tightly as she could, her face buried in the feathers atop Bumble's head. If she looked at Avery and Jasper's empty eyes one more time, she felt as though she might come apart at the seams. "This never would have happened if they hadn't come to help me."

"They knew the risks when they agreed to join us," Veda said gently, kneeling next to her. "They never would have blamed you for this."

"Shouldn't they though?" Gwen snapped, turning on Veda and grabbing her by the arm. "This didn't have to happen! I could have stayed home and lived out my miserable life without ever dragging anyone else into it. I was never worth it. None of it was ever worth...this," she choked.

Veda looked away, to the stone floor, and wet her lips with her tongue. She looked like she'd been slapped, and Gwen added that to the pile of guilt building inside her.

"That's not what I meant," she tried to say, stumbling over the words. "That's not—"

Veda placed a hand on Gwen's cheek, tears streaming down her own face. She seemed to think hard before she said, "No one accomplishes great things without suffering horrible injustices along the way. It's the cruel way of the world. You miss them. I miss them. This is a hole inside us that will never be filled, but Avery and Jasper *chose* to follow you. They *chose* to die for us. Avery was a brilliant woman and she made her choice knowing the outcome. She did it because she loved us, and she believed in us, and she believed in our cause. Jasper did too. We cannot let that be for nothing. We have to respect their choice by continuing to fight." She moved her hand from Gwen's cheek to rest it over her heart. "The dead feel no more pain; only the living can hurt this much. It's our duty to take that pain and use it to honor them."

She tapped her fingers on Gwen's chest, twice. "Do not let this break you. I haven't regretted my decision to join this cause for a moment, nor will I ever. I do not doubt that Jasper and Avery felt the same." Veda slid closer, pulling both Bumble and Gwen into her embrace. "I will fight beside you; I will help you carry this weight. Do it for them. It's not fair, but few things are."

"I'll help carry it too," Sylvia said quietly behind them. Gwen felt her clawed hand settle softly on her shoulder.

"I'll help carry," Bumble repeated.

Myev and Boris knelt on either side of her. "We will do this together," Myev said. "In their honor, we will see this through."

"Together," Boris agreed.

"It's what they would want." Ivy stepped in front of her, reaching her tiny hand out to grasp Gwen's forearm. "Don't quit yet. Please. This is it; this is what we are supposed to do," Ivy's eyes bored into hers.

Gwen could only nod, truly overwhelmed in every possible way.

***

They carried the bodies outside. Avery and Jasper first, and then they went back in as many times as it took to bring all the dead out. They pulled the sheets and blankets from the beds, carefully wrapping each body from head to toe. While some did that, the others built a large pyre from materials in the surrounding woods. They would wait with Avery and Jasper's bodies until Aiden arrived, but they had no idea who the others were and the best they could do was give them a proper send-off.

When it was done, Veda said a prayer to Reynta, asking that their souls be cradled in her warmth until they were remade into something new in their next life. Sylvia did a blessing over all the bodies and then they lit the fire, watching it swallow the strangers who also fell victim to Zachariah's cruelty. They were all silent as they felt the weight of their grief, for both their friends and those they never knew in life.

Wrapped around Gwen's leg was Jasper's multi-dagger sheath and she leaned on Avery's staff, to which she had tied the sash Avery always wore around her waist. There was blood all over it, but she would wash it as clean as she could before giving it to Aiden. Next to her, Bumble held Jasper's hat close to her chest, the brim crinkling in the tightness of her grip. They held them as if they were precious treasures, these objects that were all they had left of their friends.

After the pyre had been going for some time, Sylvia had taken Avery and Jasper down to the nearby river one at a time and gently cleaned the blood from their bodies. It seemed like she had needed those last, private moments with them. When she returned and they were once again wrapped tightly in the stark white sheets, they all settled down near the pyre, adding more wood as necessary until the bodies were gone. Eventually, the fire burned low and night truly blanketed them. They would sleep there. Aiden was due to arrive the next afternoon.

They had grown quiet when Gwen heard a flutter of wings. "I see you couldn't stay away," a familiar voice said from behind them. Gwen turned to see the raven perched in a tree. "Should have set another trap."

Rage filled Gwen as she leapt to her feet, stalking closer to the bird. "I will destroy you," she told Zachariah through the bird.

The bird laughed, a jagged cackle. "No, you won't. This organization is deeper than you could ever hope to unroot. You'll be killed before you get the chance."

"You might be right. I'm one person and we both know I probably won't live to see the end of The Brotherhood," Gwen growled, "but when I leave this world, I'm doing it with my blade in your gut. I will not leave this life unless I can take you with me, you sick bastard. That's a promise."

With that she pulled one of Jasper's daggers free from the pouch on her thigh, letting it fly towards the raven. It hit it square in the chest and it staggered before falling to the ground, the blue light gone from its eyes.

Chapter Fifteen

Sylvia heard the crunching sound of Aiden walking up the path through the trees before anyone else did and stood, stepping forward to meet him. Gwen felt her stomach leap into her throat and tried to swallow it back down. He was a thin man with long black hair that he kept tied up in a high ponytail and laugh lines around his dark, almond-shaped eyes. He froze when he saw them, anticipating the bad news he knew was coming, but then pushed through the anxiety enough to pull Sylvia into a hug anyway. He held onto her forearms as she told him.

Gwen couldn't hear their quiet words from where she was, but she watched as his knees buckled and Sylvia took on all his weight to stop him from sliding to the ground. Gwen's heart wrenched and she felt the urge to run, to go as far away from this man and his pain as possible. She felt like she had no right to bear witness to his anguish since she was the cause of it.

She watched him walk on unsteady legs to the white sheet covered bundles that held his parents and fall down next to them. He reached his shaky hands out, placing them over Jasper and Avery's still hearts.

Gently, he uncovered their faces, and Gwen was so deeply grateful that Sylvia had cleaned them up. His body shuddered and swayed as he spoke to them, too quietly for anyone else to hear. They allowed him to sit in his grief for as long as he needed until he covered them again, turned to Sylvia, and nodded, wiping his eyes with his fists. He helped them lift his parents onto the pyre they had already built and straightened the sheets they were wrapped in, removing as many wrinkles and snags as he could.

"She hated disorder," he said to no one in particular, smoothing his hand over his work.

It was the first time Gwen had heard his voice and the softness of it somehow hurt her just as much as if he would have screamed at her. More, perhaps.

He took a dented metal lighter from his pocket and set the kindling below them ablaze.

"Would you mind if I said a prayer?" Veda asked and he shook his head, so she spoke to Reynta again, asking for love and warmth and kindness for their friends in their next lives. "May they find each other again in that life," she added, "because I know the world could never be right unless they do."

"Isn't that the truth," Sylvia said, her voice low. "Their souls are made of the same stuff; their hearts beat to the same rhythm. May they find us, too, because we will miss them." She put her glowing hands over the now crackling fire as it fully engulfed them and blessed it. For just a moment, it had a green tint to it.

Bumble lifted Jasper's hat to Aiden and he took it, settling it on his head. "Thank you."

Wordlessly, Gwen handed over Avery's staff and the worn leather sheath of daggers. She had scrubbed the scarf in the creek until her fingers were frozen and raw, yet a faded brown stain still remained. She couldn't make herself meet his eyes as she gave it to him. He thanked her too and she nodded, staring at the ground.

They stepped back and settled on the grass to watch the fire do its work.

***

They were all at the small dive bar next to the inn, drinking mostly in silence. Sylvia sat at a back table fidgeting with some crocheting she'd pulled out of her bottomless pit of a bag and Gwen sat next to her, watching her hands work the bone needles. Veda's hand was warm on her knee as she stared into the distance, somewhere over the top of the bar. Bumble, never a drinker anyway, had conned Myev and Boris into a half-hearted game of cards at the other end of the table.

Nihal had barely spoken a word to any of them since the funeral, yet he'd been flittering around their edges, like a ghost who didn't want you to see them, but wasn't able to move on. Gwen watched him, waiting for the right moment to approach. He was speaking to one of the other patrons, trying to tell a story like he usually did, but she could tell his heart wasn't in it. When the stranger called it a night and left, his eyes darted around, looking for someone else to distract him. Finding no one left in the bar but their own group, he set his stein down and made a move for the door.

He was facing away from her, nearly outside, when Gwen came up behind him and gently placed a hand on his shoulder. He turned, his wide eyes filled with a mixture of grief and guilt and self-loathing and all of the things Gwen recognized in her own reflection.

"What's going on?" she asked.

"What do you mean?" He tried to smile, but it was barely a twitch of his mouth.

"You're avoiding everyone, but you also haven't left," she said directly. "Why?" She was certain she already knew the answer.

Nihal cleared his throat, unable to form the words. Gwen waited. He looked down at his hands and licked his lips. Finally, "I can't leave; I can't abandon all this. I truly believe in it and want to help, but...it was my fault. I passed on what Pavlin, or whoever he was, told me. I took you all down there. I should have been smarter about it, I just—I—"

"You were trying to help," Gwen finished the sentence for him, staring until he finally made eye contact.

He was silent for a minute, floundering, and eventually just averted his eyes again.

"No one blames you."

"I blame me," he laughed sardonically, his voice thick.

"Shit, me too," Gwen said, blowing air from her nose. She didn't know what to say; she wasn't good at this stuff. "If Veda were the one having this conversation, she'd say that blame doesn't help anyone, and then give some sort of wise speech," she finally said, a fond smile pulling at the corner of her mouth. "I should've had her do this talk, real bad luck that you got stuck with me."

Nihal snorted. Then, "You have every right to hate me."

"I don't," Gwen said honestly. "You never could have known. None of us could have, no matter what we tell ourselves in our lowest moments. I know you never would have led us into something dangerous on purpose. Plus, I know you're soft—I saw you at the funeral, all tears and snot running down into your beard the whole time."

He laughed, quick but real this time. It was the assurance he needed. "Thanks."

She ushered him over to sit at their table, she guessed so that they could all make Sylvia uncomfortable as they stared at her while she worked. No one knew what to do, but it felt good not to be alone.

It wasn't long before Aiden entered the bar and it was Gwen's turn to want to run, all of her sage advice to Nihal immediately going out the window. Veda waved him over and he settled down in the empty chair next to Bumble.

Gwen tried to kick the hamster in her brain into gear, convince it to come up with literally anything to say, but it had already done its mushy-feely duties for the day. Eventually her mouth began to move without the permission of her brain and she found herself saying, "W—will you...tell us about them?"

Aiden looked up and cocked his head. "What would you like to know?"

"Anything, I guess." Gwen took a deep breath. "It's just that—I feel like I didn't get enough time? Like I wish I'd known them for so much longer than I got to."

Aiden gave a knowing nod and looked down into his drink. "You ever been to Coral Wharf?"

"No," Gwen replied. "Heard of it."

"Yes," said Myev. "Jasper loved that shithole."

Aiden released a bark of laughter, "That he did."

"That boy never did listen to reason," Sylvia interjected. "'But Sylvia, you wouldn't *believe* the stuff you can find there!' Yeah, like yourself, with the business end of a drunken pirate's dagger in your belly."

"Oh, Auntie, who hasn't been lightly stabbed a few times?" Aiden winked. "Dad said you could get a little stabby from time to time yourself."

Sylvia brandished a knitting needle threateningly at him, grinning. "Go on, continue your story."

"Coral Wharf is where they found me, orphaned and destitute, working all day and night for this shady black market magic dealer so I'd be able to eat and have somewhere to stay...."

Aiden talked for hours, until the bartender had to ask them to leave. He told them about how Jasper had caught him attempting to pick his pocket, and how in true Jasper fashion, he'd found it endearing how Aiden had almost gotten away with it. How Avery had insisted they rescue him from the magic dealer because he was dangerous and abusive, and that they had to take him with them back to Peonia because where else was there for him to go? And even though it was her idea, she insisted it was temporary and kept him at arm's length for several months, until bit by bit, she opened up and that the first time Jasper finally called him their son, she didn't even argue. He told them about Jasper teaching him to read and Avery teaching him to fight. How on his sixteenth birthday, they gifted him with the rapier he carried to that day.

He told them story after story and Myev, Boris, and Sylvia joined in—even Nihal had met them once or twice. Even after all the stories they'd told the nights prior, still there were so many to tell. Soon they were all smiling and laughing, the entire table completely enveloped in the warm, fond memories of a pair of lives well lived. And it still hurt, a terrible ache in the pit of her stomach, and it probably would for a very long time, but Gwen thought to herself again that it felt good not to be alone.

Chapter Sixteen

They could see the smoke miles and miles away from Rivergate, huge plumes—some black and some white—rising into the sky and turning the sun into a great red eye staring down at them. "Gotta be a lot burning to make that much smoke," Aiden said, though they all knew as much without being told. He had chosen to join them on their way to Rivergate, knowing that the town could probably use all the help it could get if the rumors were true, and it seemed that they were.

The trains wouldn't go further than halfway between Golden-field and Rivergate, so they had to walk the rest of the way. It got warmer the closer they got to the coast, which they were grateful for because they'd had to wrap damp cloth around their faces to help them breathe—Gwen could only think how miserable they'd be if it was also half-frozen to their skin. Still, the smoke stung their eyes and Gwen kept finding herself squeezing hers shut as tightly as she could to try to find any small bit of relief. She couldn't imagine how the people of Rivergate felt. She envisioned them all with red-rimmed and constantly leaking eyes, voices hoarse and dry, the smell of smoke now inextricably embedded in everything they owned. Even the fraction of that which she now felt was miserable.

By the time they were less than a mile outside the town limits, the smoke was thick enough that they almost couldn't see Sylvia's contacts a few yards ahead of them at the place where they were supposed to meet.

"Follow us, the smoke is better this way," the shorter one said, not taking the time for introductions. Gwen didn't consider mistrusting them for even a second, as she thought she'd do just about anything to get out of the smoke more quickly, even though both of them were covered nearly head to toe in long coats with hoods and their faces were obscured by masks. Sylvia seemed comfortable enough that they were the right people, so they did as they were told.

The two strangers led them around the town instead of through it, hidden behind a ridge of tall rock. They moved quickly and quietly despite the roaring White River to their other side, hoping to avoid drawing attention to themselves. The person had been right—the smoke grew thinner the further they walked, as they were passing what was on fire and the wind had taken to blowing the smoke back the way they came. Gwen hoped it wouldn't switch directions any time soon.

Because of the clearer air, Gwen could see through breaks in the rocky outcropping that the town itself was the source of the smoke, much of it now just smoldering piles of what used to be homes and businesses. Several sections were still actively burning. She stared at the rubble, her body almost forcing her to stop walking to take in the sheer destruction wrought. She'd known it was bad, but seeing it was an entirely different matter.

From their vantage point on the ridge, she could see to the edge of town farthest away from them. Peonian flags—a sea of green with a proud yellow lion standing in the very center surrounded by swirling pink peonies—flew high over an army encampment. Gwen ground her teeth together, tamping down the desire to scream in fury.

Turning forward again, she saw that a huge wall loomed in the near distance, nestled up against the rock. Large sheets of metal had been hastily joined together to make a rusty but firm barrier between the hydro plant and the rest of the world. It encircled the entire building up to the cliff and a fair amount of land around it, ensuring the plant was not vulnerable from any side. The wall even went through the river and over the dam, cutting off access from that side of the building. Along the outside, at the very top of the barrier, metal grates created rickety catwalks, upon which people had been stationed every few hundred yards.

The river curled protectively around the building and then fell over a natural break in the cliffs, creating a waterfall that dropped back towards the valley Rivergate was nestled in. The water still rushed through both the dam and the bottom of the wall, so Gwen could only assume there were holes of some kind, allowing the river to continue its natural course despite the new blockage.

They approached a seam in the metal barrier and the taller of the two figures leading them raised their hands high in the air. Next to them, the shorter figure did the same, their hands very close together, and they curled their fingers as if they had hooked them around the edge of something. At the same time, they pulled their hands slowly apart and the metal seam opened, creaking and groaning all the way. They opened it just far enough for their group to enter and then quickly closed the gap. The metal sheets came back together with a heavy thud, knocking up a small cloud of dirt where they had long since torn through the grass.

They were then led towards the plant, which had seen better days. Gwen could now tell that much of the metal for the barrier had come from the tall building, which looked unusually naked and sparse, including sections where Gwen could see all the way inside. Hundreds of people milled about the encampment doing various jobs, crowded into every possible space both inside and outside the building. There were faded tents and homemade awnings lining the walls to shelter those that could not fit inside, which appeared to be a lot of them.

They were led in and even without the din of running machinery, the noise level of all the citizens trapped there was so intense that Gwen thought it was like the busiest days in the Ironforge market times ten. Every noise bounced off the walls and was magnified, and even the holes where the metal sheeting had been removed did little to ease the pandemonium. It smelled like sweat and fear and too many people crammed into too little space.

It appeared that the hard, packed dirt floor beneath them had once been covered, but even that had been stripped bare. The flooring only remained beneath the heavy equipment, unable to be easily pilfered. Gwen could see clean spots on the dirty walls where anchoring hardware had been removed high above and around the machinery, presumably to create the catwalks. The machinery was bare and still, most of the useful parts repurposed and the rest of it left to rot until the war was over. Even then, the time and effort it would take to get the place in working condition again would be no small feat. It was no longer a factory, but a hastily built fortress for the refugees of Rivergate, built out of the one thing The Council and army cared enough about not to burn.

They were led into a small, mostly empty room at the back of the building, containing only a desk and a handful of chairs. It appeared to have been an office before everything, and it was the only place Gwen had seen in the building with any amount of open space. When the door was closed behind them, the intense noise inside the plant was muffled to a dull roar and Gwen let out a breath of relief.

Now that they were here, Sylvia's contacts removed their hoods and masks.

The second they had, Sylvia threw herself into the arms of the larger person. "Oh, Tellulah," she croaked. She had been crying, but none of them had been able to tell through the cloth covering her face. She pulled away so that Tellulah could see her and signed to her, *"What horrible things they've done to your beautiful town."*

Tellulah was an owl aviseum, her bright white, heart-shaped face ringed with orange and brown feathers. Large black eyes were set above a small beak. She had wide shoulders and was very tall, only a few inches shorter than Sylvia. She signed enthusiastically back to Sylvia and once their conversation was done, she pulled Sylvia into another hug and clung to her, her weariness and grief extremely apparent.

The second person could have been mistaken for a human if it hadn't been for their soft green skin and the ring of magical black smoke that floated lazily around their head like some kind of halo. Gwen had never seen anyone quite like them. The color of their skin reminded Gwen of Jasper's hair and she felt a sharp pang in her chest.

She consciously did not look over at Aiden because despite their burgeoning friendship, she couldn't stand knowing if he felt the same.

The new person ran their fingers through their shoulder-length, navy-colored hair, which had been mussed by their hood, and then held out their hand to Gwen, who was nearest them. "Cian."

Cian had kind blue eyes and Gwen liked them immediately. If she had been Sylvia, she probably would have been able to say it was something about their aura. "Gwen."

They went through introductions and Sylvia signed the names of those who didn't know the language for Tellulah, who shook each of their hands warmly.

"What brought *you* here, Cian?" Sylvia asked. She always signed as she spoke, her hands where Tellulah could see them. "Not that I'm sad to see you, but I was surprised to hear you answering Tellulah's messages instead of Henri. Where is Henri...?" she trailed off, like she was afraid to learn the answer.

Tellulah looked incredibly sad as she responded while Cian translated, *"Henri, my friend and interpreter,"* she added for everyone else's benefit, *"was killed in one of the early onslaughts. Cian was nearby, so I asked for their assistance."*

"And when the mayor of Rivergate asks for your assistance, you don't turn them down," Cian said with a smile.

"Let's get you some dinner," Tellulah said. *"You must be starving after such a long walk."*

They followed Tellulah and Cian back out into the extremely loud communal area and deeper into the bowels of the stripped factory. Soon, the smells of roasting meat and baked bread filled the air, covering up some of the more unpleasant scents. Gwen's stomach growled in anticipation.

They approached a massive makeshift kitchen, filled with ovens thrown together from loose bricks and chunks of metal, firepits with various meats being cooked over them, and dozens of large baskets that had once been filled with produce and other ingredients, but were now looking painfully empty. More empty baskets were stacked together and lined one long wall, far outnumbering the baskets that still had food in them.

Most everyone that wasn't working on cooking the meat, which seemed to Gwen to be mostly game hunted from nearby forests, was busily churning out loaf after loaf of bread. Some were measuring out the ingredients, some kneading the dough, some carefully sliding the raw loaves into the rickety ovens, others pulling finished ones back out. Gwen could see a lot of empty flour bags and not nearly enough full ones.

"It takes a lot to feed all these folks, especially with our fields being burned," Tellulah explained. *"We've been hunting and gathering whatever we can, but it's getting harder and harder with the armies surrounding us and winter coming. They're doing their best to cut us off and we've lost several hunting parties already. We can only hope they're being kept as prisoners instead of dead."*

"An envoy my parents assigned from the Dimroot Kingdom is currently on their way with dozens of manned carriages filled with food and medical supplies," Ivy told Tellulah with Cian's help. "The group isn't cleared to fight, as we intend to keep our involvement under wraps as long as possible to make it easier to move supplies without interruption, but they have been instructed to provide whatever other aid they can before they return home. I've been keeping in touch with them through one of Sylvia's satchels. We can work together to plan the safest route for them."

Tellulah looked like she might cry. *"I can't tell you how grateful I am. When Sylvia sent word that the Dimroot Kingdom was going to assist us, I nearly passed out from shock."*

"She really did," Cian added.

"I couldn't believe she was even there *in the first place,"* Tellulah laughed softly. *"She's always found ways to surprise me, though,"* she added fondly. Sylvia smiled and looked down at the ground, shyly wrapping her arms around herself.

Tellulah led them further into the noisy kitchen, over to a group kneading dough on a large, well-abused wooden table. At the head of it was a woman clearly related to Tellulah, as they were nearly twins. The only difference Gwen could see was that the second woman's feathers were slightly darker in most places and her eyes were a warm brown, instead of Tellulah's deep black.

"This is my daughter, Lucy," she said as they approached.

Lucy looked up from her work and squealed a little. "Auntie Syl!" she lifted her hands, took a step forward, hesitated, and looked down at her messy fingers. "I would hug you, but—"

"Oh, don't mind that," Sylvia grinned, tugging the woman into an embrace anyway.

Lucy laughed and stuck her hands straight up in the air to keep them away from Sylvia's clothing, unfurled her wings, and wrapped them around her instead. "There, that'll have to do for now. I feel like I haven't seen you in forever!"

"Ah, I know, I need to make time to visit more," Sylvia agreed. "Where's Josie?"

"Bah, who knows with her," Lucy snorted. "She was supposed to be helping in here, but I haven't seen her for a few hours. She's seventeen, she's easily distracted."

"Saw her with that Remington boy shortly before we went to meet these guys," Tellulah informed her.

"Of course she was. She's also boy crazy," she informed them out of the corner of her mouth, as though it was some sort of secret, but one no one should be surprised by. "Abandoning her mother to work all day in the kitchen while she's off canoodling. Typical."

Lucy finished her dough and then assisted in gathering food for everyone, announcing loudly that it was time for her break. They walked until they found a small open space nearby to sit and eat. Sylvia and Tellulah fell deep into conversation that Cian didn't translate, as it was for no one but them, and Gwen didn't miss the way Sylvia's knee was butted right up against Tellulah's, or how she leaned forward into the woman's space, like she was being pulled.

After dinner they were given a more thorough tour of the encampment and then found a somewhat unoccupied corner outside the factory to set up their own bedrolls. After Tellulah and Cian took their leave for the night, Gwen took the opportunity presented by the relative privacy to sidle up to Sylvia. "So."

Sylvia eyed her suspiciously when she didn't continue. "...so?"

"Avery gave me some good advice when I first met her," Gwen said as nonchalantly as she could manage, which wasn't very. "She said, 'If you like her, you should tell her.'"

"And did you take it?" Sylvia asked.

Gwen laughed. "Of course not. Not at first, anyway."

"Just as I thought," Sylvia gave a droll smile and sat down on her blanket.

Gwen did the same. "But you're smarter than I am, so why haven't you?"

Sylvia, not even a little bit of an idiot, replied, "I have no idea what you're talking about."

"Mmhmm."

Sylvia tried to ignore her.

Gwen was not to be assuaged. "How'd you meet her?"

"I've known Tellie since we were young; she was one of the first friends I made when I left Marshwoods. For a long time, we were inseparable."

"Sounds cute. Tell me more."

Sylvia let out a long-suffering sigh, giving in. "I suppose I was always in love with her, but back then—" she trailed off, unable to find the words. She settled on, "It's bad now, but it was worse then."

Gwen nodded.

"So we—I—never said anything. And eventually she got married. He was a good man, Antwon, always treated her right and loved her the way she deserved to be. It was clear that she loved him too. Then they had Lucille. Spirits, little Lucy was the most adorable ball of fire, every bit as stubborn as her mom. Just as smart, too. Got herself into and back out of so much trouble. Still does, sometimes," she laughed. "I hear plenty of stories.

"Years later, Antwon got sick. They lived in Ironforge at the time and the doctors thought maybe it was the air there, so Tellie decided they would move to Rivergate, where the air was clearer. She got a job in the plant to support them. It worked for a few years, seemed like. He was still sick, but it wasn't progressing quite as quickly, and sometimes it even seemed to be going away. I actually took up healing magic because of Antwon; I so badly wanted to save him.

"I didn't succeed though, never did figure out how to stop it. I visited them all the time, tried everything I could come up with. Spent hours upon hours researching, reading everything I could get my hands on. Sometimes, when the body is really determined to destroy itself, there's nothing you can do. No magic is enough for some illnesses. I can fix a broken bone, bring two halves of a wound back together like it was never even there, but when a body has decided to rewrite itself at its very core so that it's falling apart faster than you could ever mend...."

Gwen reached out and placed her hand on Sylvia's where it rested on her knee. The woman gave her a small smile and patted the back of Gwen's hand with her other.

"Anyway, the illness got him in the end. It was a slow and miserable death, and it really broke her and Lucy, who was around twelve at the time. I asked them to come home, come live with me, but they'd made a life here and it wasn't long after that Tellie quit the plant and got involved in Rivergate politics. She was always trying to make her community a better place. Eventually they figured out how to be happy again, especially when Lucy got married and had her own little one. Tellie loved being a mother and grandmother more than anything. They had a beautiful life. And then Tellie became mayor and I was all the way up in Tall Pines. They didn't need me butting in. I guess what I'm trying to say is that it never felt like the right time," Sylvia finished with a sigh.

"Why not now?" Gwen asked softly.

"Might not make it out of this one," Sylvia smiled, her eyes not the slightest bit unkind. "Still doesn't seem like the ideal time."

"Aw, come on," Gwen cajoled, ignoring the guilt in her belly, "Doomsday confessions are the best kind."

Sylvia shook her head and smiled, "Maybe for you youngins. I'm too old and tired for that kind of drama."

"Make me a deal then."

"What's that?"

"*When* we make it out of this one, make the right time happen. You deserve the same kindness and love you heap onto the rest of us. There's no point in wasting any more years. And even if nothing comes of it, at least you'll have said it."

Sylvia was silent for a few moments, mulling it over. "I reckon you're right. It's a deal." She pulled Gwen into a side hug and squeezed tight. "You're a good egg, Guinevere Flynn, I'm glad I got to meet you."

***

There was a series of shouts and then several long blasts from some sort of horn. Cian put their hand on Tellulah's arm to get her attention and then they made the sign for *danger*. Tellulah's eyes grew wide and she leapt to her feet, immediately running outside.

"The scouts have seen something," Cian said as they all followed.

Tellulah ran to the wall where they could see a scout already clambering down the rickety ladder from the catwalks. He began to sign at her the second his feet hit the ground, panting.

"The army is approaching," Cian translated. "A large number of them, mostly on foot. There's a single person riding a horse at the front, maybe a negotiator."

Tellulah looked at Cian, *"We have to go meet them. I don't want them getting any closer to the wall."*

"Not alone," Sylvia immediately interjected. "Please let me go with, to protect you."

"We are both capable of protecting ourselves."

"Please," Sylvia said, all but begging. "Please, Tellie. I've already lost two friends to these people, almost lost another. I won't be able to live with myself if I'm not there and something happens."

"We would also—" Gwen began, but Cian cut her off.

"What if they recognize you? They could attack before giving us the chance to talk. You guys are big game right now."

"What about those cloaks you guys had when you met us?" Myev said. "Make us look like guards going to ensure your safety, cover our faces."

Cian translated and Tellulah thought it over, clearly conflicted by the idea of putting them in more danger. *"Fine. Quickly."*

She took off again, all but running, and they followed. Gwen could feel her heart thrumming in her chest as they searched out enough cloaks for all of them and left the relative safety of the wall. They walked towards the approaching soldiers quickly, trying to cut them off as far away from the wall and the citizens as they could. When they got within a few yards, the rider stopped and the accompanying soldiers moved in front of and around him, shielding him.

Sylvia's footsteps faltered. "It's...it's Regan," she whispered to Gwen. "The rider is Regan Cole."

Gwen's blood went cold and she stared, trying to memorize his face. He was human, of course, and mostly unremarkable. His mousy brown hair was thinning at the front, and he had a round face with thin lips, which were twisted into a barely concealed scowl that showed exactly how much he did not wish to communicate with them in any capacity.

Nonetheless, he called out, "I have come on the behalf of The Council to arrange the surrender of the rebel populace of Rivergate."

"Has The Council changed their position on Rivergate's freedom?" Tellulah asked as Cian translated.

He ignored her question, instead saying, "The Council has advised that they will order the army to retreat and send workers to help rebuild key areas of the city, provided the people of Rivergate stand down and return the hydro plant to working order. There need not be any more bloodshed."

"So they have not."

"The workers sent by The Council will assist in building a large community center, which The Council has generously offered to pay for, to house those that have lost their homes in the battle," Regan continued.

"You mean the homes *your* army burned to the ground," Sylvia hissed *sotto voce.*

"Are you approved to negotiate on behalf of The Council?"

"There will be no negotiation; this is The Council's final offer. They have given you numerous chances to surrender and they have been very patient. The army is prepared to take the rest of your settlement by force, as the cost of this rebellion has well surpassed the usefulness of your town's position and the hydro plant. However, they would like to avoid that, if possible, as I'm certain you would agree."

"I will have to speak to my people," Tellulah said, though her body language was clear. They would not be taking the deal.

"You have until tomorrow at noon to decide, no longer," Regan said. He turned his horse around and went back the way he came, his band of goons on his heels.

Tellulah watched until they were out of sight. *"I have bought us a very small amount of time to prepare. Come, we have much to do."*

Tellulah gathered her people as quickly as possible, packing them into the makeshift courtyard created by the tall metal walls. Cian used magic to amplify their voice to a thunderous boom and translated as Tellulah explained that the citizens would have to make what could very likely be their final stand the next afternoon. *"Anyone who does not wish to go forward may leave, get as far away from here as possible."* Her eyes conveyed her sincerity. No one rose. At that, she wasted no time in preparing everyone for what was to come. She gave each of them jobs, no hands left idle.

Ivy and Boris went with Tellulah and Cian to communicate the new developments with the groups traveling from each of their countries to help. The Dimroot Kingdom convoy would be in Rivergate within only a few days, and while their help was sorely needed, the battle could put them in serious danger. They would need a plan to circumvent the Peonian Army. The forces from Syrenmysta were also still days out and Boris urged them to go faster.

Sylvia, Nihal, and Aiden worked on moving all those who couldn't fight into the deepest, most secure sections of the building, along with all the food, medicine, water, and other supplies left. Included in that group were a handful of more elderly magic users, who would use their abilities to create a magical shield in the event that the Peonian army did manage to breach the walls and approach their hiding place. While they could not keep the shield up forever, the plan was that while the army was distracted with the shield, as many Rivergate citizens as possible would be able to escape through a cleverly hidden secret tunnel at the heart of the factory that went below ground, deep under the river, and let out somewhere in the woods behind the factory. Everyone tried to keep a spark of hope that that would not become necessary.

Veda, Bumble, and Gwen helped gather every single weapon and shield the people of Rivergate had at their disposal, and even created makeshift weapons and armor out scraps of whatever they could find. Many of the city's best fighters had already fallen in other battles and most of the citizens left had only held weapons for the first time shortly after Rivergate had been attacked. Thus, once they had been armed, they were sent to Myev to practice fighting. Tailors, farmers, bakers, artists, scholars—every able-bodied citizen in Rivergate regardless of profession had to learn how to defend themselves and each other.

"I'm afraid it's not enough," Myev said despondently as they laid down for bed later that night. "They're not warriors, Gwen, they're not ready for this kind of violence. They're so incredibly brave, but…" she trailed off.

Gwen nodded, trying to find the words, any words, but failing. They were going to get slaughtered. Everyone knew it. They were going up against a trained army which, by the sounds of it, had gained more firepower in recent days. *The army is prepared to take the rest of your settlement by force,* she heard Regan say in her mind.

Despite all of that, despite knowing the risks, Gwen hadn't heard a single person suggest Rivergate should surrender all day. Even those unable to fight had an unshakable determination in their eyes as they packed and organized. They would not have taken things this far if they were not going to follow it through. They would be free or they would die.

Myev cleared her throat. "But they will do their best," she said, visibly trying to shake off her doom and gloom mentality. "And we will help them. Wars have been won with less."

The majority of the people inside the encampment slept only a few hours, most of them too jittery for more. Gwen herself was awake well before dawn, stretching and pacing in turns in the courtyard, trying to release some of her nervous energy.

Warm arms wrapped around her waist from behind, the comforting smell of campfire smoke enveloping her. "Did you sleep at all?"

She turned in the circle of Veda's arms to drop her head into the crook of her neck, rubbing her face softly against the skin there. "A little."

"It's important to rest before battle."

"Okay, Boss. I'll keep that in mind for next time."

Veda chuckled and used her leverage on Gwen's hips to push her back so that she could press a long, sweet kiss to her mouth. Then they stood there wrapped tightly together, silently soaking in each other's strength. This would be the hardest thing they'd done yet and they both knew it. This wasn't unprepared guards versus the entire lower half of Mooncrest. This was the remnants of a half-starved, exhausted population making their final stand against a fully prepared army. They had to not only try to keep themselves alive, but also hopefully keep Rivergate alive as well. It seemed insurmountable.

"Love you," Veda whispered into Gwen's hair.

Gwen said the words back into Veda's skin, where her lips were pressed to her neck. "I'm glad you're here with me."

"Would never choose to be anywhere else."

Chapter Seventeen

With the rising of the sun, the weary fighting forces of Rivergate began to file towards the main opening in the wall. Gwen and Veda followed them, catching up with their friends. Veda, of course, picked Bumble up and held onto her until the entire crowd had made it out of the safety of the encampment and had taken their places. Only then did she place Bumble back on the ground so that Bumble could join the living wall they were creating.

Everyone stood only a few feet away from each other, creating rows and rows of flesh between where the last hope of Rivergate remained and the frontlines, where they would be meeting the Peonian army in only a few short hours. As some of the most trained fighters, Gwen and her friends took up much of the front row. Tellulah and Cian stood beside them. They all tried to hold onto the belief that, perhaps if they were lucky, the army wouldn't be able to plow through every single one of them. That they would be stopped before they could reach the walls and the vulnerable people within. If things got too bad, if the army was cutting through them too quickly, there was a single scout perched upon a catwalk inside the wall that would warn those left to flee. At least then something of Rivergate would survive.

As they waited for Regan's promised time to arrive, some of the townspeople sat on the ground, eyes always searching the horizon. Some of them stood, shifting from foot to foot, too nervous to sit still. Some paced the small area around their designated position. Few spoke. All had their weapons in front of them, fingers clenched tightly around metal, wood, bone.

Gwen, however, found herself to be surprisingly calm now that it was almost time. It was a fight they were waiting for, and she knew how to do that. They'd done everything they could to prepare for this moment and now all that was left was to see it play out. The adrenaline had honed her focus, calmed her mind in preparation for what was to come. She recognized the same dangerously calm waters inside the eyes of her friends. They would make it through this. They would. She wasn't losing anyone else.

Eventually, the sound of marching feet began to echo off the cliffs and they all resumed their ready positions. Regan came towards them with a band of armored soldiers surrounding him on foot while he rode what appeared to be the only horse. Behind them, a few hundred more soldiers marched steadily forward. A golden roaring lion's head was emblazoned on each and every chest.

"There's fewer than I thought there would be," Cian said softly.

Gwen strained her eyes to the very edge of the horizon and saw that Cian was right. A strip of green ground was still visible behind the sea of silver and gold armor. She had expected the soldiers to stretch endlessly beyond her eyesight, more always coming forward like the tide. Were they hiding further back or could she dare to hope that it was it all a bluff? If these few hundred soldiers were all The Council had actually allotted, perhaps they were in better shape than they had thought. If that were all, the citizens of Rivergate outnumbered them by quite a bit and if they were lucky, they could scrape through this despite their untrained nature. Not without casualties, but at least they wouldn't be wiped entirely off the map.

If there was truly only this many soldiers available to come to Rivergate, it could also mean that the rebellion in Peonia might have spread further than they'd heard. Perhaps they *couldn't* provide more soldiers because perhaps there weren't enough. They'd had to send forces to try to quell things in Rivergate, Ironforge, and Mooncrest at the very least. If there were more rebellions popping up, maybe the Peonian forces were too scattered. It would only be a matter of time before they regrouped, realized this fire was spreading too far and too fast for them to put it all out at once and focused their energy on the battles they absolutely had to win, but for now, if the rebellion continued to ripple outward and cause enough uprisings, it would be a great blow to The Council and Peonia.

Regan stopped a few dozen yards back, truly looking at their faces for the first time, and he laughed. "It's *you*. Didn't recognize any of you in the daylight and not paralyzed." He pointed to Myev. "I didn't recognize you without a knife in your belly. Pity." He waved them off as though they were pathetic flies, a nuisance taking up his valuable time, and turned instead to Tellulah. "What have you decided?" he called out, though he clearly already knew the answer. The mass of people lined up behind them, the weapons in their hands—those were answer enough. "Can't say fraternizing with these traitors looks good for your charming little burg."

"It does not have to be this way," Tellulah replied.

"No, it didn't. If you had surrendered, some of you could have lived."

"What you offer isn't life," Gwen snarled, unable to hold her tongue.

With that, Regan lifted his hand and motioned for the army to begin their attack. They immediately flew into action and as they did, Regan began to retreat in the opposite direction. He flicked his reins, urging his horse to move more quickly past the surging soldiers beside him. The citizens of Rivergate also rushed forward, cries of rage flying from their throats.

Gwen rapidly fell into the almost musical rhythm of battle, exploiting the weak points in the soldier's armor with practiced ease. Due to her lack of it, she was afforded quicker and more lithe movement than they were. She traded protection for speed, but it had always worked for her. It was a song she was familiar with. She'd never fought at quite this scale, but the notes were the same. Stab an opponent through the armpit—dig your sword deep into their chest so that it's quick—use your foot on their chest to pull it out when they hit the ground. Slash another enemy along the backs of their knees and once they fall, make one decisive thrust through their visor, killing them before they could even think about it. Dodge an attack. Shield yourself from one opponent with the body of another, then push them away from you and keep moving. Take a fist or a foot to the back, to the arm, to the leg. Those were fine because they couldn't cause the damage a weapon could. Brush them off. Ignore the small cuts and bruises from your near misses.

Twist.

Roll.

Slash.

Stab.

There was a kind of weird peace to giving everything over to your body, to kill or be killed. This wasn't emotion the way it had been with Vito and Ian. This was just business.

Gwen met another soldier's sword with her own as they charged her, then, gripping her weapon with only her main hand, used her other to grab onto their arm. She twirled around them and pulled their arm with her until it was pinned behind them and they were bent in half, then slid her sword down until it hit their hand and they were forced to drop theirs. She flung it behind them both, out of reach, and then quickly stabbed through the soldier's armor. It was over in seconds. She gave an unconscious millisecond's thought to their family, as she did for each of them, sorry that it had ever come to all of this.

In her peripheral vision she could see Aiden using a razor-sharp, paper-thin rapier to slide through his enemy's weak spots with almost medical precision. His blade whispered as it moved, taking his bulkier opponents down with only a few quick strokes. It was the first time she'd seen him in action and she was reminded of Avery, how every single tiny movement was so calculated, had so much purpose, not a single step unplanned. Yet his wicked grin as he did so was all Jasper, the satisfaction he got from outwitting his enemies.

She knew they would be so proud of him.

Cian was somewhere behind her. She'd caught only a glimpse of them as they used magic to create great waves, knocking their enemies to the ground. From there, huge tentacles rose from the wet ground, holding the soldiers as Cian used long daggers to finish them off. Honestly, it was terrifying, and Gwen was glad they weren't on opposite sides of this thing.

Nihal's hammer rang out like a gong as it hit the chest of a soldier and the jarring sound brought her back to herself. It was as if it was creating an unintentional war drum every time he struck. She caught Veda grinning at it as she pivoted back to Gwen's side. She had blood dripping down her cheeks and more staining her white clothing. Gwen was unable to tell if any of it was her own.

"Hey, babe," she chirped, bringing her axe down on a soldier that had followed her. The axe glowed like molten metal and it sliced through the man's armor as if it were butter, severing most of his arm at the shoulder. He hit his knees with a yelp and Veda finished the job with two more brutal strokes.

Even here, in the middle of all this violence, as she literally killed a man, Veda managed to make her heart skip a beat. "Cool trick."

"Isn't it?"

"Sylvia!" Myev hollered, running and sliding on the ground to kick the feet out from under the three soldiers coming towards her. They did not expect such a low attack and they stumbled forward in a jumble of clanging metal, tripping over each other as their momentum turned against them. Behind her, Boris finished them off with powerful strikes from his sword. Myev rolled gracefully to the side and back onto her feet, pointing to the river. "Can we follow Regan through the water?"

Sylvia, kneeling over a Rivergate citizen to heal them, finished her work and stood. "Clear the way."

They did as they were told, gathering the others and moving through the soldiers, leaving a trail of bodies in their wake. When they reached the bank, Veda swung her axe in a broad arc, channeling fire from her hands down the handle and out of the head, creating a wall of fire that would stop anyone from following them.

Sylvia lifted her hands and a large section of the water rose and flattened, like a sheet of glass, which she held still as they all stepped onto it. She briefly looked back at Tellulah, on the other side of the wall of fire. She was flying above the fray, throwing magical lightning towards the soldiers. The bolts rushed through one metal-clad person to another, causing several of them to fall to the ground, convulsing. She made brief eye contact with Sylvia through the flames and gave a curt nod. Sylvia took a deep breath and stepped onto the magical raft.

Veda pulled the wall down and Sylvia had them surfing against the flow of the river, in the direction Regan had gone. Soldiers turned their heads as they went by, hefting their swords, but quickly realizing the pointlessness of their actions. They could not enter the river—their heavy armor would cause them to get caught in the mighty current and they would drown before they could get back out.

Gwen was exhausted, her muscles burning, and she tried to breathe deeply during the few restful seconds they got as Sylvia pushed them forward. Blood flowed into her mouth from a cut on her lip where someone had caught her with the pommel of their sword and she spit it into the river. She flexed her fingers, one hand at a time, and cracked her neck.

Regan had ridden all the way to the back of his army and then some, hundreds of yards behind the rest of them, and had turned to watch the battle unfold. He looked entirely too smug and unworried. His face changed quickly when the sound of Sylvia forcing them through the water reached him, his expression becoming all bared teeth and ugly, hateful eyes. He turned his horse to retreat further just as they reached the shore and leapt onto solid ground again.

"Sorry, horsey," Ivy said quietly as she stepped in front of Gwen, throwing a blast of magical energy that hit Regan square in the chest, knocking him off the horse, who spooked and bolted. He hit the ground hard, grunting as the wind was knocked out of him.

Immediately the soldiers that had not advanced with the rest of the army, those that were there explicitly to protect Regan, turned and beset them as their leader regained his bearings. They were quicker and more thinly armored, chain instead of plate, and more skilled than those they had already faced. It quickly became clear that where their comrades towards the frontlines were battering rams, these soldiers were fine-tuned knives, meant to kill as quickly and accurately as possible. Of course Regan would keep the best at his side.

Blocking a close blow from a sword with her own blade, Gwen yelled out to Bumble, "Get to the tree!" Bumble didn't hesitate, clambering up the trunk of a tree on the riverbank until she was high in the branches and then pulling out her bow to cover them from there. She let out shot after shot, many piercing the thinner chainmail armor the soldiers wore. A few shots could drop a soldier to their knees, if they didn't kill them outright, and the others were able to more quickly finish them off from the ground.

Ivy saw this and smiled, impressed with the idea, and used her magic to lift herself into an adjacent tree. She sent out small, viciously precise bursts of energy, hitting her targets over and over again until they dropped, still as stone. Gwen even saw her using her magic to retrieve Bumble's arrows and return them to her, and she smiled.

She pulled her sword out of the neck of the man now at her feet, his blood pooling on the dirt below. Sylvia was behind her and Gwen motioned her forward, closer to Regan. She could see him at the back of the pack and watched as he spread his hands slowly in front of his body, palms down. A light mist rose from the ground and moved towards them. "He's doing something. Magic."

"Not this time," Sylvia snarled, throwing her own hands forward. A massive blast of air burst from them, nearly knocking over everyone between them and Regan with its strength. The mist was pushed behind him, quickly dispersing.

Regan hissed, annoyed, and locked eyes with Sylvia.

Several soldiers stepped between them, breaking her line of sight, but Sylvia was focused in a way that had Gwen's skin prickling. Most of the others were further away, busy with their own battles, so Gwen called out to Aiden, who was behind them.

"Can you help me cover her?"

He nodded and took up Sylvia's other side. "Let's go."

Two soldiers stepped towards them, engaging Gwen and Aiden, but Sylvia managed to continue moving, her gaze locked on Regan. He raised his hands, throwing a blue ball of fire towards her. Sylvia slapped it out of the air and towards the ground with one glowing hand. He continued to shoot blasts at her and she deflected them with razor-sharp focus. Even the few that hit her seemed to fizzle out, as if she couldn't even feel them in her current state. All that showed they'd even made contact were the slight burn marks on her scaley skin. In between, she would fire back bolts of crackling energy, which Regan worked hard to dodge. He glanced around himself, but few were left to guard him and those that remained were already deep in battle, leaving an almost clear path for Sylvia.

Gwen tried to keep her soldier busy, tried to deal with him swiftly, but she had to admit that she was slowing considerably. Fighting for any period of time was exhausting and spirits only knew how long had passed since this had begun. Her opponent was skilled and had not yet had to fight off as many as she had.

She felt her feet slipping—the grass, her sword, her clothing, her body, all covered in blood and viscera—and with every blow, she could feel herself losing ground. Her sword met his, grinding horribly as she tried to push him off her and back some, to allow her to regain her balance, to give her even a second to regroup. The soldier advanced relentlessly, knowing that he had the upper hand. He suddenly pivoted to the side as she swung and her momentum brought her stumbling forward. He then rounded on her and kicked her hard in the side, destroying any hope she had of recovering from the mistake.

Her body slammed into the ground, taking her breath. She wheezed, unable to control the spasming of her lungs, and was briefly blinded by the glint of metal in sunlight. The soldier had raised his sword, ready to bring it down on her in a killing blow. Time slowed and even though she only had a fraction of a second to think, she instinctively tried to decide which body part she could afford to lose.

Tail? An arm? Could she take the hit in her leg and keep fighting? Distantly, she tried to convince her still shocked body to roll so that he would miss the vital parts of her torso, hit something, anything, that wouldn't kill her.

And then the soldier was flying sideways as a large boot hit his ribs and his legs were knocked out from under him, causing him to drop to the ground as she had. Then Myev's axe was buried in his throat and suddenly Gwen got to keep all of her limbs both intact and functional. She let out the breath she'd just barely sucked into her clenching lungs, her chest still aching, and looked up.

"Keep going!" Myev yelled, inclining her head to where Regan and Sylvia were locked in battle, massive flashes of light colliding over and over again, creating intense booms not unlike thunder.

Gwen nodded and tried to stand. Aiden came to her and grabbed her arm, helping her rise. "I've got you." They moved together towards Sylvia, who was steadily pushing Regan back into the wall of rock behind him. Gwen took one side and Aiden the other, blocking any escape route unless he found a way up and over the cliff.

"It was you," Sylvia said as they got closer. "In the woods. I thought it was Zachariah, but it was you. Your magic."

Regan laughed, the sound ugly with spiteful surprise. "As you were meant to, but all his 'magic', *all of it,* has always been me. No magical skill whatsoever, Zachariah, but I let him take credit. I bolster him because Starlowe chose him to lead and me to follow." His voice was high and manic. A blast from Sylvia went whizzing by his ear, singeing his hair and smashing into the rock. Shrapnel flew all around him and crunched under his feet as he was pushed even further back. "But I will do as Starlowe commands because He is right, and He will not let us fail. I am the true hand of God, and Zachariah is His voice, His face. We both have important roles to play."

"Don't blame your god for your willingness to play second fiddle to a megalomaniac," Gwen snapped. "How stupid can you be? You do his dirty work and get all the blood on your own hands so that he can throw you to the wolves when he needs a scapegoat."

"You don't know him," Regan said, eyes wild. "Starlowe chose him. And he chose *me.*" He lifted his hands and the broken stones around him rose into the air. He threw them forward, raining down on them like hundreds of knives. Gwen grit her teeth and shielded her face with her forearms as they tore at her, ripping through her leathers and skin with equal ease.

"It was me, you know," Regan cried, his sudden cackle of laughter showing the blood staining his teeth. "I was the one that gave that stupid dwarf the information about the hideout. I sent your friends to die."

Before Gwen could even process the words, a scream tore itself out of Sylvia, sounding as if it had come from the very core of her being and had hurt the entire way out. Her rising hands shook as though picking up something very heavy and Gwen could feel the ground quaking beneath them. Something moved under her feet, snaking towards Regan, and suddenly massive tree roots shot up out of the grass, tearing through the ground as though it were as inconsequential as paper. They wrapped around Regan's body, covering him from toe to neck and lifting him several feet off the ground. Sylvia's fingers curled into tight fists and the roots constricted, squeezing Regan until he coughed out the last breath he had, his eyes bulging. She yanked her hands towards her body with another scream and the roots jerked Regan closer, until he was only a foot or two away from her.

Gwen had never seen her like this, so absolutely filled with animosity and anguish. She felt an instinctual, animal flash of fear at a might she could never hope to understand. Inside her benevolent, endlessly kind-hearted friend lay a power the universe granted to very few.

"You sent them to their deaths?" she asked, her voice like the blade of a knife. The sound sent a chill down Gwen's spine. She recognized it all too well.

Sylvia loosened the roots just enough for Regan to suck in a desperate breath, giving him a single chance to retract what he had said. Instead, he just growled at her.

"You killed them." It was no longer a question and her voice broke, the pain evident.

"Trained the beasts myself," he wheezed, defiant. "They're oh-so effective."

Sylvia glanced back, tears leaking unnoticed from her eyes. Her face was a question and Gwen nodded once, giving permission. That pain belonged to all of them, not just Gwen.

Sylvia then looked to Aiden. "Please do," he agreed, his voice low.

Syliva took a single step back. She then put a fist in the air and drug it down with great force. As she did, the roots sucked Regan into the ground and he disappeared beneath an avalanche of dirt. Gwen could feel the vibrations of the roots pulling him down, down.

When Sylvia released her hold, she fell to her knees and wailed towards the sky, entirely inconsolable. Gwen knelt beside her and wrapped her arms around her friend's waist. She could feel Aiden on the other side, both hands on the center of Sylvia's back, both comforting her and using her to keep himself upright.

Somehow, in the face of all of their grief, the battle had faded, and it was just the three of them there in that moment, feeling the magnitude of it. Anyone could have come up and sliced them to ribbons then and they would have let them. After everything, they didn't have it in them to stop them.

Sylvia had stopped weeping, though tears still ran down her beautiful green face, and was instead staring with blank eyes at the ripped-up ground in front of her. She shook, all her muscles violently quivering. She had killed a man—an act Gwen was sure she had done exceedingly rarely, if at all—and in doing so, had avenged Gwen's parents, Myev, Avery, Jasper, Aiden, and everyone else Regan had ever hurt.

Gwen knew the cosmic scales had tipped, just a little, in their favor, but she also knew that inside Sylvia there would only be a gnawing emptiness. Soon that space would be replaced with any number of things for a million different reasons—fear, sadness, anger, righteousness, eventually simple acceptance—but for now, she would feel hollow until it all set in.

Eventually the sounds of battle returned to them, distant but not distant enough, and Sylvia tried to stand. Her legs buckled and she fell forward. "I—I overdid it, I think. I apologize for that," she said in a small voice.

It was so very Sylvia, so ridiculously polite in a situation that no sane person should ever have expected it in, that Gwen couldn't help but smile a little. "Rest, friend. We can take a moment."

Myev came bounding over to them, chest heaving, and between gasping breaths informed them that the army further up towards the factory appeared to be turning back. "There's no one left here—Ivy's going to take us back that way—see what's going on." She pointed to where the others were already mounting another sheet of water, smaller than the one Sylvia had made. Ivy was also exhausted, not used to expending so much magical energy without the assistance of the crystals beneath her kingdom.

With Myev's help, they supported Sylvia enough to get her to the river and sat her down on the water. She pressed a palm flat to the sheet and after a few wobbly attempts, added her magic to Ivy's so that they could widen the makeshift boat enough to fit those left.

When they reached the front of the battle, they could see that Myev had been correct—the army was retreating. They made their way to Tellulah, who stood bloody and proud between the town's forces and the army as it disengaged. Someone, a commanding officer, Gwen imagined, was shouting directions at them. It was clear he had given some sort of order to retreat and the people of Rivergate were not going to pursue. They would not cause more bloodshed than necessary.

Sylvia moved to Tellulah's side and slid her hand into her friend's without hesitation. Tellulah squeezed back, but kept her eyes trained on the soldiers. They watched until they had gone back over the horizon and disappeared. Only then did Tellulah's shoulders slump with relief, exhaustion, grief—a myriad of emotions that it was now safer for her to feel. She gave herself just a moment and then Gwen saw the mask of duty take over again.

She turned to Cian and motioned for them to follow her. As a group, they moved towards the center of the remainder of their militia, Cian calling out to get their attention.

"We are safe for another day," Tellulah began. *"We have fought bravely and I am so grateful to every single one of you for putting your lives on the line to save our community. Yet we have also lost so many."*

Gwen tried not to look around them, at the bodies from both sides littering the ground. At the blood pooling below them. At their empty eyes and broken bones and shredded skin. At the bloodstained, tear-streaked faces of the living, whose mourning would last lifetimes. She wasn't ready. She had already felt too much. Soon she would make herself truly look at the cost of their war, but not yet.

"Too many of us have lost beloved friends and family members to the violence of a government that has never cared for us beyond what we can provide them. We are numbers to them, objects to squeeze dry of every last drop of productivity, but we know different. We are more than our labor. We are living, breathing souls with so much to offer. We are a community that will stand for each other, fight for each other, and die for each other."

The crowd let out a cheer.

"We will honor the sacrifices of our loved ones by continuing to fight for a better life for our children. Today we took a step towards building the world we all deserve. We helped turn the tides of history. We stand side by side with the other communities all across this country who fight the same fight. We are not alone, and we have never been alone. We will continue to show those that would subjugate us that they cannot break our spirits."

Tellulah stepped away to applause and shouts of agreement. There was so much sorrow here, yet they all knew they needed to take their scant moments of triumph wherever they could.

Chapter Eighteen

It took several days to deal with the dead. There was so much to do that teams of the Rivergate populace were out working at all hours: keeping watch, identifying the dead, cleaning them up enough to reunite them with their families for one last goodbye, digging grave after grave after grave to turn the strip of land in front of the plant into a charnel house for all of the plain, everyday folks who had never deserved to die that way. The corpses of the Peonian soldiers were gathered onto carts and dropped off closer to the scorched city, so they could be retrieved if the army so chose. They may have been enemies of the rebellion, but they too deserved whatever funeral rites they preferred.

For each person Gwen touched during the cleanup, she whispered an apology and then thanked them. She didn't allow herself to take the blame for the war anymore (mostly), but the massive loss of life still hollowed her out inside. She felt empty. So many had died here and for what? Because their country refused to respect their personhood? Because of its ravenous appetite for their resources? Because they only mattered if they shut up and worked hard? Entire family lines had ended in this battle, the last of them giving their lives to protect each other and their home.

In the faces of the dead, she saw her friends. This person had Veda's warm eyes, now empty. That one had Sylvia's shiny scales, now dull, and this one had Bumble's beautiful feathers, now soaked in blood. That person had Avery's long, soft eyelashes. The one over there had Jasper's hands and the one next to them had Myev's tusks or Ivy's hair or Boris' nose or or or.... Something inside of her felt loose, rattling around in her chest.

So she worked. It didn't take long for her muscles to feel like they were on fire as she lifted body after body, her own screaming for a break, but she continued. She helped every way she could until she fell into her bedroll at night, unconscious only seconds later. Her friends did much the same.

The first forces from Syrenmysta arrived and they helped to finish burying all the dead. Scouts later confirmed that the bodies of the soldiers were gone and the army itself was packing up to leave Rivergate. It appeared that The Council had declared Rivergate a lost cause, or at least they hoped so. They hoped it didn't mean they were regrouping for another attack later. The Syrenmysta troops remained to guard the much-diminished population of Rivergate as they recovered.

After that, the supplies from the Dimroot Kingdom arrived. Gwen saw Lucille weep silently with joy at the influx of food supplies, and on that day, she stayed in the kitchen so that Lucy could teach her how to bake bread. The repetitive motions of kneading lulled her into an almost meditative state, her brain quiet for the first time in ages. She served her friends dinner using the first misshapen loaf she made with her own two hands.

Soon, talk of moving on began to bubble up in her group, as Rivergate no longer seemed to be in quite as much danger as they had been. They heard from friends of Myev who had gone to help in Mooncrest that some manufacturing in Ironforge had resumed, powered by smaller plants in other towns, mostly those in the north. Wheatvalley, Goldenfield, and even little Windyplains had begun to rebel, effectively cutting The Council off from everything south of the White River. The army had not yet been sent to these smaller, less vital towns, as most of the forces seemed to be focused on keeping the peace in the more instrumental places like Ironforge and the richer mining towns around the Argent Mountains.

"We can create a base here, try to keep organizing from a distance, or we can travel up to Ironforge and see what we can do there." Myev said. "My people there have been keeping a low profile, waiting for instruction."

One battle in one war had still not turned Gwen into a tactical genius, so she continued to offer little to the conversations, though for Veda's sake she generally stayed present during them. She listened and tried to learn, but so much of it was completely beyond her. They decided to spend another week in Rivergate and then move to the woods outside Ironforge, to Sylvia's land, and start working on freeing Ironforge.

It was only hours later that she passed Nihal and as he saw her, his face lit up and then just as quickly became unsure. "What?" she asked, stupefied by the reaction.

"I just got news. About Zachariah's location...." he trailed off.

"Where?" She could feel a buzzing energy of some kind rising in her. Some might have called it anticipation, perhaps, but she knew that wasn't quite it. Her exhausted mind was formulating an idea based on some kind of instinct that she didn't want to examine too closely.

"I—uh—I don't know if it's a good idea to go after him based only on the preliminary intel again."

"Where?" she asked again, more forcefully.

"Listen, this time the source is more trustworthy, I've known them for years, but who says they didn't get bad information and pass it along to me?" he hemmed and hawed.

"Nihal, I won't ask again. I will string you up by your beard from the catwalks."

He chewed on his lip a minute longer. "Between Mooncrest and Ironforge. He's been tasked with directing the forces there and they've set up a camp—I have coordin—"

Gwen snatched the tiny slip of paper from his hand and opened it. His handwriting was cramped and blocky, rushed, but she could make it out.

"But we should be careful and get more confirmation before we go running in there," he continued, "and—"

"You're right," Gwen said. "Do me a favor and don't tell anyone about this yet. I want some time to decide what to do." She looked him in the eyes, tried to sell it with her face. She already knew what she was going to do. She knew it was an awful, terrible idea and she was going to do it anyway.

"Yeah, okay," he agreed. "My lips are sealed."

She walked away, her heart hammering in her chest and her mind running a marathon inside her skull as it worked out the details. It was as if the universe chose to confirm her decision when later that night, Sylvia left her bag with Gwen as she went to help Tellulah with something. "Be a dear and watch that, will you?"

Gwen waited until she was out of sight and with something an awful lot like guilt gnawing through her stomach lining, she reached her arm into the bag. There was no bottom, just never-ending space as her fingers groped and searched, bumping into item after item seemingly floating through the void as she tried to find the small jar of sleeping powder Sylvia had used on Myev. She began to panic as she pulled the tenth unwanted object out of the bag, fearing that Sylvia would come back and catch Gwen betraying her trust red-handed. *Where is the fucking sleeping powder?* she thought angrily, and then it was suddenly in her hand. She pulled it out and did not have time to be astonished by the efficiency of such a system, so she closed the bag and carefully put it back where she had found it, tucking her ill-gotten spoils into her pocket.

That night she took Veda to the woods behind the plant and across the river, laid her on a blanket, and kissed every inch of her body. She tried to sear all of it into her memory: the way Veda gasped and then laughed when her side was touched just right, the way her long, thick fingers felt clasped in Gwen's, how her breath caught in her throat when Gwen pressed kisses there. She ran her hands along every curve, slow and worshipful, so that her adoration would be clear and undeniable. When they returned, she slept soundly with her head pillowed on Veda's chest.

In the morning, she returned to the woods and searched until she found Bumble the perfect rock. Rose quartz, she thought—blush pink with a crackly little vein of white running through it, shiny in the light. She spent the afternoon baking loaves of bread, each of which she carefully, if not clumsily, carved her friends' initials into. It was shitty, as far as "thank you and also I'm sorry" presents went, but she had nothing else to offer. The next morning, while everyone else was busy and distracted, she laid the gifts on their bedrolls.

For Veda, she placed a folded-up piece of paper that said, "*You have been such a beautiful and unexpected bright light in my life. I'm sorry. I love you.*"

The one she left beneath Bumble's rock said, "*I could not have asked for a better friend. Thank you for your steadfast loyalty and your absolutely bonkers sense of humor. You made all those hard years bearable. I love you.*"

Most of the bread went without notes, except Nihal's which said simply, "*Do not tell them where I have gone. I will haunt you.*" She knew it was wrong to put him in that position, but she'd already made her choice.

She then slipped out of the gate with a group of strangers and headed north, her pace as quick as she could make it. She had to get as far away as she could before they noticed she was gone. The trains weren't running from anywhere north to anywhere south and vice versa, so she had five days walking ahead of her to reach Goldenfield, and then another day by train to get as close to the coordinates as possible. She walked with as few breaks as she could manage all day and for a good portion of the night.

She slept for only a few hours and then began again. She could barely sleep anyway with the guilt chewing her to pieces, but this was the only way to keep everyone safe. If anyone was going to die by Zachariah's hand, it was going to be her. He would not be taking another one of her friends away from her. She'd seen enough death.

Her communication satchel's beads had been glowing since sometime in the night and when she was another half-day's walk away, she braved opening it. Sylvia's voice came through. "Where are you, Gwen? We're worried about you—your notes scared us. Please answer."

She did not respond and continued walking.

At the end of her second day, she had several more messages. She opened them because apparently she enjoyed torturing herself, but also because their voices reminded her who she was protecting.

Another from Sylvia. One from Bumble. One from Veda asking where she was, sounding the most scared Gwen had ever heard her. "Please be okay," she whispered at the end.

When she awoke, it glowed again. This time, the tone had changed. Veda was furious. "Nihal finally told us where you're going, the little snake. How could you? I can't believe you would leave us without a word and put yourself in danger! For Reynta's sake, you're not stupid, Gwen, you know this is a terrible idea! How could you go behind our backs like this, I mean really?" Gwen tossed the satchel in her bag, muffling the sound, and began walking again, letting the rest of the rant play out without listening.

In the morning: "Please stop and tell us where you are," Veda pleaded. "Wait there, we'll come to you. It's not fair that you're going to do this without us. We're your friends and we deserve to see this through with you."

In the afternoon: "Gwen please, I'm begging you. I love you. Don't do this."

Two, left that night: "We're coming for you, whether you like it or not. You could make this easier and tell us where you are." The second was quieter, Veda's voice wretched, "I wonder if you even have your satchel anymore—maybe all of this is pointless. Did you throw it in the river? Leave it back in Rivergate somewhere? Maybe you threw it into a fire. I'm so fucking mad at you. I thought you wanted *us*. I thought after all this you were going to go home with me and we were going to build a life. How could you throw that away? How could you—" her voice cracked— "how could you abandon me after everything we've been through?"

Gwen didn't know anymore why she kept opening all these messages when they just made her feel like tearing her heart out with her bare hands. Maybe she just missed Veda, the ache like a living being taking up all the space in her chest, and even if Veda was angry and sad, Gwen still wanted to hear her voice.

Maybe she *should've* thrown the satchel into a fire.

She didn't.

She'd picked up a map in Goldenfield and by the time she was almost to the coordinates, her legs were sore and stiff from the ruthless pace she'd kept, despite the rest she got on the train. Her body felt bruised and cold down to the marrow. She hadn't spoken in days and her eyes were red and dry from tears she'd never admit to anyone. She was not in fighting shape, but she wouldn't allow that to stop her.

She crept up near the encampment and watched until the night, when most of the inhabitants laid down to sleep. There was a single building, a plain and unadorned cabin, which stuck out like a sore thumb with all of the canvas tents surrounding it. No doubt Zachariah was there, too good to sleep on the ground like his minions.

The cabin was not very wide, but was almost three times as long. There appeared to be only one story and she could see a single entrance at the front. There were always two guards patrolling around the building and another two standing in front of the door. She tried to memorize their routine and paid attention to when they switched. Just before they were due to trade off, she snuck into the camp, silent as a shadow, and hid out of sight until the new guards took over.

She only had time to do it once, so she had to get it right. She waited for the walking guards to turn the corner of the building and approached the side. There was a stack of crates there, which she used to boost herself onto the roof. Slowly, keeping as low as she could, she crawled towards the front, hoping her dark skin and clothes would be enough to make her all but invisible. She waited until the patrolling guards passed the door and rounded the corner again before she poked her head over the edge, above the door guards, and dusted the sleeping powder down over them. They fell like bricks.

She leapt down, her knees screaming in protest, and pulled out the lockpicking kit she'd stolen from Bumble. She was nowhere near as good as her friend and she struggled, becoming frustrated as the tools did little more than scratch at the lock and jostle around. She could hear the walking guards approaching her, so she flattened herself against the front of the building and when they stepped in front of her, she blew more dust into their faces. They went down as quickly as their friends, and Gwen sent a mental thank you to Sylvia and also to the universe for her luck. She returned to the door, took a deep breath, and kept at it with the picks. Finally, the door opened and she slipped into the dark hallway inside, closing the door behind herself.

She slinked towards the rear of the building, sword in hand, where she could see a light emanating from under a door. She opened it without pretense and there he was, at the back of the room, seated at an overly extravagant desk. Zachariah looked ever so slightly impressed, but carefully controlled any surprise he may have felt.

It was the first time she'd actually ever seen the man and he truly was just a man. He had pale skin, intense blue eyes, a beard cropped close to his face, and well-combed salt and pepper hair. If she'd seen him in the streets, she'd just assume he was just another run of the mill wealthy human man, not the person who had haunted her all her life and killed so many people she cared about.

"I see my multiple warnings didn't take," he said simply.

She responded by levelling her sword at him.

He stood from his chair, sighing as if he were being horribly inconvenienced by her. "I take it the guards aren't coming to help me?"

"Nope."

"Where are your friends?"

She didn't answer.

"Afraid I'll kill even more?"

She remained still as a statue. She wouldn't allow him to bait her.

Zachariah's own sword was in its scabbard and hung on a hook behind him. He pulled it free, no hurry in him, and turned back towards her, the metal glinting in the light from the fancy electric bulbs illuminating the room. The sword was thinner, smaller than hers. Expensive and probably made specifically for him. Built for speed, not force.

He continued to speak, though she didn't respond. "Kind of you to wait for me to prepare my weapon. Could have just come right at me, killed me at my desk." He dropped into his stance, finally ready. "Would that make even a violent street urchin like yourself feel dirty? To kill an unarmed man? Ah, but V—"

"Holy *fuck*," Gwen finally said, interrupting him. "You never stop talking—you must really love the sound of your own voice. I truly am beginning to regret not just running you through the second I set eyes on you."

He looked annoyed at the interruption.

She sensed his movement only a fraction of a second before it happened and managed to step out of the way as he lunged at her. He was certainly quick. He pivoted before he hit the door, turning and coming at her again and again, giving her no time to adjust her own stance.

She backed up, parrying each of his blows, but he was pushing her towards the corner. She slipped behind his desk instead, using her foot to kick it and send it towards him. He moved out of the way before it could hit him and the desk tilted and wobbled, but ultimately stayed on its legs. They circled each other around it, eyes locked.

Zachariah wasn't talking now, eyes focused on the hunt.

Her reach was longer, so she stepped closer to the desk and lashed out at him. The tip of her sword caught the sleeve of his shirt as he dodged, ripping it. His upper lip curled with distaste and he shoved the desk out of the way.

As he did, she swung again, and he barely pulled his sword up in time to block her. She put her other hand against her blade and put all her strength into it, hoping she could force him to lose his grip. He dropped low and managed to squirm away, sword still in hand. As he was forced to retreat to regain his bearings, she followed him forward. He was now being herded towards the corner she'd almost been put in and he knew it, but there was no way out. Zachariah hit the wall and she swung again. He batted the blade aside, but with his range of motion suppressed, he only managed to send it a few inches away and upward. It sliced into his shoulder before the tip of it was buried in the wall behind him.

He hissed and reached out with his good hand to shove her backwards. Gwen was able to keep ahold of the handle of her sword, but only barely, as the wall resisted letting it go. She stepped backwards as he switched his weapon to his offhand, the wound to his shoulder stopping him from effectively using his primary hand.

They looked at each other for just a moment before he darted at her again. His blows were less smooth with his offhand, but the sheer force of the rage in his swings knocked her off balance again. Distantly, she regretted pushing herself so hard to get here and not resting before she engaged him. Veda had said she wasn't stupid, but she was. She really was.

He supplemented the blows with a quick kick to her shin and she felt her knee buckle. She hit the stone floor hard and felt her sword leave her hand as her knuckles bashed into the floor with her full weight behind them. Gwen tried to grab her sword again, but he kicked it away underneath the desk.

She rolled to her back so she could see him and scuttled backwards, but not in time. His sword came down towards her chest and she lifted both hands, catching it mostly on the flat sides, but not quite perfectly, and the blade bit into the skin of her palms. Grinding her teeth, she twisted it to the side, surprising him and causing him to lose his own grip. She flung it aside and heard it hit the wall somewhere, metal clanging.

Zachariah wasted no time diving at her, his face red with anger. His fists found the shoulders of her jacket and he slammed her body into the floor, her head bouncing off it again and again. *Don't black out, don't black out,* she told herself forcefully as her vision blurred and darkened. The blood coming from her hands was making her grip too slippery to get a solid hold on him, causing her to scrabble ineffectively at his forearms.

Gwen bucked as he pulled her up again, causing him to fall off her, and kicked backwards. Spreading her arms, she reached for anything she could and made contact with something cold. She heaved it at him without looking. The heavy metal paperweight had fallen off the desk when she'd kicked it, but now it sailed through the air and hit him in the face, opening a gash in his cheek. He fell to the side with the force, yelping.

Gwen pressed against the wall and clambered to her feet, her hands leaving smears up the wallpaper. Grabbing a few bottles of ink, a small ceramic vase, and several books off a nearby shelf, she pitched them towards him, one after the other. In her haste, most of the objects missed, shattering on the floor, and he batted the books away like they were insects. The last bottle of ink hit him in the chest, spraying black down his shirt.

His face like thunder, Zachariah pulled a dagger from underneath his pant leg and rushed wildly at her. He slammed into her and they went careening into the wall, the dagger sliding into and along her upper arm. Gwen cried out as it hit bone. He had her pinned against the wall, his forearm over her chest, and his face was inches from hers.

"Do you think your cause is righteous?" Zachariah roared, spit and blood flying from his snarling lips. "Do you think God cares about you? Do you think he'll allow this pathetic rebellion to succeed? To let you murder the true, rightful owners of this country?"

"I didn't ask your god," Gwen growled through her teeth. "I don't care what he thinks."

He pulled the dagger from her arm and buried it in her gut, once, twice, three times, before he left it in and pressed all his body weight into it. She gasped, but then bit down hard on her tongue, refusing to scream again. If this was it, she didn't want him to have even an ounce more satisfaction.

Gwen locked eyes with him. She was fading, but she wasn't done yet. She flailed her knee blindly towards his groin and felt it hit home. Zachariah instinctively pulled away, leaving the dagger in her stomach. Ignoring the pain, she yanked it out and quickly twisted to slam him back against the wall while he was distracted, one hand on his chest and the other around his throat. He choked, his eyes bulging.

"Where's your god now?" she growled. Her nails were piercing the skin on his neck, she was gripping him so tightly. "Why won't he strike me down? If you ask me, either he's not here—maybe not anywhere—or he *won't* save you because he despises you and what you've turned him into as much as I do."

Zachariah coughed, a ragged, desperate sound, and pulled at her forearms. His face was darkening and his legs were writhing, frantically trying to get enough force to knock her off him. Despite his proximity to death, she could still read both pride and hatred in his eyes as he looked back up at her. She couldn't stand it a moment longer.

Gwen brought her mouth closer to Zachariah's ear. "How does it feel to be so well and truly alone?" Blackness was growing at the edges of her vision, the blood pouring from her abdomen thick and warm, and she was getting colder by the second. "If I'm dying today, you're coming too."

With the last of her energy, she plunged the dagger into his own stomach and twisted it, sliding it upwards and opening his belly. She let go of his neck when she felt viscera like feverish, wet snakes spilling out of him, and allowed him to fall to the floor. Zachariah coughed once and then was silent.

That was it.

He moved no more.

It was over.

She stumbled backwards, hitting the desk with the backs of her legs and falling gracelessly onto it, surprised at the sob that tore itself out of her chest. He was gone. Her lifelong bogeyman, one of the most important men in the country, had been taken from this world as unceremoniously as any other person. No god intervened, the heavens did not burst open and send lightning to punish her, no angels sang out for the loss of him. He was just a man and he had been breathing and now he was not. It was as simple as that.

She'd made her peace days ago with dying here, but she had to admit her body was afraid. Bodies were like that, she figured—all instinct, with very little care for the convictions of the mind. Tears slipped down her cheeks and her hands shook as she wiped them away. She didn't know why she bothered.

Images of her friends flashed through her head and for the first time since leaving, she truly regretted that she was there by herself, bleeding out on a rich man's floor. She missed them so much that the ache in her chest felt worse than the aches everywhere else. She'd betrayed them, but at least they'd all be safe a little longer. She didn't know if it was the right choice, but it was the choice she had made and she didn't get to try again.

Despite that knowledge, in that moment, with her hands warm and slippery with both Zachariah's blood and her own, she thought she might have chosen differently if she'd known how lonely this would feel. She didn't want to be alone anymore. She'd always thought she was good at it, but she'd been spoiled. It was hard to go back to being alone once you'd had a taste of love.

She slid to the floor, unable to stop herself, and fell to the side. This was really it; she'd done it. She'd kept her promise, at least. She looked out at Zachariah's open, empty eyes across from hers. Then the darkness won.

Chapter Nineteen

Consciousness came to her slowly, begrudgingly. She felt like she was under water, swimming upwards, but making little progress. It felt like days passed this way until finally she cracked her eyes open. All she could see was red and orange. She thought she might still be dreaming, delirious, but then realized it was fire. She squinted, trying to focus. Not just any fire, but Veda.

Veda smiled at her, crooked and watery. She was holding one of Gwen's hands with both of hers. "Welcome back."

Gwen tried to speak, but couldn't figure out how. She settled for a shaky nod and squeezed Veda's hand.

"I'm so fucking pissed at you."

Gwen let out a ragged laugh, but the sound turned into a cough and she regretted it, her stomach aching with the movement. "I take it I didn't die," she finally rasped, for lack of anything more intelligent to say.

"Don't get too excited," Veda said, "I might kill you yet. Add another few holes to your pincushion ass body."

Gwen smiled, trying not to laugh again. Veda had a new bruise across her left check, angry purple and red, and her bottom lip had been split, now covered with a thick, ragged scab. Gwen tried to reach up, but her arms felt like lead. "Your face," she said, still the epitome of brilliance.

"Do you think those guys just let us waltz in and retrieve your idiot body?"

"Ah."

"They were real riled up, too, when the guards you knocked out woke up and realized what had happened. Good thing we weren't far behind you."

"How?" Gwen asked, a bit shocked. She'd really pushed herself to get there as fast as she had.

"Lucky for you we were able to get a couple carriages from a farmer a few miles outside of Rivergate with some money Tellulah gave us. We took turns driving and didn't stop unless someone's bladder was going to explode or the horses needed rest. We pushed them insanely hard–I feel really bad for them. I'd also barely slept or eaten since you left, so I could take a lot of shifts. Was probably going on 32 or more hours without sleep by the time we rolled up to the camp, and had barely slept the days before that." Veda said.

Gwen opened and closed her mouth, unable to properly respond. She thought about deflecting, making a joke about sleeping before battle, Boss, but decided not to push her luck. What she really wanted to do was apologize, but her eyes were still unreasonably heavy and every time she blinked, her head swam. She tried so hard to keep them open and on the woman in front of her. Gwen squeezed Veda's hand again, hoping that said enough until she could say more.

"Yeah," Veda said, squeezing back. Then, "Guys! She's up!"

Soon the room was filled with bodies. Her friends surrounded the bed she lay on, except Bumble, who was, of course, in the bed with her. Even Aiden and Nihal were there, though the dwarf kept a wide berth from Veda. Gwen assumed she'd made some pretty colorful threats towards him.

"You lost more blood than me," Myev said, punching her shoulder a little too hard. "Way to show me up."

"Oh!" Sylvia exclaimed, "Do be careful!" She pushed Myev aside to pull the bandages off the wound on Gwen's arm to check that the friendly gesture hadn't caused any new damage. "Those magic-resistant blades they have, I swear," she began to mumble under her breath as she poked and prodded. "You have to be so careful...."

"Oops," Myev said over Sylvia's fussing, blushing a little. "Sorry kid."

"S'okay," Gwen smiled up at her.

"Your bread was tasty, but a pretty shitty apology," Ivy informed her.

"I thought so too," Gwen agreed in a slurred murmur.

"Good thing you lived so that you can make up for it."

"One million rocks," Bumble grouched. "Good ones. The best."

Gwen squeezed her as tightly as she could with the arm Sylvia wasn't currently looking at.

"You almost got me killed, pulling a stunt like that," Nihal told her, thumbing towards Veda.

"I'll apologize when I'm coherent," Gwen managed to say with great effort. "Promise."

"All right, get out, everybody shoo," Sylvia said, replacing the bandages and flapping her hands. "She's not dead, but she still needs rest."

***

The next week consisted of about a thousand lectures, twice as many heartfelt apologies, and four billion hugs. Gwen accepted all of it with dazed gratefulness, as she hadn't actually expected to be here for any of it.

They spent the time it took her to heal at the home of Myev's friend, Thea, who owned a farm outside of Ironforge and had taken them in while Gwen healed. "I have friends too," the woman said, fake wounded, when Gwen expressed surprise that it wasn't another one of Sylvia's seemingly endless contacts. Thea was kind and generous and they did all the chores they could for her farm while they were there. Even Gwen, who Sylvia wouldn't allow to do much, helped where she could.

During a break, Gwen was sitting on the wraparound wooden porch attached to the old farmhouse and enjoying the midafternoon sun on her face. She could feel the chipping paint and soft wood underneath her palms, the gentle fall breeze rustling through her hair. The trees here were mostly deciduous, unlike those in the Tall Pines Forest, and their leaves had all turned orange and brown and yellow. Many had fallen already, creating a thick blanket on the ground that crunched when anyone crossed it.

Such crunching alerted her to the presence of another, though she didn't bother opening her eyes. Veda's scent hit her as the woman sat beside her and without a thought, she leaned sideways into her. It was such a short time ago that just that casual show of affection would have scared her half to death.

"Hey," Veda said softly.

"Hey."

"How are you feeling?"

"Good. Sylvia said my body still has work to do, but it feels just like it always did."

"Good."

They still hadn't really talked about it. They'd talked about how stupid she'd been, how much she'd scared them, how she was never to do it again. They hadn't talked about the betrayal of it all. Veda had not withheld affection from her, but Gwen could sense that something was stuck within her, holding her back.

"Tell me what you're thinking."

Veda mulled it over a few seconds more. Then, almost a whisper, "How could you leave me behind like that? I know you're going to say to protect me, but I thought—I thought we were a team."

The pain in Veda's voice made Gwen sit up and open her eyes, to face full-on the hurt she had caused. She threaded her fingers through Veda's and pulled the hand to her lips to press a dry kiss there as she tried to come up with a coherent answer that wouldn't sound trite. "After Avery and Jasper, after the battle, it became even clearer to me what I now had to lose. In the beginning of all of this I was scared to let anyone become that important, but it happened anyway. And I told myself, it's fine I can protect them, and then it became clear that I couldn't."

"I didn't ask you to protect me, I asked you to be my partner."

"You're right, I fucked up. Plain as. I did what I thought I needed to do for myself, and I accomplished my goal, but I'd basically given up on everything that actually mattered. I went in there expecting to die and I almost let go of my—my family, even though that's what I was trying to save in the first place." She cleared her throat, swallowed the emotion. "But I killed him and now that chapter's over. Hell, that whole book is done. I don't want to be that person anymore, the one who thinks she has to be all alone."

"We don't have to keep it up," Veda said after a long while.

"Keep what up?"

"This war stuff. We could find somewhere to lay low. Go back to Vulcaria."

"Oh, don't chicken out on me now," Gwen offered her a lopsided smile.

Veda rolled her eyes, "I mean it."

"No, you don't. You could never walk away from something you care about, could never leave all the hard work for someone else."

She sighed. "Yeah, I guess that's true."

"You were right all along anyway. This is a battle we've got to fight. I thought change had to happen all at once and that none of us were big enough for that, but you, Rivergate, Dimroot—all of it showed me that change is caused by individual people waking up and choosing to do the right thing day after day. We might as well keep being some of those people, make the world a little better if we can. I'm all in now, there's nothing else to distract me."

"That's a different tune."

"Mm," Gwen agreed. "Almost dying taught me a few things."

Veda wrapped her arms around Gwen's shoulders, buried her face in her hair, and held her tight. "Well, I'm glad to hear it."

***

The trees parted and they entered the clearing where Sylvia's cottage sat. Breeze and her children were hard at work in the garden, but when they called out, the children tossed down their tools and ran towards them to dole out numerous child-sized hugs. Gwen felt like it had been several lifetimes since she'd last seen them.

She lowered herself onto the grass and laid back with her head on her pack to watch them run and play, both her and the children officially relieved of their duties for the next few hours at least.

Veda laid beside her, eventually rolling to face her with her head pillowed on her arms. Gwen moved onto her side and reached out, running her fingertips along Veda's jaw, her thumb across her soft lips. "I love you, Veda Aalish."

"I love you, Guinevere Flynn."

Soon, they would have more battles to fight. There would be blood and heartbreak and fear, but they would face everything together, all of them, as a team. One could never know the suffering the future may hold, but today, they had this. It was a warm day for fall and they laid there together, unable to help dozing off and on, until the sun began to droop in the sky and the cool night started to set in. Sylvia called out from the doorway of the house that they could use a few extra hands to prepare dinner and so they finally sat up.

"Come on, our friends need us."

Pronunciation Guide

Disclaimer: I am, unfortunately, monolingual. I have tried to learn other languages and I have failed miserably. As much as I would *love* to speak all of the beautiful languages that inspired the names of locations and races in Engadi, I cannot. Therefore, I did my best to listen to the way the words were pronounced and used that to create my place and race names. The pronunciations are based on how they sound to my ears, but there's a very good chance I'm wrong on several or all of them. If you know better, feel free to pronounce these names better than I ever could and know that I both respect and envy you!

Character Names:
Veda Aalish - [VEY-DUH EYE-LISH]
Myev [MEE-EHV]
Naiavara [NAI-UH-VER-UH]
Eren [AIR-EN]
Nihal - [NEE-HALL]
Cian - [KEE-AN]

Places:

Engadi – from the Zulu word *ingadi* (garden) - [EN-GAH-DEE]

Vulcaria - [VUL-CAR-EE-AH]

The Dunes

Vedvik Dunes – from the Estonian word *videvik* (twilight) - [VID-VIK]

Apelgor – from the Russian words *апельсин* (orange) and *город* (city) - [AH-PEEL-GORE]

Syrenmysta – from the Russian words *сирень* (lilac) and *место* (place) - [SEER-REE-EN-MEE-ES-STA)

Krasyngavan – from the Russian words *красный* (red) and *гавань* (harbor) - [KRAHS-KNEE-GAH-VAHN]

Stragrevat Pustynya – from the Russian words *нагревать* (heat), *страдания* (suffering), and *пустыня* (desert) [STRAW-GREE-VAHT POOHS-STEEN-YA]

Zhidukh Istochnik – from the Russian words *Жизнь* (life), *дух* (spirit), and *источник* (fount) - [ZHEE-DUKH EES-TOCH-NICK]

Marshwoods

Maraisespirit - from the French word *marais* (swamp) and *esprit* (spirit) - [MAH-RAY-ESS-PREET]

Epaisquet – from the French word *épais* (thick) and *bosquet* (grove) - [EE-PEHS-KE]

Tourtrou – from the French word *tournée* (round) and *trou* (hole) - [TOOR-TROO]

Perais – from the French word *perdu* (lost) and *marais* (swamp)- [PEAR-AY]

Charriche – from the French word *charpente* (timber) and *riche* (rich) - [SHAR-REESH]

Bhollaisca

Bhollaisca – from the Irish word *bholláin* (boulder) and *scáth* (shadow) - [BOW-LASS-CAH]

Creagtra – from the Irish word *creagach* (rocky) and *trá* (beach) - [CRAHG-TRAY]

Scoitalamh - from the Irish word *scoilt* (split) and *talamh* (land) - [SKAHLT-TAHL-MUH]

Glastonnta – from the Irish word *glas* (green) and *tonnta* (waves) - [GLAHSS-TAWN-TUH]

Clobrisead – from the Irish word *cloch* (stone) and *bristeoir* (breaker) - [CLAWGH-BRIS-EAD]

Muarbol

Muarbol – from the Spanish word *mucho* (much) and *árbol* (tree) - [MOO-AR-BOWL]

Quilcasa – from the Spanish word *tranquilo* (quiet) and *casa* (home) - [KEEL-CAH-SAH]

Grandesagua – from the Spanish word *grande* (large), *descendente* (falling), and *agua* (water) - [GRAHN-DES-AGWA]

Quenabos – from the Spanish word *pequeño* (small) and *bosque* (forest) - [KEHN-AH-BOHS]

Bebol – from the Spanish word *bebé* (baby) and *árbol* (tree) - [BEH-BOWL]

Alcanpropi – from the Spanish word *alcanzando* (reaching) and *propina* (tip) - [AHL-CAHN-PRO-PEE]

Races:

Aviseum - from the Latin word *avis* (bird) - [UH-VEE-SEE-UM]

Bovillum - from the Latin word *bovillus* (bovine) - [BO-VEEL-UM]

Canieum - from the Latin word *canis* (dog) - [CAH-NE-UM]

Drakoso - from the Greek word δράκων (dragon} and the Greek word πρόσωπο (person) - [DRAYK-OH-SO]

Felineum - from the Latin word *felis* (cat) - [FEH-LEE-UM]

Fyrdiav - from the old English word *fyr* (fire) and the Italian word *diavolo* (devil) - [FEAR-DE-AHV]

Laisarnne - from the French word *lézard* (lizard) and the French word *personne* (person) - [LE-SOHN]

Lepeum - from the Latin word *lepus* (rabbit) - [LEH-PEE-UM]

Sliman - [SLY-MAN]

Other:

Starlowe – from the German words *stark* (strong) and *lowe* (lion) - [STAR-LOOH-VAH]

Loweans - [LOOH-VEE-ANS]

Reynta - [REIGN-TUH]

Bahen – as it appears [BAH-EN]

Acknowledgements

As most of us do, I have many people to thank. Nothing in this life is done without community—I truly believe that.

Specifically, thank you to Andrea for being the first person to read this book in its raw form. Your belief in me and willingness to edit for me meant more than words can say. Thank you to my husband, Tom, and my friend, Case, for reading this story to make sure it was ready to be published. Case, I also thank you for always being my biggest cheerleader in my creative endeavors. Thank you, Noelle, for answering my many, many questions about how to do this whole author thing! Thank you, Zach, for coming up with the names for pretty much all of Peonia and thus creating the naming scheme I continued on everywhere else. Also, thank you for letting me bounce ideas off you during the early stages of writing this—without you I may never have gotten here.

Thank you to Case, Tom, and Misty for allowing me to borrow your characters (Boris and Jasper, Cian, and Naiavara, respectively) to help flesh out this big ol' world of mine. I had a lot of fun with them.

In general, thank you to my mother and grandmother, without whom I wouldn't be alive many times over. Thank you for always being excited by my creative pursuits and encouraging me to be the best weirdo I can be.

For the third time I will thank my husband, who puts up with more than any mere mortal should be capable of. (He says it's not that bad, but I regularly wake him up in the wee hours of the morning to remove spiders from the house, if that tells you anything about what it's like to be married to me....) I truly don't know what I'd do without you.

Thank you to all of my other friends—you know who you are (and you are too multitudinous to list)—for listening to me ramble about this story over the years. I have finally finished getting the brainworms onto paper now, aren't you proud of me?